MORGAN COUNTY PUBLIC
110 SOUTH JEFFERSON ST
MARTINSVILLE, IN 46151

P9-CDX-780

FIC
WOO

Woods, Janet.
Secrets and lies

SECRETS AND LIES

Recent Titles by Janet Woods from Severn House

AMARANTH MOON
BROKEN JOURNEY
CINNAMON SKY
THE COAL GATHERER
EDGE OF REGRET
HEARTS OF GOLD
LADY LIGHTFINGERS
MORE THAN A PROMISE
PAPER DOLL
SALTING THE WOUND
SECRETS AND LIES
THE STONECUTTER'S DAUGHTER
STRAW IN THE WIND
TALL POPPIES
WITHOUT REPROACH

The author invites comments from her readers
via her website:
www.janet-woods.com
or by post:
PO Box 2099
Kardinya 6163
Western Australia

SECRETS AND LIES

Janet Woods

This first world edition published 2012
in Great Britain and in the USA by
SEVERN HOUSE PUBLISHERS LTD of
9–15 High Street, Sutton, Surrey, England, SM1 1DF.

Copyright © 2012 by Janet Woods.

All rights reserved.
The moral right of the author has been asserted.

British Library Cataloguing in Publication Data

Woods, Janet, 1939–
    Secrets and lies.
    1. English – Australia – Fiction. 2. Family secrets –
    Fiction. 3. Love stories.
    I. Title
    823.9'2-dc23

ISBN-13: 978-0-7278-8181-6 (cased)

Except where actual historical events and characters are being
described for the storyline of this novel, all situations in this
publication are fictitious and any resemblance to living persons
is purely coincidental.

All Severn House titles are printed on acid-free paper.

Severn House Publishers support The Forest Stewardship Council [FSC],
the leading international forest certification organisation. All our titles that
are printed on Greenpeace-approved FSC-certified paper carry the FSC logo.

Typeset by Palimpsest Book Production Ltd.,
Falkirk, Stirlingshire, Scotland.
Printed and bound in Great Britain by
MPG Books Ltd., Bodmin, Cornwall.

Welcome
Dallas O'Connor
Latest and much loved addition to my family.
Arrived on earth
June 2011

One

Esmé Carr adjusted the pleated knee-length skirt of her dress and cast a critical glance over the portions of her body reflected in the small mirror held by her room-mate, Minnie James.

'It's not too short, is it?'

'It will be if Matron sees it.' Minnie set the mirror back on the chest of drawers. 'Pale pink looks good on you, and I like the crystal beading. You've got long legs to show off.' She sighed, 'I wish they were mine . . . your hair, as well.'

Drawing a brush through her brown curly bob, Esmé laughed. 'Funny . . . I always wanted to be a blue-eyed blonde, like you, and you have lovely fair skin to go with it. It's a pity we couldn't do a swap now and again.' Stretching her lips into an oval, Esmé outlined them in light rose to match her nails, and then rubbed them together. It felt good to be out of her starched uniform and be able to dress up. 'Chad was quite taken with you when he met you. I do wish Matron had allowed you to come.'

Minnie blushed. 'Oh, don't be silly, Esmé. Chad isn't interested in me. He has his training to do and it takes years to become a doctor. I was flirting with him, that's all. He's so sweet, dependable, and too stodgy for me, like a favourite teddy bear. Besides, I want to go to Australia.'

Esmé was sceptical. 'We're in the middle of a depression.'

'There's always work for nurses,' Minnie scoffed. 'Come to Australia with me.'

'What about my family? I promised Chad I'd work for him after he's fully trained.'

'We don't have to stay abroad forever. It would be like a long holiday with a sea voyage at either end. Think of all that sunshine and the beaches, and lounging on the deck between ports, while the crew lust after us.'

It sounded tempting, if the end bit was left off. Esmé had no intention of being gossiped about, and she doubted if Minnie would enjoy it, either.

'To be honest, I'll be relieved when my brother finishes medical school.'

And not least because her twin had dominated her life since they'd spent several years in a London orphanage together. He'd taken on the job of being her protector then, and it had become a habit. Between Chad, her brother-in-law, sister, and the matron, sometimes Esmé felt *managed*, as though she had no mind of her own.

She rolled her stockings up and attached them to the suspenders dangling from her garter belt. 'Seams straight?'

'Perfectly. Are those stockings silk?'

'They are. They were a Christmas present from my sister. There's another pair in my drawer if you want to borrow them.'

'Don't tempt me.' Minnie opened the cupboard door. 'Wedge heels or T-strap?'

'T-strap.' Esmé pulled on her coat, hat and scarf then thrust her feet into a pair of silver shoes that Minnie dusted off and held out to her. 'What's the time?'

'Time you were gone. You know how punctual Dr Elliot usually is.'

'Only too well.' Picking up her bag Esmé headed for the door.

'Have a nice time,' Minnie called after her. 'Think of me swotting away for my midwifery exam while you're sweeping all the young men off their feet on the stroke of New Year.'

Esmé grimaced. 'It will mostly be older men. I might be able to find one for Matron.'

Minnie giggled. '*He* would have to be a hero. She told me I should have paid more attention to the lectures, and if I fail the exam a second time I won't be given another chance.' She shrugged. 'That would be a pity, because I love delivering babies, and that's what I wanted to specialize in. They're so sweet and helpless. I suppose somebody has to be on duty and look after the patients over New Year, though.'

Esmé didn't add insult to injury by telling Minnie the matron was right. All the same, she felt sorry for her friend.

Outside the nurses' quarters it was cold. A silver crescent of moon was diffused in the misty air. Longfleet Road was deserted in both directions, except for a man on a bicycle. He rang his bell noisily at a cat padding across the road. Instead of running, the cat went into a crouch, and froze, forcing the man to divert. He swore as he turned the corner, the handlebars wobbling.

It seemed odd going home on a Thursday evening, even if it was New Year's Eve, and it was an unaccustomed luxury to have the whole weekend off. She supposed her brother-in-law had pulled a few strings, and she felt guilty.

The hedge outside the building across the road was rimmed by frost. From a lit window over a shop came the faint, catchy song of *Ain't She Sweet*. Giving in to impulse, Esmé stood under the street light and did a tap dance to keep her feet warm. Perhaps she should have become a showgirl. She grinned as she thought of the scandal that would have caused.

When she was young she'd wanted to make dancing her career, and had imagined herself gracefully flitting across the stage on points, wearing a tutu, or leaping into the arms of a young muscled god. A year of dancing lessons convinced her she didn't have the strength or dedication required. She wasn't bad at tap though, and she enjoyed ballroom dancing.

If she couldn't be a famous dancer, then she'd have liked to live on a farm surrounded by animals to care for. She'd thought of becoming a vet, but nobody had taken her suggestion seriously, not even her sister, Livia.

Chad had taken it upon himself to point out what she already knew . . . that they had no money of their own, and besides, they'd long ago decided that he'd be a doctor and she a nurse. Both were good, solid professions, and their sponsors, Livia's first husband, the late Richard Sangster and her second, Denton Elliot, had provided the means to ensure they were educated properly to that end.

'We can't let them down now, can we?' Chad had said, sounding horribly stuffy and responsible, and . . . well, as Minnie had said, slightly teddy-bearish. And she giggled at the thought.

She heard the sputter of the engine of her brother-in-law's

Morris Oxford and did several ragged pirouettes on the spot, thinking, Matron would give her a good dressing-down if she saw her.

She flopped into the seat next to Denton when he drew up beside her. 'You're late.'

'Sorry, I had an emergency, so got myself a quick bath and shave at the hospital afterwards. I'll only have to change into my dinner suit when we get home.'

Her nose wrinkled. 'Ugh . . . no wonder you smell of carbolic soap.'

He grinned at her. 'There are worst things to smell of. Why the hornpipe on the pavement?'

'It was to keep myself warm whilst I waited. I also wondered what Matron would say if she saw me, and was hit by a sudden burst of rebellion. So I flirted with danger, found the nearest limelight and kicked my heels up a bit higher.'

'It's a gaslight . . . not lime.'

'You're being terribly correct. I'm going to stay out of your way tonight.'

'I can't help it, poppet. I've been conditioned since birth to be dogmatic.'

'Woof,' she said.

He suddenly remembered Minnie. 'We've forgotten your friend?'

'She failed her midwifery exam, so Matron wouldn't let her come. She has to work on the mater ward and swot in her spare time.'

'Is Matron that bad?'

'She can be a bit fierce, but she has to be, I suppose. It will be nice to be out from under her eagle eye for a short time, and I've earned my belt buckle, at long last.'

Denton produced a bit of a smug grin. 'You have your specialist certificates, as well. I'm proud of you Es. Matron turns out well-trained nurses.'

'She's diligent, I'll give her that. My friend, Minnie, is a good practical nurse, and she loves the midwifery side. She finds written stuff a bit difficult. Most of us daren't put a foot wrong with Matron, and sometimes, having you for a brother-in-law is a decided disadvantage. If I do something wrong she purses her lips, stares down her nose at me and then goes "tut-tut", like a hen about to lay an egg. Then she says, "I wonder what our esteemed colleague, Mr Elliot, would say to *that* if he saw you." As if you'd be interested when I dropped a kidney dish on the floor. You're not interested, are you, esteemed colleague?'

Denton laughed. 'Not in the least.'

They took the road that crossed the swampy area at the edge of the harbour, where the mist curled upwards to dew the windscreen. It was often misty there, but Denton knew the road like the back of his hand and he drove slowly, his eyes on the gravel at either side of the tarmac so they didn't end up in the mud.

'I should have stuck with dancing. I wanted to be Anna Pavlova when I was small.'

'Who knew such dreams of fame gathered cobwebs in Esmé Carr's sensible brain? In this day and age you're better off working in a safe profession with long-term prospects.'

'Do you think I'm too old to have dreams, Dr Denton?' She had called him that when she was a child so she didn't get him mixed up with his father, who was also a doctor . . . and she still did on occasion.

'None of us are too old. I once yearned to be a train driver.' He picked up speed when they were through the mist, smiling at what must seem like a ridiculous notion to him now. Then he surprised her with, 'Sometimes I still get an urge to drive a steam engine. They make such a nice clacking sound on the rails. And I love it when I'm lying in bed and the whistle blows in the distance.'

'I'll buy you a clockwork train for Christmas, and a whistle to go with it. How's Livia been keeping?'

'When I rang her earlier to say we might be late, your sister was in a panic trying to decide between orange satin with coffee lace inserts, or burgundy lace with a handkerchief hem.'

'I hope she wears the burgundy lace. It's pretty, and it will match my outfit, so we'll look good together.'

He laughed. 'The mysterious logic of the female mind never fails to astound me, poppet. I just hope the caterers provide a decent dinner. I'm starving.'

Laughter bubbled from her. 'Well, I can safely say your mind might work in mysterious ways but your stomach is predictable. I think it will be a cold buffet supper.'

He groaned. 'I haven't eaten since breakfast.'

'While you're changing I'll dash into the kitchen and find something to keep you going. There's bound to be some broth to heat up. And I'll make you a ham and cheese sandwich.'

'You're a sweetheart, Esmé.'

She rummaged around in her bag. 'I've got some humbugs if that's any help. I know you can't resist them.'

'It will certainly give the blood sugar a boost. May I enquire how long they've been in there?'

'No, you may not, but they're not quite antiques. They're still in the original bag, though they've melted into sticky blobs and the paper is stuck to them.'

'A bit of paper bag won't kill me. I've eaten worse.'

'Really . . . what was worse than paper bag?'

'I ate a fly once. It was during a riding lesson and I was out of breath. The fly flew into my open mouth.'

'Ugh!' Shuddering she found the humbugs, popped one in his mouth and another in her own. The car was filled with the sound of sucking and slurping as they tried to outdo each other.

Esmé laughed first. 'If only your juniors could see you now.'

'If you don't tell them, I won't tell Matron about you.'

'There's nothing to tell; I'm totally boring.'

Denton chuckled. 'Yes, well . . . you can't help that, I suppose.'

They settled into a comfortable silence as they went through the crossroads at Upton and followed the headlights into the tunnel of light they made. Hedges grew tall on either side of them, reaching out with clutching hooked fingers.

Esmé was looking forward to the comfort of the Elliot home. 'It seems forever since I last saw everyone.'

'I'm pleased to say they're growing like a crop of spring weeds, including you and Chad. I'm expecting great things from your brother . . . and from you too, young lady. You're a good nurse, the cream of the graduates, I'm told, so try and forget all that dancing nonsense. Look on it as exercise rather than a career.'

There was a flicker of annoyance in her, squashed when she remembered that Denton had given herself and Chad a home. 'I think I'm a little too old to train for ballet now, don't you?' She kissed his cheek, and laughed. 'Never fear, you darling fuddy-duddy, I'll do what's expected of me. I'll become the ghost of Florence Nightingale herself, if that will help.'

'Mmmm . . . just don't hover around the patients with your lamp. We want to keep them alive, not frighten them into the next life.'

She gazed at his profile. Denton had been the nearest thing to a father that she and Chad could remember, and she loved him dearly. 'Denton . . . did you ever regret taking the three of us on?'

He gave her a quick look. 'Good gracious! What an odd thing to ask me. You do like putting a chap on the spot. What would you do if I said yes?'

'Curl up and die.'

'We can't have that, can we, with you looking so pretty. If you want the truth, your sister became the love of my life from the very first moment I set eyes on her. It was on a train.'

'Is that why you like trains?'

'Could be. Livia was wearing an awful grey suit and a hat with drooping pheasant feathers. She was on her way to London to visit you and Chad. One of the feathers snapped, and I kept it with me all through the war to remember her by. You and Chad were part of the package.'

'You've forgotten Meggie.'

He laughed. 'No I haven't. Who can overlook Meggie when she's Livia's daughter? And now we have the boys, as well. I was an only child, so I always wanted a big family to make up for it.'

'Did you mind that Livia married Richard Sangster?'

He nodded. 'I pretended not to, but it hurt like hell when she married Richard, even though he was my best friend. But I knew he was dying, and under the circumstances it felt mean to deny him some happiness by being churlish about it, and punching him on the nose. He did love Livia, and it was for the best.'

'I liked Richard. He was so brave and jolly. Livia told me she loved both of you at the same time.'

'Yes . . . she probably did. Livia has a soft heart.'

'She loved you the most, Denton. She said Richard was a will-o'-the-wisp type of love that would probably have burnt out, but you were always her soulmate, and she knew you'd always be there for her.'

'You make me sound awfully dull.'

'Nonsense. Chad and I adored you. You spent time with us and played lots of games. We wished you were our real father.'

He flicked a glance her way. 'Thank you for that nice compliment, your late parents would be proud of you all, you know.'

'Why don't we have anything to do with Major Sangster any more? After all, he is Meggie's grandfather.'

He sighed. 'You asked your sister the same question, I understand. What was her answer?'

'She said she didn't want to talk about it.'

'Then it's not fair of you to expect me to break a confidence, and I advise you to let sleeping dogs lie, as Livia wants. That's my last word on the subject.'

And judging from the impatient tone of Denton's voice, Esmé knew it was. 'Sorry,' she murmured. All the same, he'd made it clear that there was some underlying problem they avoided. It was jolly curious, and she thought about it often.

He changed the subject, his handsome, rugged face softening. 'Can I book a dance before your card gets filled.'

'Which dance . . . tango or Charleston?'

Denton laughed at the thought. 'Good Lord; I'm not quite that ambitious. If you value your feet a slow foxtrot will do me nicely . . . the slower the better.'

He honked the horn as they rounded the bend.

Home was a slightly shabby red brick building called Evesham House, and named after the village. Evesham House had half-panelled wooden walls and large fireplaces. Bits had been added to it from time to time, so it fell together in a comfortable heap of mismatched bricks and windows. Sometimes the house rattled if the wind was strong enough.

The Elliot house was situated not far from Blandford, along with a clutch of other houses. It included the shuttered Foxglove House, and Nutting Cottage, where Major Henry Sangster lived. A mile away on the other side of the village was the home of Andrew Elliot, who was Denton's father, and also a doctor.

Esmé's sister, Livia, had a chintzy, country taste in furniture, though nothing really matched, and although the house never looked completely tidy, everything seemed designed for an active family to relax in – a house that didn't mind displaying its dusty corners.

Dressed in their pyjamas, the three younger children of the family came rushing down the staircase except for thirteen-year-old Meggie, who rode down the banister rail with a wide grin on her face.

'One of these days you're going to hurt yourself,' Livia told her for the umpteenth time since Meggie had discovered how to ride down the rail safely. But when Esmé's eyes sought out those of Denton they were filled with amusement, and he winked at her, because she and Chad used to do the same.

They exchanged hugs and kisses, and Adam said, 'Come up and tell us a story, Aunt Es.'

Swinging Meggie on to his back and tucking Luke and Adam under each arm, Denton gave Livia a smacking kiss on the mouth. 'Hello, my darling . . . I'm home.'

'As though I hadn't noticed. As usual, pandemonium reigns the moment you walk through the door.'

'Who's Pan D. Moanium? Have I met him?'

Esmé giggled and Livia laughed, as Denton headed back up the stairs weighed down by the trio clinging to him. He dropped them in a heap on the landing, and fussed with a big black dog that had come out of the kitchen to follow them up, and now greeted his master's acknowledgement with a slurp of its long, pink tongue.

'I'll be up to tell you all a story in a minute,' Esmé shouted after them, and headed for the kitchen to see to the promised sandwich.

Dressed in the burgundy gown, Livia followed after her and watched as Esmé grabbed an apron. 'Don't tell them a ghost story else they won't settle. What are you doing in the kitchen?'

'I promised to make Denton some soup and a sandwich. He had an emergency and that put his schedule out. He hasn't eaten since breakfast, but he's had a bath.'

'Yes . . . I can smell the soap.'

'I told him it whiffed but he just laughed.'

Livia's smile brought a shine to the surface of her brown eyes. 'I'll never turn my man into a dandy and I'm used to the smell. I've already made a sandwich for him. It's on the tray, and the soup is on the stove. I heard the car coming. Denton always honks at the corner, to let me know he's nearly home.'

'I'll take his supper up and settle the kids down while you welcome your guests, if you like, Livia. Is Chad coming?'

'He said he is. Did you see the caterer's van on your way? They're very late.'

'No . . . they're probably a bit behind seeing as it's New Year, and anyway, they'll be coming from the other direction.'

She left the supper tray on the table outside the master bedroom, rapped on the door to let Denton know it was there and then headed for the children's rooms.

Meggie had her own room. It was a bright shade of sunshine yellow, and had a flaming red quilt on the bed with an orange sunflower. Meggie was not a child who suited pink.

She tucked the boys into bed and kissed their cheeks and then sat on Adam's bed with Meggie snuggled against her. 'Now . . . what will it be?'

'A ghost story, you make up such corkers,' Luke said.

'Not tonight, your mother doesn't want me to give you the willies.'

Luke made a moaning sound and Adam put his head under the blanket, shouting, 'Shut up, Luke, else I'll tell.'

'The owl and the pussy cat,' Esmé said firmly, hoping she could remember the words to the Edward Lear nonsense rhyme.

'The owl and the pussy cat went to sea in a beautiful pea green boat.'

Adam piped up, 'They took some honey and . . . and . . .'

'Plenty of frogs legs and bats wings to eat and they turned green and got seasick all over the boat,' Luke said, hanging his tongue out and making heaving noises.

'They did not.' Adam scowled at his older brother. 'Besides, I did that last time Aunt Es read it. You're a copycat. '

'No I'm not.'

'Yes, you are. Besides, it's a nursery rhyme.'

'And you're both acting like babies.' Meggie sighed. 'Stop arguing at once. *Boys . . . honestly!*' was huffed out in an exasperated sigh. 'Allow Aunt Es to recite it otherwise we'll be here all night. Go on Auntie, and don't let them interrupt. I'll sit on them if they do.'

Issued with her instructions, Esmé started at the beginning again, and by the time she got to, 'they danced by the light of the moon', the boys were nearly asleep.

Kissing them both, she tucked the covers under their chins and walked Meggie through to her bedroom. She looked around for the cat, and found Whiskers in his usual place, asleep in the doll's pram. He was getting old, she thought when he gave a sleepy but irritated 'meow' as Meggie tucked him in.

Both pram and cat had been a gift from Livia's first husband to Esmé. Richard Sangster had bought Chad a dog at the same time. Bertie had died the previous year and they'd buried him in the garden. His place in the family had been taken by the tall, but gentle, black curly-coated retriever called Shadow.

Meggie looked like Livia with her dark hair and eyes, though there was more than a touch of Sangster in her. 'Will you teach me to dance the Charleston tomorrow?'

'I thought I'd taught you that one.'

'You did. But my hands keep getting mixed up with my knees when I do that crossover bit, and I bang them together.'

She laughed and gave her niece a hug and a kiss. 'It is a bit tricky. We'll go through it again tomorrow. Goodnight, Meggie Moo. I love you.'

'I love you too.' Meggie yawned unconvincingly. 'Leave the door open a bit so I can listen to the music on the gramophone. I wanted to attend, but Mummy said I wasn't old

enough, and would have to wait until I was sixteen, but that's
years away. I am old enough, aren't I?'

'Not if your mother says you're not. Stop being such a drama
queen.'

'That's what Daddy said.'

'Then everybody else must be right, except you.'

Meggie gave an offended snort. 'Honestly! Everyone always
sides with Mummy. Just wait until I'm old, like you, I shan't
invite *anyone* to my parties.'

Esmé grinned. 'They'll be quiet parties then, and nobody
would want to attend anyway.'

Her cross patches never lasted long, and Meggie giggled.

Esmé went down, in time to see her brother shedding his
coat. With him was a lanky looking man with a tumble of
dark unruly hair.

Chad hung his coat on the hallstand and beamed a smile at
her. He wasn't very tall, but was handsome with his soft, but
astute brown eyes and wavy hair. 'What-oh, sis! You're a sight
for sore eyes.'

Chad looked tired. 'Have you been burning the candle at
both ends?'

He nodded. 'At least I've graduated with enough marks to
take me into medical school. I've got to keep up with my
studies if I'm to succeed.'

His single-mindedness worried Esmé. 'What if you don't?'

His eyes told her the thought was alien to him, so did the
short huff of impatience he gave. 'You should know me better
than that by now, Es. Failure is not part of my nature. We were
given an opportunity to better ourselves, and it shouldn't be
wasted. We'll never be out of work once our training is over
. . . and from what I hear the depression is going to worsen,
and will dig deep. Not a good time to be unemployed. Be glad
that, despite everything, Livia managed to marry well and didn't
leave us in that home we were in. I shall do the same.'

Despite everything? Married well? It seemed an odd thing
for her brother to say. Esmé sighed and gave him a hug. 'How
mercenary of you, Chad. Livia loved Richard Sangster, that's
why she married him, and she adores Denton. She didn't marry
either of them to enable you to attend medical school.'

'Of course,' he said, colouring a little. 'I didn't mean to suggest anything else.'

'It's a terribly romantic story, and both men were heroes. I shall only marry for love, too. I won't care if he's well-off or not. And I hope you do the same.'

'You will care when you and your brood of children are starving in a backstreet slum, and you're begging on the street and have nobody to turn to.'

'Who's starving in a backstreet slum?'

Esmé turned to see Denton behind her, and wondered how much he'd overheard. 'I am, apparently. I said I wanted to marry for love, and Chad immediately placed me in a slum dwelling with a dozen starving children to support.'

Denton held out a hand to Chad, grinning. 'Welcome home. Don't worry, when Esmé gets into that state we'll rescue her and the dirty dozen. You know, your sister has more sense than you give her credit for, Chad.'

Chad looked slightly dubious, and then gave a small smile. 'If you think so Denton; it depends which sister we're talking about, I suppose?'

Esmé gazed at her twin for a moment, almost dumbstruck. 'You made a joke, Chad. It was a pitiful one, but a joke nevertheless. Congratulations.'

His companion chuckled, a warm rumble. His clothes hung loosely, as if somebody had picked him up, shaken the wrinkles out and hung him back on a hook. She offered him a smile so he wouldn't feel excluded, and he winked at her.

Hah! He was full of so much confidence that she was left feeling ruffled.

'Make the most of it, sis. In the meantime, I'll work on a better joke for next year.'

She laughed, and placed a kiss on his cheek. 'Don't strain yourself, Chad. Now, I'm not standing here in the cold indulging in idle talk all night. You haven't introduced your friend, and I want to join the party.'

'This is Leo Thornton. He's at a loose end and will be off home in a month or so. He's a fairly decent chap so I've brought him home. Leo, meet my sister, Esmé, and my brother-in-law, Denton Elliot.'

A firm handshake was exchanged with Denton and there
was a murmured, but respectful, 'I'm pleased to meet you, sir.
I've heard a lot about you.'

Denton nodded. 'Welcome.'

A pair of vivid blue eyes regarded her from a face that looked
as though it smiled a lot. He gave her a lopsided grin and
drawled, 'G'day, Es . . .'

She blinked.

'Australian,' Chad said, reading her mind. 'Leo lives on a
station.'

'Oh, I see.' Though she didn't see at all. 'That must be quite
noisy with the trains.'

Leo chuckled. 'You'd call it a farm here, I reckon.'

'Oh . . . *that* sort of station. How absolutely wonderful; I've
always wanted to live on a farm. Do you have rabbits?'

'Do we have rabbits? I'll say we have rabbits, hundreds of
the little b—' Chad's quiet cough interrupted and Leo grinned
at him before offering her a smile that was both apologetic
and charming. *'Blighters.'*

A cheer went up as they entered the room and they were
drawn into the partying crowd. Mostly it was the neighbours
who'd been invited, but they had grown-up sons and daughters
who intended to have a good time.

There were also a couple of doctor colleagues and their
wives, and horror of horrors – Matron! In an olive-green dress,
which was only minutely less severe than her uniform, she was
with a tall, thin gentleman who resembled her. Her brother,
Esmé imagined. She couldn't ever remember seeing Matron
without her cap starched rigidly into its severe kite-shape. Her
hair was a pretty, light shade of brown, and curly, as though
it was rebelling against the severity of the rest of her.

She slid Denton an accusing glance and he grinned and
winked at her.

It would be rude to ignore Matron, even if she'd dared to.
She crossed to where they stood and smiled, because she didn't
like feeling at a disadvantage on her home ground. 'Is there
anything I can get for you, Matron?'

'No dear, we're fine. May I introduce my brother, Percival.
He's a headmaster. Percy, this is one of my girls, Nurse Carr.'

Percival looked perfect for the role of headmaster in his round wire-framed glasses. He sported a neatly trimmed salt and pepper moustache and smelled of peppermint cordial. She took the hand he offered, thinking he had a nice smile.

He said, 'Ah yes . . . one of Hilda's best, I'm given to understand.'

Esmé offered Matron a slip of a smile. Compliments were hard to come by from her, so even a second-hand one was worth having.

Matron's glance settled on Esmé's hemline. 'Hmmm . . .' was all she said, and although the younger guests mostly wore their skirts knee length, Esmé felt as though she were naked. She gave a nervous giggle.

'A nurse is only as good as her tutor,' Denton said gallantly, coming from behind to rescue her. She watched Denton wrap the woman around his little finger. 'I'm pleased you could come, Hilda. How pretty you look. You must save me a dance.'

Matron simpered. 'I'm surprised you managed to get away.'

'I couldn't keep a beautiful young woman waiting for me, so I left the patient open on the operating table, and will stitch him up tomorrow after breakfast.'

'Dr Elliot! You wouldn't do such a dreadful thing. I believe you've met my brother.'

'Hello, Percy. How have you been keeping? Es, my love, there was a problem with the caterers being late, and Livia needs a hand setting up the buffet if you wouldn't mind.'

She escaped with relief and headed for the kitchen, where her sister was struggling with plates of this and that. She picked up a soggy water biscuit with a sardine attached and gazed at it. 'Good grief, this fish looks as though it died six months ago. Do you need a hand, Livia?'

Livia snorted and giggled at the same time. 'I'm beginning to think Denton is having a bad influence on you.'

'He's buttering up the matron at the moment, and she's falling for it, hook, line and sinker.'

'Perhaps we should swap him for the sardine then. Talking of butter, there doesn't seem to be enough food to go round. What do you think? I'm sure I ordered more than this, but I can't find the list.'

'I'll make an extra platter of sandwiches to be on the safe side, if you like. So much for hiring caterers to save time.'

'There was a dreadful mix-up. First they delivered the food to Nutting Cottage, and that awful old man sent them to Foxglove House. He knows very well the place is boarded up. Eventually they found us, and delivered, but there was nobody to serve it. Now I've got to try and make it look pretty. I'm sure I ordered some caviar.'

'There's a tin in the larder left over from Christmas. I'll tip it into a glass bowl, and make some toast fingers. Haven't we got some cake doilies in the drawer? We can fancy things up with those?'

Relief came into Livia's eyes. 'Why didn't I think of that?'

'Because you've got yourself in a tizzy.' Esmé took out a dozen eggs and placed them in a pan of water on the stove to boil.

'I'm sure the major did it on purpose because he wasn't invited.'

'Stop talking and let's get on.' Esmé took out a loaf of bread and slid it to her sister. 'Cut it into thin slices and butter it while I prepare the filling.'

'You're being awfully bossy, Es.'

'I know, that's what comes of being a nurse.' Opening a tin of salmon she drained it, mashed it up then spread it on the bread and added some mustard and cress that was growing on damp blotting paper in the larder. One of Meggie's attempts at gardening, she supposed, and hoped it was edible.

She sliced off the crusts and cut the sandwiches into fingers, leaving Livia to arrange them while she investigated the pantry further. The remaining half of the Christmas cake was cut into squares, and a sprig of holly decorated the top.

Livia gazed dubiously at it. 'Perhaps we shouldn't. Holly berries might be poisonous.'

'Only if you eat several at once. Have you invited the old man?'

Livia offered an emphatic, 'Certainly not.'

'I remember old Major Henry as being a nice old man. Why don't you ever invite him? He's Meggie's grandfather, isn't he? One of these days she'll put the two Sangster names together. You know what she's like. She'll want to know why she hasn't been encouraged to socialize with her grandfather.'

'You forget that Denton adopted Meggie when she was a baby. Although she knows who her father is, she thinks of herself as an Elliot. I'll tell her when she's sixteen and old enough to understand things better, that's soon enough.'

'What if she learns of the connection before then . . . from Major Henry himself perhaps?'

Livia smiled. 'If he as much as breathes a word of it I'll turn him out of the cottage, and he'll have nowhere else to go. This conversation is now at an end, Esmé. As I've told you before, it's none of your business. Pass me a sprig of parsley, if you would.'

Amid an atmosphere of slight awkwardness, Livia took the eggs from the stove, plunged them into cold water and began to peel the shells from them. Cutting them in half she laid them on a bed of parsley.

Esmé noticed the exasperation in her sister's eyes. There was more to this than met the eye. She knew it. 'If you ever need someone to talk to in confidence, I'm all grown-up now.'

Livia looked her straight in the eye. 'Then act it. I have Denton to confide in. From the goodness of his heart, he took you and Chad in and treated you as part of our family. You've done well and we're proud of you, but don't think that responsibility has always been easy. Although you're still welcome in our home now you're able to support yourself, I'd like to remind you that you're Meggie's aunt. As such, you have no say in my daughter's upbringing. Is that understood?'

Livia had never been so straightforward with her, or so resentful-sounding. In one fell swoop she'd built a barrier between them, and it hurt like hell. Tears pricked her eyes. Everything Livia had said was true,

Esmé nodded and said into the frosty atmosphere, her voice thick with unshed tears, 'You couldn't have made it clearer, Livia . . . sorry. I wasn't trying to interfere, and you know I'm grateful for all you've done for me. So is Chad.'

They rarely quarrelled, and eventually Livia heaved a sigh. 'I didn't mean it Es. I know you have a special relationship with Meggie . . . you helped her into the world and she adores you.'

'No . . . you were right. I've taken you and Denton for granted. When you took Chad and me out of the orphanage it was like having a mother. Then there was Richard Sangster, who was so wonderful to us while he lived – and then darling Denton, who we adored at first sight, and still do. I'm a selfish pig.'

She was folded in a fierce, brief hug. 'You know you're always welcome here, Es. I don't know what I'd do without you.'

'Yes, you do . . . you have Meggie and the boys to keep you busy.'

There was a brief pause, and then, 'Yes, I do have the boys . . . and Meggie.' Livia arranged the sandwiches on a tray and picked up the plate. 'Come on, let's take this food through into the dining room, else we won't get to eat it until next year.'

As they went out with the trays there was a scuffle at the top of the stairs, and a movement in the shadows.

'Is that you, Meggie?' Livia called, her voice sharpened by the thought that her daughter may have overheard something she shouldn't have.

There was no answer, but after a moment Shadow came down the stairs. He gave a stretch, his chest flattening against the floor in an elegant bow, his back end rearing high in the air. Going to stand by the front door, he gazed expectantly back at them, tail wagging.

'You certainly pick your moments to go outside,' Livia grumbled. 'I'll be back to open the door when I've got rid of this food tray.'

The rug had been rolled up and removed leaving the parquetry floor exposed, which made an ideal surface for dancing on.

The younger people gravitated towards each other and soon the gramophone was going at full blast as they energetically applied themselves to the latest dance tunes from the Jack Payne orchestra, while the older generation sailed more sedately around the floor in matched steps.

Esmé didn't allow Matron's presence to lessen her enjoyment of the party as she lost herself amongst the other swirling short skirts.

Champagne corks popped. Somebody grabbed her hand when a Charleston started, and Leo Thornton rumbled softly into her ear, 'Chad said you're a dab hand at this. Let's give it a go then.'

He was loose-limbed and uninhibited, and soon they had a circle of people round them as they all frantically applied themselves to releasing their pent-up energy. Matron was jiggling around on the outskirts, tittering into her champagne.

It reached a crescendo with a countdown from twenty, and as the clock struck midnight everyone shouted 'Happy New Year!'

Leo's timing was perfect. As the clock finished chiming he took her into his arms and kissed her. Considering he'd hardly spoken to her all evening it was rather a long and intimate kiss, but she enjoyed it.

Then someone came between them. 'Don't keep her all to yourself, Leo.' She parted with the Australian reluctantly, blushing a little when Chad grinned at her and kissed her cheek. 'Be careful of Leo, he's got a way with women,' he said against her ear in a voice loud enough for Leo not to have missed. Esmé had the feeling he was warning Leo, rather than her.

Everyone hugged and kissed each other and welcomed in 1934 with *Auld Lang Syne*.

Esmé wondered what the New Year would bring, apart from the fact that she and Chad would officially become adults. Perhaps she *would* go to Australia with Minnie for a couple of years on a working holiday. If Leo was staying for the weekend, which he probably was, she could ask him about the place.

By the time she returned Chad would be well on his way to becoming a GP. Dr Elliot the elder had promised to employ him during his holidays so he could gain some experience, and Esmé had planned to work for them. She gave a tiny sigh. Oh dear, the future seemed all very dull and safe. She must make sure she never married a doctor, because she was up to the ears in them already. Then, when her eyes met Leo's and he grinned, and winked at her, she thought: Well . . . she could always be persuaded to change her mind if need be.

Six months later, when the air was perfumed with flowers and the country was a choir of summer colours, Esmé's life took an unexpectedly dramatic turn.

Two

Esmé concentrated on the button she was sewing on her blouse, only half listening to Minnie's prattle.

The first half of the year had sped by. As usual, there had been scandalous rumours about the Duke of Windsor and Mrs Simpson. In January over 10,000 people had attended a rally in London, arranged by the Blackshirt, Oswald Mosley. There were scuffles, and violence. More recent news was that several squadrons were to be added to the Royal Air Force, as part of a new defence programme.

'Defence of what?' she asked Denton.

He shrugged. 'There's a lot going on in the world, poppet. It's better to be prepared, in case there's another war.'

Esmé didn't like thinking about war, because she remembered what the last one had done to Richard Sangster.

Having passed her midwifery course, Minnie was doing time in emergency, and bubbling over with gossip of the latest medical mishaps. 'Liam Denison was brought into emergency after he gashed his arm. He's such a nice man, and is the entertainment director on a ship. He was about to audition dancers when he had his accident.' In her usual friendly and open manner Minnie had struck up a conversation with him.

Esmé was more reserved than her friend when she was at work, aware that her behaviour would reflect back on her brother-in-law. She bit through the cotton, murmuring, 'How did he cut his arm?' Not that she was all that interested, since drama wasn't hard to come by in the emergency ward.

'He slipped in some liquid on the bathroom floor, put out his arm to stop himself from falling and it went through a mirror. It took eight stitches, but there was no nerve damage, thank goodness. It's exciting having a dance director in the hospital, even if he is an outpatient.'

'You think having a dance director who loses his sense of balance getting out of the bathtub is exciting? I pity his partner.'

'It could happen to anyone. He's really nice, and handsome; sort of neat and well-muscled, like a greyhound.'

'And here was I, thinking it was his arm you were looking after.' Esmé smiled at Minnie's enthusiasm until Minnie handed his card to her. In embossed blue on white it stated: *Liam Denison. Director of Entertainment. Blue Horizon Line.* There was a drawing of the front end of a ship in the corner.

With studied casualness Minnie said, 'Liam indicated he might be able to get me a job as a children's nurse on board the ship he's on. All it will take is a phone call, since they haven't finished interviewing crew. The ship is called *Horizon Queen.* Isn't that romantic?'

'You'd be on the ship to work, not as a passenger.'

'Yes . . . but we'd get some time off. The ship doesn't sail for eight weeks, which would give us time to work out our notices. He was in Poole auditioning a couple of dancers when he had his accident. He said they weren't suitable. I told him he should audition you. So he's going to.'

'You must be crazy. I'm not a trained dancer. Besides, I've more or less accepted the ward nurse's job here.'

'They can get someone else for that. And you don't have to be a trained dancer because he wants a ballroom dancer. Liam said his partner would have to do a demonstration dance with him, and then teach the dance to the passengers. Just think, Esmé. We could go on a cruise, and end up in Australia. He said being a nurse would be an added bonus since you'd be expected to do other jobs on the ship, such as help out in the doctor's surgery, or the dining room – anywhere you're needed. Do say you'll come Esmé. We've always talked about going to Australia, and this way we'll get our passage paid at the same time.'

Going to Australia was something Minnie had wanted, rather than herself. All the same, the idea had merit. It would be an adventure. It wasn't as though she wouldn't know anyone there, and she smiled when Leo Thornton came to mind.

Caution crept in on her. 'I can't just go off with a man I don't know. My family would be furious.'

'Oh, for goodness sake, Esmé Carr, you do jump to conclusions. You wouldn't be going off with a *man* you'd simply be changing your job. Besides which, I rather fancy this man myself, so hands off.'

So far Esmé never had time to fit a boyfriend into her life. She'd never gone looking for one and assumed it would all just happen one day . . . courtship, love, marriage and family. There had been the occasional approach from a young doctor or a patient, which hadn't been encouraged. Her training had never been disrupted by the emotional pull of falling in love, unlike Minnie, who seemed to fall in love with every other man she met. Her life had been calm in comparison, well, almost.

Boring was a good word to describe it, she thought. Sedate, even. Her stomach was already awash with nerves at the thought of stepping out of her safe little world, and her instinct was to refuse. 'I'll think about it.'

'Not for too long. He's leaving in a day or two. He wants to see you tomorrow if you're interested. It's our day off and I said we'd meet him at the tea dance at Bournemouth Pavilion.'

'You could have asked me first.'

'What better way is there to find out if you can dance? And don't say you've got nothing to wear. Ordinary clothes will do, and you've got that blue suit with the side pleats and scalloped collar.'

There was no harm in going to the tea dance, she thought, since it wouldn't be the first time.

Minnie borrowed one of Esmé's dresses and her spare pair of silk stockings, and off they went, catching the Bournemouth bus from outside the hospital.

It was a warm afternoon, and the pier stretched out into the sparkling sea. Deck chairs littered the sand, and although it was only the beginning of summer, quite a few people paddled with their children or built castles in the sand.

Across the road from the beach, people strolled unhurriedly arm in arm in the gardens, and in the flower-beds the blooms opened their colours to the sun. The stream sparkled as it made its way through the gardens to the sea.

Liam Denison was about twenty-three, with blue eyes. Those

eyes widened and he stared at her for several seconds without saying anything, which was rather disconcerting. The grin he eventually offered her was wry, and slightly self-mocking. 'Miss Esmé Carr, I take it.'

'It's nice to meet you, Mr Denison.'

'Likewise.' His friend was introduced as Eric Blair. Quiet and polite, he had a flop of straight brown hair.

There was a faint sense of familiarity about Liam, as though they'd met before, though Esmé couldn't remember where.

'Have you had any dance training, Miss Carr?'

'I did a year at ballet school when I was thirteen. It was an interest rather than a desire to become a classical dancer. I prefer ballroom dancing. We had lessons at school, but it was more of a free-for-all. Most of my dancing experience comes from family parties and dance halls.'

His sigh had a dismissive sound to it, and Minnie leapt to her defence. 'Esmé can dance really well.'

'So you said. But she's an amateur, and I'll need to judge that for myself. If you don't mind, Miss Carr, I'll ask you to dance with Eric first. I want to see how you move from a spectator point of view. Can you foxtrot?'

He'd chosen the most difficult dance, and she didn't blame him. She could dance it well. But as he'd pointed out, she was an amateur. 'You're throwing me in at the deep end, are you? I know all the dances, including Latin American. Most of the student nurses go to the local dance hall on their night off. However, I don't want to waste your precious time.' She picked up her bag.

'No . . . wait! I'm sorry if I've upset you. It was unintentional.' He shrugged. 'Stay.'

When she placed her bag down on the table, he smiled at her. 'What about tango? I want to choreograph one as a demo dance.'

'I know the basic moves. I love the tango; it's dramatic, and I'd be eager to learn something more advanced.'

'Good. Now, you do realize this is not permanent, don't you? My regular partner is also my fiancée, and she'll be rejoining me in time. We'll have to leave Pam in England, because she's broken her ankle.'

The two men exchanged a glance, and although Esmé wondered why, she said, 'Broken ankles take a while to heal. I hope your fiancée soon improves.'

As soon as the music started, Eric led her out on to the floor. He was good. He kept her in a firm hold as he led her through the foxtrot, so even the most intricate of steps came easily to her.

There was a spattering of applause for the band before they went into a quickstep.

'I think she'll do,' Eric said, leading her back to her seat.

'I told you so,' Minnie said.

Liam nodded. 'So you did, Miss James.'

'I thought I told you to call me Minnie.'

He said easily, 'It's best to keep things on a professional footing. Formality will be expected on board during working hours, and it becomes a habit. We're there to serve the passengers, not to enjoy ourselves.' He turned to Esmé. 'Your footwork and timing isn't bad but you're a bit stiff at the moment. We'll see what your tango is like, Miss Carr.'

'I'm stiff because I haven't danced for a while.' She wondered why she was making excuses to him, when she didn't care if she got the job or not. 'Is your arm up to it?'

'Be careful with it, and follow my lead,' he said, as he took her out on to the floor.

'You should be resting it until the stitches are out,' the nurse in her said, and he smiled. 'I won't tell the doctor if you don't. It's well bandaged, and it's almost healed.'

Once again, her partner's professionalism saw Esmé through, and she appreciated the difference having a good dancing partner made. Liam Denison was sensible enough not to demand anything too dramatic on this occasion. But she forgot her feet when they found the passion in the tango music. Absorbing it she concentrated on the story in the music, and when they finished dancing and he took her back to the table, the other dancers applauded.

She blushed. 'Oh, my goodness.'

Liam grinned. 'You'd better get used to it.'

'You looked as though you were besotted with each other,' Eric said. 'Be careful Pam doesn't see you dancing like that with another woman.'

When Liam laughed, Minnie looked peeved.

There was an interval for tea, when they talked over general things. 'Your dancing needs to improve, but that will come with practice, since you anticipate and follow well. Believe me, you'll be rehearsed until you're perfect, and half-dead from fatigue. You trust me, which is a good thing because you will need to in some of the lifts.'

'I enjoyed dancing with you both.'

'Good. We'll go through the contracts with you.'

'But . . . I haven't had time to decide yet.'

He looked puzzled. 'I thought that was why you were here . . . to be auditioned. I must know now, otherwise I'll have to find somebody else, and quickly. We'll have to rehearse quite a lot before the ship sails.'

'Oh, for goodness sake, don't be such a ninny. For once, do what you want to do, not what your family want you to do.' Minnie dug her in the ribs with her elbow. 'Of course she'll come, won't you, Esmé?'

'If it would put their mind at rest, I'd be quite happy to meet your family,' Liam said. 'When's your next day off?'

'Next Tuesday.'

'Oh, come on, Es. If you won't come, I'm not going either. Say yes, then tell them after.'

She gave in to her friend, realizing she was allowing Minnie to make up her mind for her. 'Yes . . . all right . . . I suppose so. I'll want to read the contract first.'

'You're showing good sense, Miss Carr. Don't forget food and quarters are included.'

The wage was more than she earned at nursing, and like Liam had said, she wouldn't have to pay bed and board, which was a bonus. There was a huge sense of relief as well as a dollop of trepidation . . . for she still had to tell her family.

'You'll need at least three evening gowns and some dance shoes,' Liam said, as her pen hovered over the signature line ready to descend.

Esmé's face fell as she remembered the empty spaces in her wardrobe. As a nurse she had no need for evening gowns. The long uniform dress with its starched collar and cuffs, the black stockings and shoes, were uncomfortable. It would be a relief not to have to wear it. 'If I buy three gowns it will take all of my wages, and I'll probably never wear them again afterwards.'

'We should have taken that into consideration.' Eric smiled. 'There's a shop across town that sells second-hand clothing. They should have something suitable. How about you buy her a gown, Liam? She can buy the others for herself.'

Liam Denison nodded.

It was a small shop front, with dressing rooms behind a curtain at the back, and a room with a sewing machine. Clothes hung on a rack. A woman came forward, a smile on her face. 'Can I be of help?'

Esmé found herself swept along by the excitement of it all, and she was sure she owed a fortune when they'd finished, but the cheapness of the gowns surprised her.

'Well that was a waste of time,' Minnie complained on the bus back to the hospital. 'I didn't even get to dance.'

'It was an audition.'

Minnie looked puzzled for a moment, and then she giggled. 'Didn't you fancy either of them?'

'I think they're both very professional and polite. Liam Denison is a wonderful dancer and I hope to enjoy a good working relationship with him. Besides, he's got a fiancée.' Her forehead wrinkled at the thought that they'd met before, but it was fleeting as well as elusive.

The enormity of what she'd done suddenly hit her. 'Oh Lor! Now I've got to face my family.'

All the same, she was excited. For the first time in her life she'd made an independent decision about her future . . . well *almost* independent, since Minnie had arranged it all and she'd just gone along with it. And, when all was said and done, the cost for the gowns wasn't as high as she'd first imagined it would be, and her wage was much more than she'd earn at the hospital . . . and higher than Minnie's.

That hadn't gone unnoticed by Minnie, who grumbled, 'Why are you getting more than I am, when my job carries much more responsibility?'

'I have to maintain a wardrobe, I suppose. I've already spent a week's wages on clothing.'

Minnie cheered up at that. 'At least we'll have a free company uniform, and the nurse's outfit looks smart with the white dress and the blue company badge and blazer. All we have to do now is hand in our notice and tell our families.' She grinned. 'Mine won't give a damn, but good luck with yours.'

Esmé's face fell. 'Matron first?'

The pair nodded. 'We'll do it together now . . . after you,' Minnie said.

'No, after you, since it was all your idea in the first place.'

Matron let them know in no uncertain terms that she was *not* happy, and the news reached home before Esmé did.

Her sister was furious. 'You've thrown in your job? Are you insane, Esmé? We spent all this time supporting you through your training, and you just walk away from it without giving us another thought.'

'On the contrary, Livia, I gave the family a great deal of thought when making this decision. It's not as if it's for ever, and I'll have my training to fall back on.'

'But a dancer . . . on a ship . . . goodness knows what kind of people you'll be associating with.'

'Passengers who can afford to go on cruises mostly, I expect. I've invited my employer over to meet you.'

'When?'

'Tomorrow afternoon. The dance director is coming to tea with his friend.' She handed over a box. 'I bought a fruit cake for the occasion.'

Livia hardly gave it a glance. 'You could have given me more notice.'

'Oh, you needn't go to any trouble. I'll do everything.'

'It's no trouble,' Livia snapped, then wailed, 'I don't know what Denton will say.'

'He's already had his say. I told him, and I'll tell you. I think the ear bashing he subjected me to was totally unfair.'

'Why didn't he ring and tell me?'

'I asked him not to. This is my business, and I wanted to tell you all myself. I had it all planned in what I thought was a fair order. Matron first, and then Denton, before it got round the hospital and he heard it second-hand, and then you.

'But Matron chewed my ear off, and she went running to

Denton, who did the same to you. Now it's your turn. No doubt you'll ring Chad and he'll have a go at me, too. Well, get it over with because I doubt if you'll have anything new to add. It's become a big drama with everyone feeling slighted. For God's sake, Livia, all I've done is change my job. Didn't you ever change yours?'

'No . . . I was sent from the orphanage to become a maid at Foxglove House, and until I married Richard I worked my fingers to the bone, and my wages went to help look after you and Chad.'

Esmé summoned up some courage. Livia was resorting to emotional blackmail. It wasn't fair, and she wasn't going to stand for it any more. 'It wasn't my fault we were in the orphanage, and it's wrong of you to use it as a lever every time I try to be independent. It's not as if I'm going away for good. Once Liam Denison's dancing partner is able to perform I'll probably take up nursing again. I've got the address of a nursing agency in Australia.'

'But a boat . . . our parents died in a boating accident.'

'It's a ship, not a boat.' Though she tried to stop them, tears damned up in her throat and she choked out. 'You'll be telling me you sacrificed yourself to Richard Sangster in marriage on my behalf next. You didn't, did you?'

It seemed as though the world held its breath. Livia stared at her, face pale and stricken. Over the sound of the clock ticking away the seconds she whispered, 'That's a filthy thing to say. Is that what you think?'

Esmé knew she'd gone too far. 'No . . . God no! Why are we arguing like this over a damned job? I won't take it. I'll stay home, and that will please every one. In time I might be able to repay the debt you seem to think I owe you.'

'You have no home.'

'What are you talking about? Of course I have a home.'

'No, this is my home . . . mine and Denton's.' Tears scalded her sister's cheeks. 'You want independence; it's yours for the taking. I'll need your room, anyway. I think I'm expecting another child in the spring.'

'Oh, Livia . . . I didn't know.' She placed a hand on her sister's arm, only to have it shrugged off.

'Of course you didn't know. I hardly know myself. I'll be going to pick the children up from school soon. After that I'm going shopping. Be gone by the time I get back. You can use the case from the storeroom for your things. And if that fly-by-night and his friend turn up tomorrow, I won't be in.'

'Don't worry; I'll tell them not to bother, in case they disturb your smug little world.'

Livia slammed the front door shut when she left, in fine temper.

'You know you don't mean it, Livia,' she shouted after her.

'I most certainly do.'

As the car drove off Esmé began to cry. She was crushed by the outcome of this argument, weighed down by the heaviness of it on her conscience. God only knew how Livia felt.

Whiskers came down to weave around her ankles. She picked him up and held him, purring against her chest.

'I might not see you again for a while, Whiskers, but Meggie will look after you.'

When she told Minnie of the argument, her friend shrugged. 'Thank goodness I haven't got any relatives telling me what to do . . . well, only my disapproving stepmother, who intends to leave everything my dad provided her with to her own children. She thinks I'm a flighty creature who will come to no good, and she can't wait to get rid of me.' Minnie giggled. 'She could be right.'

'My sister will come round when she cools down,' she told Minnie later.

But Livia didn't. She didn't accept her calls, and Denton took his annual leave. Matron was barely civil to them both and the following few weeks were filled with gloom.

A lump of misery settled in Esmé's stomach.

She went out to Evesham House, but the place was empty, except for the cleaning lady, who told her, 'Mrs Elliot was looking tired and run-down. Her doctor has prescribed an iron tonic, and her husband has taken them off to Cornwall for a week's holiday. I'm giving the place a thorough clean through while they're away. I thought you'd have known, Miss Esmé. You usually go with them on family holidays.'

'Not this time. I'm starting a new job tomorrow. I'll write

my sister a letter while I'm here.' She left a note for Meggie and the boys, as well, promising to send them postcards.

She rang Chad from the nurses' quarters. He was in a hurry, but he gave her the usual lecture. Annoyance flared in her. 'I don't need this, Chad. I just wanted to say goodbye. Wish me luck, would you. I'd like to know there's someone left in the world who actually wishes me well.'

'Of course I do . . . we all do, because we love you. But you can't blame anyone but yourself, since you've put yourself outside of the family.'

It sounded to her as though they were putting her outside.

'You know, Esmé, the least you could have done was let people know of your plans beforehand.'

'I thought I had.'

'But not until you'd decided.'

'It happened too quickly. I was offered the job and had to make a decision right away. You do see that, don't you Chad?'

'If you can make your mind up that fast, you can change it just as easily.'

'I've signed a contract. Besides which, I don't want to change my mind.'

'Dancing . . . who would have thought.' He sighed. 'At least you've got a worthwhile career to fall back on . . . something the family needn't feel ashamed of.'

'Ashamed, why should they be? Anyone would think I was going off to become a Parisian cancan dancer.'

'You're not, are you?'

He sounded so horrified that she gave a short huff of laughter. Or was it a sob? She was so choked up she couldn't tell the difference. 'You know, Chad, you're an awful snob at times. What's wrong with being a cancan dancer anyway? Sometimes you forget we were raised mostly in an orphanage.'

'No, Es, I'll never forget that. I hope never to experience that sort of poverty again. Which reminds me . . . do you have enough money? I haven't spent any of last month's allowance yet, and you can have that if you like. It will be something to fall back on if you need it.'

And just as she'd decided to dislike her brother, Esmé thought. 'That's kind of you, Chad, but I have my wages and some savings, enough for my fare home. Besides, there's nowhere on a ship to spend money, and my board is provided.' She sniffed back her tears.

'Don't cry, Es. I'm a born worrier, and so is Livia. As for the orphanage . . . we may have been raised there, but by her actions Livia raised us above it. She'll come around eventually.'

Esmé sensed another talking-to on the way and interrupted, 'Well, I mustn't keep you from your lecture. Goodbye, Chad.'

'Good luck, sis. I know you think I'm a stick-in-the-mud, and I am. But I envy you your courage in doing this. Let me know where you are now and again so I won't worry. And be careful that friend of yours doesn't lead you astray. She's got a flighty way with her.'

'So has your friend . . . Leo, his name was, as I recall.'

'He thought you were the cat's whiskers.'

'He has good taste, then. Goodbye, Chad. Be good.'

'I haven't got time to be anything else,' he said gloomily.

Tears trickled down her cheeks.

'For goodness sake, will you stop weeping. It's not as though we're going for good,' Minnie said, when Esmé got back to the room. 'Let's get packed.'

At the last minute Matron turned up. Her glance fell on the suitcases and her lips pursed. 'I can't say I'm pleased to lose two of my best nurses, but good luck to the pair of you. Nurse Carr, Dr Elliot asked me to give you this before you left.' She placed an envelope in Esmé's hand and kissed them both on the cheek. 'Off you go then, girls; the bus will be along in a minute, and you'll miss the train if you're not careful. Remember to be polite, modest and good, at all times.'

'Yes, Matron, thank you, Matron,' they said together out of habit as she marched away.

Minnie stuck out a tongue at the matron's retreating back, and then gave Esmé a wide smile. 'No more of *her* lectures . . . Ship ahoy, my hearty!'

Esmé didn't open the envelope until they were on the train, and pulled out a wad of five pound notes. Minnie whistled as she counted it.

Esmé dear,

I couldn't let you go off without wishing you luck. It was selfish of us to try and prevent you from running your life as you see fit. Don't take Livia's rejection to heart. She loves you dearly, as do we all, and I know she'll come to regret the argument between you.

Take care of yourself and come back safely. The money is a gift in case you need something to fall back on.

Bon voyage, poppet.

Denton

Livia hadn't forgiven her yet, that was obvious, but her sister had a stubborn streak. In the heat of the moment they had said things to each other that would have been better left unspoken, but Livia would come round eventually.

Minnie rolled her eyes when Esmé began to cry all over again.

Three

The novelty of being at sea soon wore off. By the end of the first week every bone and muscle in Esmé's body ached.

'Working my passage isn't worth the effort,' she said, groaning as she bent to spread salve on her feet. 'The next five weeks are going to be hell. If we'd paid our fare we could be on the receiving end of the service instead of providing it.'

'All right for those with money to spare, I suppose. I didn't have wealthy relatives to fall back on.'

'They're not wealthy, just . . . *comfortable*, I suppose. They're like everyone else. My brother-in-law works for a living, and he works long hours.' She winced as her probing finger found a new blister on her heel and a rough patch on the joint of her big toe. 'Dash it all, I've got a callus, and it will ruin my stockings.' So much for the glamorous life of being a dancer, she thought.

'You'd better get used to them. At least you haven't been seasick, like me. Now I know how pregnant women feel.'

Esmé watched as Minnie applied her make-up. 'Aren't you going to bed?'

'No . . . six of us are going to have a drink and play cards with Wally. He says I bring him luck.'

'He probably says that to all women. You should be careful of him, Minnie. He's a heartbreaker. That charm he displays strikes me as too practised and insincere. How are you going to get six of you in one of these little cabins?'

Minnie sighed. 'We'll use one of the benches in the galley. Are you jealous, then?'

'Jealous of what?'

Minnie shrugged. 'Because I make friends easily, I suppose. You don't join in anything, but keep yourself to yourself. Then you criticize the people I befriend when I try to enjoy myself. You're welcome to join us, you know.'

'All I've ever said is that you should be careful of Wally.'

'Is it because he's an Australian?'

Leo Thornton came into her mind and she smiled. He was an Australian, and she'd liked him a lot. He'd been so friendly and open. 'Why should that bother me?'

'Wally thinks you're a bit of a snob.'

'Who cares what he thinks? I've heard he's a womanizer, and I just don't want you to be hurt, that's all.'

'I like him, Esmé. I like him a lot. He told me he's inherited a sheep station in the country, and he might move there, settle down and prospect for gold. I'm hoping he'll ask me to go with him.'

Oh Lor, she hadn't considered that the flirty Minnie might have fallen for him. 'I'm sorry. I didn't mean to upset you. And of course I'm not jealous of your ability to make friends. Why should I be?'

'Because I attract men and you don't . . . you can be reserved, and that keeps people at arm's length. It must be your upbringing. You'll end up the very image of Matron if you're not careful.'

'I doubt if Matron would ever dance in a ship's salon, do you?'

'I'm surprised that you lowered yourself enough to, with your background.'

Minnie had forgotten it had been all her idea. Esmé didn't want to argue with her. She gave a light laugh when she thought of the orphanage, something she kept to herself. Not because she was ashamed, but rather, it was something she'd rather forget.

'I wish I had *time* to make friends. I work split shifts. Liam Denison keeps me busy rehearsing when I'm not setting tables, and I'm lucky if I get five hours off in the afternoon. Then I have to socialize with the guests every evening, and the men tread all over my feet. By the time bedtime comes I ache all over and all I want to do is sleep.'

'You should try saying no. The pair of them use you up, and you're allowing them to. You're getting thin from all that exercise you do. If I were you, I'd complain.'

Peeved, because she thought she'd left such advice behind, Esmé offered Minnie a dirty look. 'You're not me. I like being kept busy . . . and I like Liam.' She liked him because he kept his distance . . . too much distance sometimes. She didn't know what to do about the feelings she had towards him, or whether it was simply their close bodily contact. There was something remote about him and she certainly wouldn't act on Minnie's advice.

'Pardon me for interfering,' Minnie said. 'Do I look all right?'

'You look perfect . . . that's a pretty dress.'

'It's yours, and I borrowed it, as you very well know. Stop being so sarcastic.'

The casual statement was too much and Esmé glared at her as she climbed into the top bunk. 'Yes, I know. Have you ever thought of asking me before borrowing something?'

'You've never minded before . . . besides, you were nowhere to be found.'

'I expect I was eating my dinner; and I have minded before – I just didn't say so. Turn the light off when you leave, and try not to wake me up when you return, please.'

'Oh, do shut up Es, you always get ratty with me when the curse is due,' Minnie muttered, loud enough for Esmé to hear. The door shut with a definite thud.

Sighing, Esmé hung out of the bunk and clicked the switch, plunging the cabin into darkness. She didn't want to argue with Minnie, and felt guilty for being mean to her, but sometimes she overstretched the bounds of their friendship.

Minnie was untidy . . . she left her clothes where she dropped them, and worse, left Esmé's clothes where she dropped them, too. She felt as though she spent half her life picking up after her friend. Minnie was right though, the monthly curse was due.

She lay for a while, listening to the engines pushing the ship through the water. The crew's quarters were situated near the stern. Their cabin was smaller than the room they'd shared in nurses' quarters.

The sound of her heartbeat pounded loudly, as though its pulse had adjusted to the sound of the engines and was helping to drive the ship forward, instead of being the engine designed to power her body.

It must feel like this to be in the womb, she thought – or a tomb perhaps. Both reminded her of parents she couldn't remember, who'd died in a boating accident when she and Chad were only two years old.

She wished there was a window, but they were below the waterline. The air being pumped through the vents was warm and slightly moist. Her bunk was an arm's length from the deck-head, so she could reach up and touch it. Sometimes she felt claustrophobic, and longed for a window so she could allow a cool, fresh breeze to blow inside. Turning on to her side she gazed at the thin line of light under the door, which was the only way out of the small dark space that pressed in on her. She wished she hadn't come on this voyage, which seemed never-ending.

During the night she thought she heard stealthy sounds, as though Minnie had returned and was trying not to make a noise.

'Don't turn the light on,' she murmured. The next moment the door closed with a faint click. She tossed and turned, waking the next morning to find that Minnie's bunk hadn't been slept in.

Esmé showered and dressed then tidied the cabin. Her suitcase had slid partly out from under the lower bunk. She'd just finished straightening it up when the door was flung open and Minnie came in. She was still in Esmé's dress, and her hair was in a tangle.

'Where have you been all night?'

Minnie avoided her eyes. 'Since when were you my mother?' She opened her locker and began to toss clothes on to the bed, eventually murmuring, 'Where do you think I've been . . . with Wally.'

Shocked, Esmé stared at her. 'You've only known him for a few days.'

'So what? He's fun.'

'Aren't you going to get a shower?' she managed to stammer out, as Minnie dragged her dress off and threw it to her.

'I haven't got time. I overslept. Thanks for the loan. It will need washing; I spilled something on it, and the seam came undone under the armpit.'

The something was brown, greasy, and smeared; as though Minnie had spread the stain trying to wipe it off. It was at the neckline, so she'd be able to sew an artificial flower over it if she couldn't get the stain out. But she would have to sponge the perspiration with white vinegar and wash it before she tried to repair it. Perhaps the woman who worked in the laundry would allow her to use the sewing machine. The armpit seam had frayed, and was damp with perspiration.

Resentment bit her. 'Why don't *you* repair it?'

'I don't have time. If I'm late for work, that shrew in charge will chew my ear off. She's worse than Matron ever was.' Snatching up the company uniform Minnie hurriedly donned it and pulled a comb through the knots in her hair.

She caught Esmé's eyes, and then giggled. 'Oh, don't look so shocked, Es, I was only joking. Nothing happened, though that's not to say he didn't try. I told him I had the curse, and then some of us went to his cabin with a bottle of wine. I fell asleep, and everyone was gone when I woke, including Wally.'

'Be careful. We still have five weeks to go, and you don't want to get yourself into trouble.'

'Oh, don't worry. If Wally wants me, he'll have to put a ring on my finger first.'

'And would you marry him?'

'I might,' she said casually. 'He's quite well off. His parents own a hotel. And he inherited a sheep farm from his uncle.'

Minnie wasn't usually so mercenary. Why was Wally working on a ship instead of tending to his sheep? Esmé thought, then realized she was as guilty of interfering in Minnie's life as she'd accused her friend of being in hers. She sighed. 'Let's not quarrel.'

'It's this damned cabin. It's too small and stuffy. I heard a rumour last night. They say the ship isn't paying her way and she's going to be laid up. The crew will be paid off when we reach Australia.'

'We have lots of passengers.'

'Only booked on the outward run. Many of those in the economy section are migrants, and they cram them in. Anyone would think they're in first class, the way they order you around. And they rarely tip.'

Esmé didn't comment. She and Liam danced for passengers of every class, and they were mostly nice people, nothing like Minnie's experience.

Esmé left her dress with Betty Jones, the obliging laundry woman. Given an experimental, but gentle tug, the seam frayed even more. 'I'll see to it, love. The sleeve seam will never hold. I could take the sleeves out. With you being a dancer and all, it could be your Charleston dress. It would be a shame to waste it.'

'Thanks, Betty. I'm really a nurse by profession. This is a sort of working holiday.'

'I can't say I blame you. The way the world is going, it's best to have a job you can fall back on. There's always work for nurses.'

The Depression hadn't had much effect on Esmé so far. She knew there was one, but had been shielded from it by her family, and their expectations that she'd carve out a meaningful career for herself. They had been right.

Esmé asked Liam Denison about the rumour later that morning.

He smiled. 'The same rumour happens every time we sail.'

She shrugged. 'I only came to keep Minnie company. She wants to stay in Australia for a while, but being alone without family scares me. This way we can see Australia first.'

He laughed. 'It's too big a country to see in one hit. I expect the company would employ you permanently if you wanted to come and go. I'm not sure about Minnie. The nurse in charge doesn't like her. She thinks Minnie has the wrong attitude.'

'We went through training together. She's a good nurse who is highly qualified, but she doesn't take to authority kindly. She needs to be in charge herself.'

Liam nodded. 'Let me know what you intend to do. I don't want to lose you as a partner, and believe me, your body will soon get used to the exercise. It didn't take long for the stars to fall from your eyes.'

'I don't think I had any illusions. Though you've worked me harder than I expected.'

'You needed it. Do you have a job lined up in Australia?'

'I have the name of a nursing agency to contact.' She wouldn't stay in England and leave Minnie to fend for herself, if Minnie decided she wanted to stay in Australia for a while. Her friend was full of ideas, but she didn't think of what might lie ahead in the future. 'I believe there's work available for nurses.'

'I wouldn't count on it, love. There's a depression on. Do you have a place to stay, and savings to fall back on?'

He sounded concerned, and she smiled at him. 'I expect we can find somewhere cheap to board until we find work.' She remembered the money Denton had given her, now hidden inside the toe of a silk stocking in her suitcase. She wasn't going to tell anybody that there was over one hundred pounds in her suitcase – enough for the fare home for both Minnie and herself if things went wrong.

'There are a fair few first class passengers on board, so there will be tips to divide between us, as well. That includes the band and the singer, of course.' Unexpectedly, he took hold of her hands, 'You look pale, are you up to it today?'

She nodded. 'I've got a bit of a headache, and didn't have time for breakfast.'

'Well, make sure you get some lunch.' He took a bottle of aspirin from his coat pocket and shook two pills into her palm, following it up with a glass of water from the jug they kept at hand. 'Right, let's get on now. We'll practise that rumba I taught you the other day. You need to get a bit more of a rolling motion into your body. This is a dance of lovers. The female is a temptress, teasing the man with her body. Pretend I'm Adam and you're the snake.'

The more they danced the more aware of Liam she became. His body was a warm sinuous column she twisted around. He took her hips in his hands and drew her close against him.

It didn't take much to imagine she was teasing him. She loved dancing with him, and melted against him, forgetting everything, and fighting off her inclination to move against him. Although well aware of the working of the human body, she'd never been so physically close to a man before . . . never experienced the raw need and the physical fusion of body and mind.

They rehearsed for two hours, and then Eric came in to remind her it was time to help set the tables.

'Can you manage without her today, Eric? Esmé needs some fresh air, so I thought I'd take her for a stroll round the deck, then she can have the afternoon off to catch up on her personal chores before the show tonight.'

'I told you we were working her too hard.'

'So you did.'

The fresh air was a wonderful tonic. The sea was a moving carpet of dark blue, stretching to a paler horizon where it met the sky. The ship's wake was a frothy track fading into the distance. Several of the passengers were up and about. An exercise class was going on. People sat in deckchairs, soaking up the sun, and they smiled and nodded to them as they strolled.

How odd that they were a small floating island in such a large, moving mass of water.

The day felt different from the ones that had gone before, as if she'd left the nurse in her behind and had settled into her new career as an entertainer. She could almost see her name up in lights, which was odd, because she'd never been that ambitious.

Liam glanced down at her, smiled and linked hands. 'I don't think we need to rehearse quite so hard now. Take half an hour to come up on deck every day, else you'll begin to feel as though you're in prison. The captain doesn't mind if the entertainers socialize with the passengers . . . unless we get too close. And they don't like the staff forming relationships when they're on board, either. For her own good, perhaps you should remind your friend of that.'

She looked down at their linked hands. 'Perhaps I should remind you that you have a fiancée with a sprained ankle to go home to . . . Jane, isn't it?'

He chuckled. 'I told you Jane had a broken ankle, not a sprain.'

'You also told me her name was Pamela. Why the deceit?'

He didn't deny it. 'I didn't want any romantic complications from you, or any complications with that friend of yours, especially. And in case we hadn't worked out as dancing partners, having a fiancée recovering from a broken ankle would have given me an excuse to let you go.'

She laughed. 'I hadn't realized you were quite so devious. I'm contracted for the one return journey. I doubt if I'll fall in love with you in that time,' she said, imagining she might get over this schoolgirl-ish crush she had on him by the time they got home, for she certainly wasn't in love. 'As for dancing . . . are we compatible?'

'What do you think?'

'I think you're the best ballroom partner I've ever danced with, and you make me look like a better dancer than I am. You can let go of my hands now.'

He released her, and gazing through slightly-hooded blue eyes that reminded her of Meggie's, said, 'You're better than average, and you have good legs. What if I told you I'd like our relationship to go further?'

'Are you telling me that?'

'Yes . . . I think I am. I like you a lot, despite your hands-off manner. You're fire and ice, Esmé. You have a passionate heart beating inside you.'

'You said you didn't want any complications.'

'I was wrong. Since I met you I've discovered that I do.'

'We haven't known each other for five minutes,' she said, then admitted, 'I enjoy dancing with you, and I'm aware of the tension that such close proximity creates. What happened to your last partner? I take it you had one.'

'She met someone and got married. That's why I was in Poole, for her wedding, and to audition someone to take her place. I think we can relax a bit when we're together now. You can call me Liam, if you like.'

'I'd prefer to keep our partnership a working one. It's hypocritical of you to question my friend's morals, while on the other hand, expecting me to loosen my own. I don't want to become anyone's lover, however attractive they are.'

He grinned at that. 'I was referring to your friend's gambling habits. Wally's a con man. She's trying to impress him. He'll fleece her of everything she's got, and then ditch her. I hear he's jumping ship when we get to Australia.'

She sighed, saying practically, 'Poor Minnie . . . she hasn't got much of her own so it shouldn't take long.'

'As for you becoming my lover . . .' Laughter spilled from his mouth, but it was uncertain.

'What's so funny about it?' she snapped, her headache forgotten.

'You know more about me than you think, and you've got it all wrong. I have no interest in entering a casual relationship. I'm making plans for my future.'

Another person wanting to run her life, was her first thought, but the sigh she gave was almost inaudible. 'What are these plans?'

'I haven't thought them through properly yet . . .' He cleared his throat. 'The thing is, Esmé, I'd rather like you to become my wife in the future . . . I think.'

Arrows darted about in her stomach at this unexpected development, and there was a small, yawing sensation in the pit of her stomach. Was she ready to take such a step? 'I hardly know you.'

'We could easily change that.' In the shadow of the lifeboat he inclined his head and gently kissed her mouth. It was a chaste sort of kiss, as though he'd plucked one from a jar labelled 'sterile'. But then, she hadn't had much practice at kissing.

'I need time to consider,' she said, surprised beyond measure to think Liam might have deeper feelings for her than he'd let on. So far he'd displayed himself as a pale shadow of George du Maurier's Svengali.

Her own feelings were ambivalent. She was certainly attracted to him physically, and had been from the start of their working relationship. But now he was attainable her instinct screamed caution.

'I wouldn't expect anything less.'

He kissed her again, then he turned and walked away, leaving her bereft of breath and lost for words. Her hand went to her mouth and she gave a little smile, wishing Livia were there to talk to. Her sister would surely have forgiven her by now.

Four

The house was quiet except for the tick of the clock, the occasional hiss and snap as a knob of coal flared in the kitchen stove, and Meggie's snuffled breathing, for she was recovering from a cold.

Her mother and brothers were out walking Shadow. Meggie had watched the cleaning lady leave and had thought about what she intended to do as she set the kitchen table for tea with buttered buns and some fruit cake. They wouldn't be back yet.

The argument she had with her conscience didn't last long, but still she felt guilty as she went through to her stepfather's study. It was cold in there after the warmth of the kitchen, and a shiver ran through her body.

The key to the bureau was in the lock, though her stepfather hadn't bothered to lock it. The document box itself was on a table. It glowed within the inner fires of the various wood used in its creation, and the intricate design of inserted veneer plums, grapes and pears attached to a twisting vine. Her mother, enthralled by its beauty, had placed the winning bid for it at the church fête, against spirited opposition. She had given it to her stepfather for his birthday.

The box was locked, but the key was kept in the bureau. Finding it, she opened the box and gazed at the papers inside. They were filed in alphabetical order.

She pulled out an envelope marked certificates, and found her birth certificate. She'd been born in Nutting Cottage and named after her two grandmothers. Margaret Eloise Sinclair Sangster. It was a grand name, but she couldn't remember being called anything but Meggie Elliot. *Mother, Olivia Sangster (Widow). Father. Richard Sangster. (Deceased).*

Denton Elliot had adopted her.

There were other certificates, birth, marriage and death. Richard Sangster's father was Henry Sangster; his mother had been called Margaret Sinclair, before her marriage. They'd lived in Foxglove House on the other side of the village; the big house that was boarded up. Her real father had been born there.

Was Major Henry Sangster, who lived in Nutting Cottage, her grandfather? She wondered about it. He must be, though her mother wouldn't have anything to do with him. If he was mentioned she changed the subject, or pretended she hadn't heard.

Aunt Esmé had referred to him as Meggie's grandfather at the last New Year party. The sisters had been talking in the kitchen, and her mother had told her aunt to mind her own business.

There was a noise out in the hall and she froze. She'd be in trouble if she were caught. Heart thumping in alarm, she quickly replaced the documents, locked the case and replaced the key in the bureau.

It was a cold, grey day and drizzle drifted across the sky. She hoped her mother had taken the umbrella. As she straightened, a glance out the window showed the postman disappearing through the gate. Relieved, she left the study and closed the door behind her. She hadn't learned anything more than she'd already been aware of. She was curious to know why she had always been discouraged from seeing her own grandfather. But there was always another day.

In the hall the family umbrellas jostled for position with several walking sticks in the vaguely oriental, and very ugly green and orange glazed pot her mother had bought at some jumble sale. The sticks had come with the pot, and her mother said they belonged together. Somehow, the pot and its contents suited the house.

There were letters in the wire basket . . . three of them postcards from Esmé. Meggie's had tourists in pith helmets riding on donkeys in Suez. There were camels on the two for the boys, with impossibly arched necks and their noses in the air as they gazed at the camera with disdainful expressions.

'Superior creatures,' she murmured, and read the messages

as she went to the kitchen to put some milk on to warm. She placed the postcards on the dresser. It was the usual tourist stuff designed for a stranger's eyes to consume.

The letter got a thorough scrutiny from her. It was addressed to Major Sangster at Foxglove House. Her stepfather usually dealt with the mail destined for there. Often, they were bills of some sort. She'd never wondered why he paid Foxglove House bills before. Now she did. The letter had an American stamp and a faint smell of perfume lingering about it. It would give her an excuse to visit him.

Her mother would punish her if she found out, though. The squirm she experienced at the thought was swallowed by her sense of adventure and curiosity. A lecture couldn't hurt her, she supposed.

Meggie's thoughts were interrupted when Shadow gave a deep-throated woof from outside. Guiltily she slid the letter for the major in to her pocket. She poured the milk into two glasses and stirred. Boys and dog came rushing through the door, Shadow to slurp noisily at the water bowl, and the boys reaching for their mugs of Ovaltine.

'Where's Mummy?' she said.

They gazed at her, their cheeks glowing from the exercise, their upper lips decorated with milky foam. 'Mummy got a bit puffed out and is resting on the tree stump. She told us to go on.'

That was a five-minute walk away. 'I'll take her an umbrella. Don't eat all the buns while I'm gone, and be careful Shadow doesn't steal any. There are some postcards from Aunt Es for you on the dresser.'

'Wizard!' Luke said as she left.

Her mother had made progress, and wasn't too far from the gate. She looked as pale as a sheet, and Meggie's heart lurched.

'What is it, Mummy?'

'Something's wrong . . . I'm bleeding, and I felt a bit dizzy. I didn't want to scare the boys.'

'Bleeding . . . have you cut yourself?'

'No, love . . . it's coming from inside me. I think I'm losing the baby.'

Panic flickered at her, but she managed to control it for her mother's sake. 'I see . . . are you sure it's not one of those monthly period things you told me about?' She'd not experienced one yet herself, but her friend Susan had, and it had sounded horridly messy.

'Yes, I'm sure. They stop coming when you are expecting a baby. That's how you know you're having one, you see.'

Meggie didn't really see. She knew nothing about babies except they grew inside a woman's tummy and made her look rather an odd shape. How inconvenient having that big bulge at the front must be. She had no idea of how babies got out. Her friend at school said they came out through the mother's belly button, to which Meggie had scorned, 'That's silly. Boys have got belly buttons, and they don't have babies.'

Come to think of it, she didn't know how babies got in there in the first place. It was all so intriguing, but now was not the time to ask her mother, who had a small trickle of watery blood running down her leg into her shoe.

'As soon as we're indoors I'm going to lie down on the couch. Fetch me some towels, a flannel and a bowl of warm water. Then go upstairs and get me those sanitary napkins I showed you. They're in my dressing table drawer. But first, I want you to phone your grandfather. Tell him what's happened and ask him to come out.'

'What about Daddy?'

'We'll let his father call him, if need be. They understand each other's language.' Her mother's fingers brushed against her cheek. 'Don't you worry, Meggie Moo. Everything will be all right. I just wish Esmé were here. She was always so calm and capable, even when she was your age. She helped me give birth to you when she was only twelve.'

There was a twinge of resentment at her mother's use of the pet name. That was her aunt's name for her. Meggie had overheard her mother telling her father of the argument they'd had before her aunt left. Her mother said she'd been angry and upset, and had driven Aunt Esmé away. Maggie hoped she'd come back because she missed her.

The drama surrounding her own birth was something Meggie was well aware of, and because of it she had a strong sense of kinship with her aunt. It was closer than the bond she had with her mother. Sometimes, she caught her mother looking at her as if she were a stranger to her, and wondered what she was thinking. Now, her thoughtless words made Meggie feel as if she wasn't capable. After all, any fool could use a telephone.

Knowing this was not the time to upset her mother, she did what she was directed to do. Summoning the doctor, she fetched the bits and pieces her mother needed to clean herself up with. She didn't like seeing the blood; it made her feel queasy. She didn't think she'd like to be a nurse when she grew up, like her aunt.

She thought that she'd rather like to be a famous writer, like Agatha Christie. Her mind went to a summer house in a cottage garden. The air was balmy and dandelion seeds floated through the air. In her imagination, Meggie inserted a piece of paper into the typewriter and picked out on the keys, *Death by Dandelion Wine*. Speeding up, the machine clacked words at a fast rate on to the page and paper began to fly from it. Two seconds later she wrote: *The End*. She ripped the paper from the machine, placed it on top of the manuscript, and then smiled. Imagination was a wonderful thing. Perhaps she'd write a letter to Agatha Christie and ask her what came next.

'Stop daydreaming and empty the water on the garden, please, Meggie, and then put that towel and flannel to soak in cold water while we're waiting.'

The dandelion seeds dispersed, along with the typewriter and manuscript. Perhaps it would be better if she learned how to type before she tackled a novel.

When she came back from her task, she asked her mother, 'Would you like some tea and a buttered bun . . .? That's if the boys haven't eaten them all. They were as ravenous as wolverines in winter.'

Her mother gave a bit of a high-pitched giggle and bit her lip. 'I'd better not. Have you packed my bag in case I need it?'

'I'll do that when the doctor arrives. He shouldn't be long now.'

The doctor arrived within ten minutes. His wife, Helen, came with him. Suddenly superfluous, Meggie was sent from the room to keep her brothers amused.

They were amusing themselves, oblivious of the drama taking

place downstairs, and playing marbles accompanied by various boy noises and protests of, 'That's not fair, it was my turn.'

'Try and be a bit quieter. Mummy isn't well and your grandfather has come out to see her.'

They looked up from their game, the expression in their eyes more alert than alarmed as they searched her face for clues.

'I'm sure she'll be all right. Stay here out the way. I expect Grandma Elliot will stay and look after us till Daddy comes home.'

They relaxed and went back to their game, believing her because she was older, and because they didn't want the insecurity of worrying about their mother's health.

She went through to her parents' room, and laid out all the things her mother had told her to. Spare nightwear and underwear, toiletries and slippers – where were the handkerchiefs kept? *The Sittaford Mystery* by Agatha Christie was next on the list. Her mother had received the book for a Christmas present, and had kept it for her lying-in time with the new baby. It was on a shelf in the wardrobe.

Only now there might not be a lying-in, and her mother would be terribly sad if something bad happened to the baby. Meggie wouldn't know how to comfort her, for they'd never had the ease of physical closeness that her mother enjoyed with the boys, and besides, she never knew what to say when other people became emotional.

The handkerchiefs were in the other dressing table drawer. As she lifted them, a photograph was revealed underneath. It was Richard Sangster. Her father was tall and handsome in an army uniform, his cap tucked beneath his arm. Her stepfather stood beside him, equally handsome and slightly taller.

She gazed at Richard Sangster, taking in his direct gaze, his smile and his fair curls. His smile was like sunshine, and there was a little stirring feeling inside her. Why couldn't it have been Denton Elliot who'd died, and Richard Sangster who'd lived?

Immediately she felt guilty. She adored her stepfather. Gently, she kissed the images of both men and put the photograph back.

Helen Elliot was waiting at the bottom of the stairs. She

looked harassed as she took the items from her. 'Goodness, girl, I was just about to come looking for you. Stop dawdling now; go and wait at the crossroads for the ambulance to come, in case they take the wrong turning.'

'Will my mother be all right?'

'Well there's a silly question; how would I know? We'll just have to wait and see.' Her expression softened. 'Try not to worry, dear. It won't help.'

'Who will look after Adam and Luke?'

'I'll stay here until their father comes home.'

'I can get the dinner ready if you like,' Meggie offered, determined to be helpful, because after all, she was nearly grown up. 'We're having beef casserole and dumplings. The casserole just needs warming through with the dumplings on top. There are carrots and sprouts, and I can boil some potatoes and mash them.'

'Goodness, you are little miss efficiency, but let's get our priorities right. Off you go now to keep a lookout for that ambulance. We'll worry about dinner later.'

Meggie's face heated. Grandmother Elliot was good at using sarcasm to dilute a compliment. She didn't like her much. But then, she wasn't her real, flesh and blood grandmother.

And later, Helen took over the dinner, and then reorganized the kitchen to her liking, cleaning the shelves and tut-tutting over the task.

'You needn't do that,' Meggie said. 'You're puffing yourself out, and Mummy always leaves it to the cleaning lady.'

Helen awarded her observation with a frown, and a terse, 'As I see. My son was brought up in a clean home, young lady, and I'll be the judge of whether or not I'm . . . how did you put it . . . puffed out.'

Their father didn't come home for dinner, and the boys were so worried they ate their sprouts and carrots without complaint. Meggie told them a story about angels, to prepare them in case their mother died.

Afterwards, she helped her brothers say their prayers, which would save her having to say her own separately, later on. 'Bring Mummy and the baby home to us safely,' she prayed, her eyes teary.

The boys started to sniffle.

'Amen,' she said loudly, and they copied her. Because she felt holy at that moment, she thought she might become a nun when she grew up. Remembering the sober black robes they wore, the next second she abandoned the idea.

When she went down Grandmother Elliot was asleep in a chair.

Making her a cup of tea, Meggie served it with a slice of Madeira cake.

Grandmother Elliot woke with a start. Her fuddled glance fell on the tea. 'Thank you, dear. Are the boys asleep?'

'Yes.'

The telephone in the hall rang.

'I expect it's your stepfather.' Grandmother Elliot was the only person who referred to him that way, at least, to her face. 'I'll get it, dear.'

'Denton . . . is everything all right?'

'I see . . . yes, the boys are organized and settled down in bed . . . Meggie is still up. No, it was no trouble. Would you like to speak to the girl?'

Meggie nearly tripped over the edge of the carpet getting to the phone. 'Hello Daddy, is everything all right?'

'It's bad news, I'm afraid, Meggie love. Your mother has lost the baby. He was too small to survive.'

So, she would have had another brother. It was sad that he hadn't survived, but she hadn't seen him as a person so he didn't seem quite real to her. 'And Mummy? What about her . . . she's not going to die, is she?'

'Good Lord no.'

An image appeared in Meggie's mind of the three of them standing round Mother's grave with their father. Their mother flew overhead in floating, filmy white garments. She had a spread of luminous wings and her hand clasped the podgy fist of a cherub. As a final touch, her imagination placed a golden trumpet in her mother's mouth, so she could blow a fanfare to order St Peter to open the gates to heaven – if he happened to be on gate duty. On second thoughts she removed the trumpet. Her mother wasn't very musical.

Meggie didn't want her mother to go to heaven yet, so she

stopped that train of thought and concentrated on what her stepfather was saying.

'Mummy's a bit tired and sad, but she'll be all right in a day or two, and should be home in about a week if all goes well. I won't be home tonight. Can you manage?'

'Yes . . . Grandmother Elliot is here. I'll make the bed up in Aunt Esmé's room for her, and put a hot water bottle in the bed to warm it. Give Mummy my love, and from the boys, as well. They've been really soppy, but ever so good.'

'Tell them, well done. Goodnight, sweetheart. Sleep tight.'

'Goodnight, Daddy. I'll do my best to be helpful.'

She made the bed, filled a hot water bottle and found a nightgown for Grandmother Elliot to wear.

The woman sniffed the air in Esmé's room like a bloodhound, and announced, 'This room smells damp.'

'It's just cold, I think. There's a radiator, and I've opened the valve to let the hot water fill it, so it's beginning to warm. It will take a little while longer to warm the room, though. I wish I'd thought of it sooner. The room hasn't been used since Auntie Es left, you see.'

'Well, yes, as one would imagine.'

'I've put a hot water bottle between the sheets, and the blankets and eiderdown are warm and cosy; straight from the top of the airing cupboard. If you'd prefer, you can sleep in my bed, but Shadow has learned how to open the door and sometimes he makes himself comfortable on the bed and wakes me up. He's jolly clever.'

'No . . . this room will do,' Grandmother Elliot said hastily. 'Besides you've been sniffing all evening and your bed will be filled with cold germs.'

'My cold is nearly better.'

Grandmother Elliot ignored the snippet of information. 'We'd better make sure the windows and doors are locked, and the fireguards are in place. There are too many people wandering about the countryside these days.'

'Daddy said they're looking for work. It's the Depression.'

'Some people use it as an excuse. Our hen house was raided the other day and two of my best layers were stolen.'

'We lost some cabbages and potatoes from the garden; they

were probably taken by someone with children to feed. If they'd knocked at the door Mummy said she would have given them something. Daddy agreed with her.'

Grandmother Elliot snorted. 'Goodness. Thieves are thieves, whatever the circumstances. Livia would be better off making them work for it. The windows need cleaning, and the garden gate is hanging off its hinge.'

'All the same—'

'If these people are encouraged you'll wake up one morning to discover you've been murdered in your bed.'

Meggie giggled, because Grandmother Elliot must surely have meant it as a joke.

But she hadn't, for she said quite severely, 'What's so funny?'

'Well . . . how can you wake up if you've already been murdered?'

'Ah . . . yes . . . well of course, it goes without saying, doesn't it. I was making a joke, and you're being too clever by far. Off to bed with you, now.'

The thought of intruders kept Meggie awake and alert to every crack and creak until after midnight. When the clock in the hall chimed midnight she pulled the eiderdown up around her ears, so if someone sneaked in to murder her she wouldn't hear them coming. Even so she jumped when Shadow pushed the door open and settled on the end of the bed with a heavy sigh.

'Pest.' Drawing her knees up to give him the room he required, she felt thankful she had someone to guard her. She just wished her bed was bigger . . . or that Shadow was smaller!

Five

Meggie got the opportunity to visit her father the following weekend.

Grandmother Elliot had upset the cleaning lady by insisting that the house be cleaned from top to bottom. The cleaner worked sullenly, making aggrieved little remarks when Grandmother Elliot was out of earshot.

'I'm only staying because your mother's sick, poor lady. Very polite, Mrs Elliot the younger is, and she never criticizes my work. That old biddy says, "Clean this, scrub that, iron this, polish that," as though I don't know how to do my own job. She's an old fusspot, and I don't get a moment's peace from her.'

Meggie sympathized, since she got the same treatment, but she didn't think it wise to encourage the cleaning lady by agreeing out loud. Just as well because Grandmother Elliot appeared.

'Make your bed, dear. And don't leave the sheets all creased. I must teach you how to do neat hospital corners. When you've finished you can make the boys' beds and pick up their clothes.'

'My mother wants the boys to learn to keep their own room tidy.'

'Boys aren't very good at domestic chores.'

'Mother said that's an excuse, and they'll never be good at anything domestic if they don't practise it.'

'Did she now? As far as I'm concerned the men are the breadwinners, and the women stay at home and provide a comfortable environment for them to relax in.'

'Times are changing, Grandmother Elliot.'

Meggie was subjected to a long stare that would have been intimidating, had she been easily intimidated. 'Yes, they are, but answering back is still a tiresome trait, especially when it comes from a child. It must be the Sangster in you coming out.'

Meggie's ears pricked up. Any information was better than

none, even if it was of a mean and gossipy value. Grandmother Elliot didn't disappoint her.

'Richard Sangster always had a smart tongue on him, right from when he was small. But then, his mother came from a long line of Scottish aristocrats and the Sangsters always thought they were a cut above the rest of us. You would be aware of your Sinclair inheritance, I suppose?'

Meggie learned a lot from listening to gossip, and she'd heard the Sinclair inheritance mentioned a couple of times, when she wasn't supposed to be listening to the adults' conversation. She muttered in a vague, casual manner. 'Oh yes . . . the inheritance.'

Her curiosity was gnawing a hole through her skull now. What about the inheritance?

'Foxglove House used to be such a lively place when Margaret Sinclair Sangster was alive. That was before the last war, of course, though goodness knows, we seem to be heading for another one. After Margaret's accident the inheritance went downhill, I understand. Now the house is shuttered tight. Goodness knows, you'd think the Sinclair trust would let the place instead of allowing it to run down. When it becomes yours, you'll never be able to afford to keep the house up as it should be kept up.'

When it became hers?

The phone rang. 'That's probably the gardener. I want him to take that lilac out and plant a tree in its place.'

Drat Matthew Bugg for ringing at such an inconvenient time, just when she was learning something new! 'My mother loves that lilac, you know. The fragrance drifts into her bedroom when it's in bloom.' Grandmother Elliot wasn't listening, and anyway, her mother would sort it out in her own way, once she was home.

When Foxglove House became hers? The snippet of information stuck in her mind. Should she ask Grandmother Elliot to tell her more?

But she had gone to answer the telephone, and Meggie heard her say, 'Oh, it's you, Barbara. Thank goodness I can sit down and have an intelligent conversation. I'd forgotten how tiresome children can be.'

'So could grandmothers,' Meggie whispered darkly under her breath.

Shadow appeared, carrying his leash in his mouth, his tail wagging, and not in the least bit shamed by his beggarly behaviour.

'Sit,' she said, and went up to see the boys, the dog following closely after her in case she forgot him. He wagged his tail when she frowned. 'I thought I told you to sit.'

He sat.

'I'm taking Shadow for a walk, boys . . . coming?'

Her brothers were busy, engrossed in what they were doing, which was carefully pasting bits and pieces on a card . . . a welcome home gift for their mother. It would join the other cards they'd made her over the years, their felicitations carefully captured in a box that once contained her mother's favourite Oxfords . . . little scraps of love hoarded in a shoe box.

The boys looked up at her, saying together, 'Must we?'

'It's not compulsory.' In fact she'd rather have the freedom of going out alone. 'Leave some space on that card for me to write a message, if you would.' She fetched the letter for the major and headed out into the day, Shadow still carrying his leash.

The stark lines of winter were beginning to paint over what remained of autumn. There was a faint smokiness in the air, as if someone was burning the dead leaves. Those that still littered the ground were picked up by miniature hurricanes and swirled about in whirling blurs of ochre.

Foxglove House was her inheritance? Was it possible? Yes, it probably was, she thought. If it had belonged to her father then it would have been passed on to her. What about Major Henry, though? Her fingers ran over the envelope in her pocket.

She slowed when Foxglove House came into view. It stood tall in its neglected grounds, and cast a long shadow. She imagined its dark and dusty interior, the probing gleams of light momentarily piercing the cracks in the shutters, but not lingering long enough to allow the ghosts to escape and introduce themselves.

The house was a closed book to her, yet it contained her story. One day she'd discover what it was and record it in her diary. She might even write a book. She liked writing.

Nutting Cottage was a bit of a walk, so she took the leash from the dog and picked up pace. She should have borrowed her Uncle Chad's old bicycle, but then, the inner tubes would probably have perished after all this time.

A thin trickle of smoke came from Nutting Cottage chimney. It was a pretty cottage with roses growing round the door. Her mother owned it and Major Henry lived in it. Yet the two never spoke. How odd it all was.

It was with some trepidation that she knocked at the door. She felt like a traitor to her mother. There must be a good reason why she would not allow this man to intrude into their lives. Alarm speared her. What if he was a murderer?

Her heart pounded when the door opened and she felt like running. At the same time, her feet refused to move.

He was wearing a russet red cardigan with brown plus fours, grey socks and carpet slippers. The brightness of his cardigan surprised her. It seemed young and flamboyant, as though he hadn't noticed himself growing old inside it. In comparison, his pink scalp shone through thin white hair.

She didn't know what to say, but he did, and his voice was kind of clipped. 'Hello. It's Margaret, isn't it? I've seen you walk past now and then. How lovely. I wondered when you'd find time to visit a lonely old man.'

He stood aside to allow her entrance and her feet obeyed the gesture. Shadow glued himself to her side, and the cottage swallowed them when the major shut the door. It smelled fustily of burned on grease and stale sardines, as if the windows were never opened to let the fresh air in. 'You know me then?' she said.

'Of course . . . of course. It's Richard's girl . . . my . . . *granddaughter.*'

There, that had confirmed what she'd always known, deep down.

'I've brought you a letter that came from America,' she said, as he ushered her into the sitting room, and she placed it on the sideboard. 'The postman delivered it to our house.'

Shadow commandeered the worn, multicoloured length of the hearthrug, turning round three times in some doggy ritual before sinking on it with a sigh.

'It was nice of you to deliver it personally. You'll stay and have tea, won't you? There's fruit cake.'

'Thank you, sir, but I should be getting along. I'm walking the dog.'

He raised an eyebrow as he took in Shadow. His eyes were astute as he gazed at her, and he offered her a conspiratorial smile that made her feel slightly uncomfortable. 'I don't think the dog will mind, will you, boy?' Shadow raised his head to look at him and thumped his tail before going back to sleep again. 'The thing is, will you? I'll go and make the tea. You make up your mind whether to stay or go. The door's not locked.'

She gazed around the room she was in. There was nothing sinister about the comfortable chairs and occasional tables. An upright piano fitted in an alcove with a small display of photographs on top.

There was a picture of her father in his uniform. He looked handsome. There was a close up of a woman's face. She picked it up and gazed at it. The woman was perfectly breathtaking.

To Henry. Love always, Rosemary Mortimer, was dashed in black ink across the bottom. That was the name on the back of the envelope she'd brought him.

She was still looking at it when she heard him returning. Quickly she set the photograph back on the piano and took her seat. He carried two cups of tea and slices of fruitcake arranged on a plate, all balanced on a small tray. Setting it on the small table between them, he seated himself in a wing-backed chair.

They stared at each other for a moment, then he said, 'You look like your mother.'

'My mother thinks I look like my father.'

He huffed with laughter, but it had a hollow sound. 'Who do *you* think you resemble?'

'Myself . . . Meggie Elliot.'

'You're a Sangster,' he pointed out.

She didn't want to take sides. 'Yes. Dr Elliot adopted me, and gave me his name.'

'Why?'

She laughed at the rapid exchange between them. He was

sharp-minded for an old person. 'I don't know why. I imagine my mother wanted him to. Perhaps it was because my aunt and uncle grew up in the same house and they're called Carr. It would be awfully confusing having people with three different surnames living in the same house.'

'Have you asked her?'

'Good Lord, no. Mother would bite my head off.' She nibbled the edge of the fruit cake. It was stale. 'Who are the Sinclairs?'

'Ah . . . so that's why you're here. You want to know about your legacy.'

'Is there one?'

'Yes . . . the Sinclairs are your grandmother's side of the family. Goodness knows what's left of it now. The Depression is deepening, I believe. You'd have to contact the lawyer who handles it. His name is Simon Stone of Anderson and Stone.' He stood, opened a drawer and rummaged around inside it. 'Aha! I knew I had one.' He handed her the lawyer's card. 'Keep that in case you need to contact them. There's still the house, of course, but they had to let the gardener and the housekeeper go. If the maintenance isn't kept up the building will deteriorate.'

'Are you talking about Foxglove House?'

He smiled. 'I am. You should ask your mother about it.'

The house belonged to her then. Lor, what a monstrosity to inherit! She didn't know whether the knowledge was welcome or not. 'My mother won't tell me anything about the past. She won't even discuss it. If she forgets she never talks about it, and mentions it by mistake, she clams up like an oyster. It's unfair!'

'Yes . . . I suppose you would think that.' He gave a soft chuckle. 'Oysters don't clam up. Clams do.'

'What do oysters do then?'

'They close.'

'Oh . . . I see.' She didn't really. If clams could clam, why couldn't oysters oyst? She must ask her stepfather. He loved ridiculous questions that gave him an excuse to come up with ridiculous answers.

They exchanged a grin and she ventured to say, 'Grandfather . . . I swear I won't ask you anything personal, but if you happened to tell me anything I shouldn't know, wild bears wouldn't make me tell on you.'

He patted her on the knee. 'You're a girl after my own heart. In the war I used to be in intelligence, you know. I could show Foxglove House to you, I suppose. I still have a key somewhere.'

She smiled at that, saying eagerly, 'When?'

'How about next week? After school on Thursday, would be a good day.'

She nodded, gulping down her tea, along with her disappointment. She'd rather have seen over the house now, and a week seemed as long as a year.

Swallowing her disappointment, she stood, feeding the stale cake to Shadow at the same time. When she held out her hand to the major, he shook it.

'I'd better go before someone comes looking for me, I suppose. You won't tell anyone I was here, will you? If my family finds out they won't let me visit you again.'

'Good grief . . . I won't breathe a word. There's no love lost between your mother and myself as it is . . . still, that's water under the bridge, and best if it stays there. It will be our little secret.'

Rather disappointing, since she was itching to ask him what the trouble had been about. He was so sweet though, and she couldn't imagine why her mother didn't like him. But it was early days.

'I'll leave the back door to the house open next Thursday. There are some unshuttered windows upstairs, to allow the light in. But you'd better bring a torch,' he said.

'Goodbye, sir, you needn't get up.'

He lowered his voice, making it sound like a game. 'I thought I might go to the gate to make sure the coast is clear. You can't be too careful . . . they might have spies posted.'

She laughed. 'Don't forget to read your letter. It's from America. Could I have the stamp when you've read it? My brothers save stamps and they haven't got many. '

'Take the stamp with you. The letter is from my second wife . . . Rosemary Mortimer. She ran away to Hollywood and acts in films.'

Meggie couldn't stop her eyes widening. 'Gosh . . . how awfully thrilling to have been married to a film star.'

'Rosie isn't a star. From what I can gather she's had a few bit parts. And, believe me, dear, it wasn't all that thrilling being married to her. Looks mean nothing.'

Tearing the stamp from the envelope he handed it to her and threw the unread letter on to the fire.

It seemed like a decade until Thursday came round.

Meggie's mother arrived home on the Monday and her mouth tightened a little when she saw the rearranged furniture and the pristine tidiness of her home.

'How clean and tidy it looks, but you shouldn't have gone to so much trouble,' she said, sounding so warmly sincere that Grandmother Elliot smiled smugly. Meggie marvelled that her mother could lie so well.

Meggie hugged her, firstly, because she was glad to have her home, and secondly because she felt a twinge of conscience that she was going to deceive her. Still, it couldn't be helped. Her hug was abandoned when the boys came racing in and took over.

Grandmother left final instructions for Meggie – to make sure she did her share of the chores – and for the boys – to mind they kept quiet while their mother rested.

Everyone hugged each other with the relief of parting when Denton drove his mother home.

The atmosphere disappeared with her and her mother gave a big smile the next day. 'It doesn't feel like my home, but Grandmother Elliot meant well.'

'Shall I make some tea while you rest?' Meggie offered.

Her mother picked up an ornament and placed it back in its former position, and then rearranged the recently colour-coordinated cushions into some sort of confusion.

Outside the floorboards creaked. She smiled and punched a dent in the largest cushion before she threw it at the armchair. 'Denton likes that one for his back. As for resting, I'm through with it. You've no idea how tedious it is to lie in a hospital ward. Your father was an absolute bully. Everyone jumped to do his bidding, and I had to do as I was told. I've quite gone off him.'

'It won't do you any good, since you're stuck with me,' Denton said, grinning as he popped his head round the door and blew her a kiss.

'I might go outside and do some weeding, Dr Elliot. Do I have your permission?'

'Yes, my love, but take things easy else you'll end up back in hospital.'

'What happened to my lilac?'

He looked puzzled. 'What lilac?'

'You mean you've never noticed the lilac bush under our bedroom window?'

'I thought it was a fir tree.' He spread his hands in mystification and left for the hospital – but not before offering Meggie a wink. It was clear he had no intention of being put in the position of having to take sides.

Livia sighed. 'Can you believe that?'

Meggie giggled. 'No . . . he was teasing you. Grandmother Elliot insisted that Mr Bugg dig the lilac up and plant a tree in its place. I tried to stop her but she insisted on having it her own way.'

Her mother's lips pursed. 'I see. She means well, but I do wish she'd stop interfering.'

'Mr Bugg kept the lilac roots and planted them in a pot. He said it could be replanted elsewhere and it would grow again in the spring.'

'I brought that from Foxglove House and grew it from a cutting. It was to remind me of your father. He loved the scent of lilac.'

Which was why Grandmother Elliot wanted to move it. She probably saw it as an insult to her son.

'Doesn't Daddy mind?'

'No . . . it was Denton's idea. Richard was his best friend.'

Wasn't she a living reminder for them both of Richard Sangster? Meggie's smile faded as her mother headed to the telephone and dialled the gardener's number.

By evening, a considerably shortened shrub was reinstated in its original position and the fir was planted in the pot.

'It will serve us for Christmas if it survives,' Livia said.

Thursday finally came. There was an air of waiting about

Foxglove House. Downstairs, stripes of light and shadow slowly moved as the lowering sun sent dim and dusty beams of light through the shutters.

Dust sheets covered the furniture, some of them reaching out scarily, like ghosts, as though they wished to touch her or claim her as one of them.

But she didn't feel as though she belonged to this house – the home of the current Sinclair heir. *Her house!* She'd been kept in ignorance of this family, a name that was now hers alone, as though she'd become a family of one. Resentment intruded. Her grandfather explained that the house wasn't really hers. It could never be hers, even though she was tied to it. She could never sell it, just pass it on to the next Sinclair if there was one. Was she to meekly assume responsibility because some dead ancestor had declared she must? Everything in her rebelled against it.

There was a grand piano in the drawing room, uncovered, for the dust sheet had slid off. She ran her fingers over the keys and dust flew.

'My wife, Rosie Mortimer used to play that. She sang as well. She had a lovely voice.' He sounded almost wistful.

'I'm learning to play the piano, though I'm not very good yet.'

'You can play for me, if you would.'

She seated herself and clumsily played some exercises. The instrument badly needed tuning.

She laughed and closed the lid over the keys. 'Perhaps we should put the dust sheet back over it, and your memories too,' she said. 'It's a lovely piano. I wish I had one like it.'

'It's your piano, my dear. This is your house and almost everything in it belongs to you. It's part of the legacy that was passed down through those with Sinclair blood. It comes from your grandmother's side of the family. From Margaret it went to Richard, and then, when my son died it became yours.' He pressed a door key into her hand and her fingers curled around it in possession. 'This is yours, come here any time you like.'

'I understand that my father was a hero.'

'Yes, he was.'

'You must miss him.'

'Yes . . . it was a great blow when he died.'

'I should have liked to have known him. What was he like?'

'He was charming . . . always laughing. I didn't do him justice. I was ashamed of his illness. I didn't understand him, you see. Your mother did . . . she made him happy.'

Meggie drew in a deep breath, a sad one, because the atmosphere in the house was vibrating with pain. 'Why don't you get on with my mother?'

'Why doesn't your mother get along with you?'

Puzzled, she gazed at him. He couldn't possibly know what her relationship with her mother was like, and besides, it wasn't true. She did get on with her for most of the time. 'I don't understand what you mean.'

Silence pressed against her ears, held there by her own muted breath.

'We cannot speak of this,' he whispered, and the pain in him throbbed around her. His fingers pressed against his temples. 'I shouldn't be here.'

As he walked away, she said, 'You're my grandfather. I like you.'

He turned, tears trembling in his eyes. 'You don't know me, sweet girl. I have something wrong inside my head. I died once . . . I wanted to die, but I couldn't, so I stayed alive. Now I just exist from one day to the next. I must go. Pretend you never met me, Meggie. Let the dogs lie undisturbed.'

She couldn't understand what he meant by that, but his words made her uneasy. Perhaps he was insane.

She heard the door close and was left alone inside the house. Her house! The enormity of such a gift was too much to take in. It was a museum that belonged to an era, and to a life she couldn't imagine.

She didn't go upstairs but stood at the bottom, gazing up to the landing, where light streamed in through the window and patterned the dirty upstairs darkness.

She softly whispered her father's name. 'Richard Sangster.'

There was a crack in the upper reaches of the house and her heart thumped. She ran through the hall into the kitchens, and found the back door. It wouldn't open. She rattled it back and forth, panicky, feeling as though she was trapped inside with some imaginary danger.

'Ghosts can't hurt me, they don't exist,' she said loudly, even knowing that they did, because she could feel them trying to claim her as a Sinclair. They retreated into indistinct, grey shadows.

Making an effort she calmed herself, twisted the knob a little more, and then heard the tongue click clear of the groove. As she closed the door gently behind her she thought: The next time she went to Foxglove House she would not allow her imagination to get the better of her.

Six

Now Liam had made his move, Esmé became aware of him as a man, and he was attractive. She still knew very little about his background, because he rarely spoke about himself.

'You have an Irish name, are you Irish?' she asked him one day as they were taking time out from rehearsing.

Blue eyes lit on her, and they were guarded. 'That's the first time you've asked me anything about my background. Does that mean you're interested?'

She shrugged. 'Only to the extent of the question.'

'You certainly don't give a man much room in which to move. Am I Irish, you ask? No, I'm not. Do I sound Irish?'

'No.' She waited for him to say more but it wasn't forth-coming. 'Is that all you're going to say?'

'I answered your question to the extent it required.' He laughed when she stuck her tongue out at him. 'My name is William and I shortened it to Liam. I thought it sounded better than Will, and would make a less common professional name than Bill.'

'I knew someone called Billy once. You look a bit like him.'

The expression in his eyes sharpened. 'Where was that?'

She shrugged, not quite looking at him, because Livia had said it was better to keep quiet about their time in the orphanage. People would immediately think you were less than they were, if they found out. They came from a perfectly good background – probably better than most. Their father had been a parliamentary secretary and their mother a dress designer, until they'd died in a boating accident.

She fobbed him off with a vague, 'It was at school, I think. I can't really remember him.' Her curiosity was pricked. 'Tell me more about yourself. What made you take up dancing?'

'It's the only thing I did well. My ambition is to go to

America and I've been saving most of my wages. When we return to England I intend to apply for a position with the Cunard line. We dance well together, Esmé, and there's no reason why we shouldn't go to America together, as a partnership.'

She'd never had any ambition beyond finishing her nursing training before, and she gave a slightly doubtful laugh. Dancing for a living wasn't as glamorous as she'd thought it would be. 'America . . . truly?'

He nodded. 'I'm acquainted with someone who might be able to help. He directed a stage show Eric and I were in before it folded. He might be able to get us on the *Aquitania*, even if it's only in the chorus line.' His voice was as enthused as his smile. 'She sails the North Atlantic route. You said you could tap dance a little, and so can I. We could work tap into our routines. With legs like yours, and with your looks . . .' He shrugged. 'We could become a husband and wife act. Liam and Esmé Carr-Denison.'

'Carr-Denison?'

He looked sheepish. 'The Americans seem to like double-barrelled names, and they like the English, especially blue bloods. You could reinvent yourself with a title.'

She laughed at that. 'I'm definitely not royal, and besides, I'm not a very good liar, and I'd rather be myself.'

'You could still be yourself. You have good manners and one of those soft, ladylike voices that encourages respect. Most of the crew refer to you as Lady Esmé behind your back. You could use it as a stage name.'

'Do they . . . how very odd. Why don't you reinvent yourself?'

He didn't answer her question. 'Lady Esmé and Liam Denison is a catchy title for dancing partners. I've been so in awe of you that I could barely drum up the courage to approach you. I know I'm not nearly good enough, but —'

Sensing something vulnerable in him then, she placed her finger over his mouth. Liam Denison was not the confident creature he made himself out to be, and she smiled. 'You didn't make a bad job of it, considering the short time we've known each other, and just Liam and Esmé Denison will do fine.'

A gleam of a smile chased the anxiety from his eyes. 'You mean . . . you'll marry me.'

'We could be engaged, but I don't want to rush into marriage, so not until we get back to England. I want my family to attend my wedding, and I'd like to meet yours.'

His chin came up slightly. He had a small cleft in it, and was a handsome man. The female passengers flirted with him, as well as the women staff members. He kept his distance, spending most of his spare time with Eric, who shared a cabin with him, and who acted as their choreographer.

'I haven't got any family left. I had a younger brother once, Tommy, his name was. He died when we were children, in the Spanish flu epidemic.'

An image of the orphanage was a fleeting, unpleasant and unwanted thought. Her body had been burning and her head had spun every time she moved. She'd been listless and whimpering and suffered from bad dreams in the infirmary bed, where she'd been soaked in her own sweat.

Chad had been there. He'd been sick too, but he'd made her drink, forcing droplets of water into her mouth and telling her, 'The flu took Tommy. I'm getting better and so will you, because you're my twin, and if you die, I'll die too.'

Absolute nonsense, of course, but they'd believed it then. Something surfaced in her mind, a flash of memory that seemed important, but eluded her before she could catch it.

'I'm so sorry about your brother. I survived the illness when I was a child. What about your parents?'

He shrugged and his eyes flickered away from her. 'Gone . . . both of them.'

She assumed their death had been caused by the influenza outbreak as well. 'I lost my parents when I was small, too, and can't remember them. My sister and her husband gave my brother and me a home, and she made sure we had a good education. My brother is training to be a doctor now.'

'You were lucky to have someone to look after you.'

'Yes, I suppose we were.' A strong wave of homesickness swept over her and she could almost smell the fragrant perfume of fields alive with poppies and cornflowers drifting in the wind. But, no, it would be winter in England now. The hedges and trees would be bare, and there might be snow on the ground.

And in a few short weeks, spring would bring Livia's new baby into the world. She was longing to see it. She knew her sister well enough to be certain Livia wouldn't hold a grudge for the argument they'd had. The ship might be due back at its dock in time for the birth. She hoped so.

Meanwhile, ahead of her and just two days away was Melbourne. The sea sparkled in the sunlight and the air smelled of salt. Half the people in England would be wishing they were in her shoes, sailing on a passenger liner somewhere on the ocean, and soaking up the sun, whilst she was doing the opposite with little twinges of homesickness.

Following Melbourne they'd sail across the Bass Strait to Tasmania, and then on to Wellington in New Zealand. There they'd pick up passengers and mail before heading back to England.

Where she'd become Mrs Denison if the marriage went ahead! A thousand butterflies came alive in her stomach . . . or were they wasps? She couldn't make up her mind whether it was excitement or a kind of dread!

Liam's smile was a mile wide, as if he had no qualms. 'I'll buy you an engagement ring when we get to Australia . . . make us official. Can we keep it a secret between us, else people will talk.'

Her smile felt forced. 'Does that bother you?'

He nodded. 'Normally, it wouldn't, but it would be better if nobody knew about it. The shipping company doesn't like on-board affairs.'

She nearly pointed out that it wasn't an affair, but an engagement, which was a promise to marry. Surely that was entirely honourable.

Later, she shared the secret with Minnie. Her friend shrugged and looked askance at her. 'Well, you're a fast worker, I must say. How long has this been going on?'

'Oh, stop it, Minnie. Nothing's going on.'

'You knew I liked him; but all this time you've worked on him behind my back. What about the fiancée he'd left back home?'

She didn't want to tell Minnie that Liam had invented a girlfriend to protect himself from predatory females like her. 'I haven't worked behind anybody's back. Besides, you said you liked Wally. You can't have all the men on board . . . though from what I hear it's certainly not through lack of trying.'

Minnie's eyes began to glitter and her fingers became claws that scratched at the empty air. 'Well, meow. You can be a right bitch at times. What have you been saying behind my back?'

'So can you. I haven't said anything, it's what others are saying.' Her voice softened. 'We've been friends a long time, Minnie; don't let's spoil that now. I know you don't mean anything by your flirting, whatever impression other people get. You've forgotten that being on a ship is like living in a small village. Everyone gossips about everyone else.'

'Oh la-di-da! How very kind of you to advise me of that fact, dear. Just because they call you Lady Esmé it doesn't mean you're the bee's knees. You don't know anything about me. As for Liam Denison, you can keep him. See if I care. He's a bit of old rubbish that floated to the top because he happens to be able to dance. Wally said Liam's deep, and he doesn't trust anyone . . . so he's probably got something in his past to hide.'

Which might hold a grain of truth. It was hard to get Liam to talk about his past or his background, and he'd lied to her in the beginning about having a girlfriend. But he'd put her straight about that, and she believed him.

Despite her strained relationship with Minnie, Esmé wasn't entirely comfortable with her decision to become engaged, since it was a commitment. She couldn't help wondering if anything else would go wrong after they'd docked at Melbourne.

It was a brilliant day, the sky a cloudless infinity of blue, and the air bursting with sunshine and warmth. The dockside bustled with people. Carts and cars came and went, piled high with luggage. Passengers were herded into queues. Babies screamed, children ran around getting used to their land legs, and mothers scolded.

Esmé thought she saw Minnie amongst the jostle of people,

but it couldn't have been because the crew wasn't allowed ashore until the passengers had disembarked. She lost sight of the woman when a man got in the way.

After she'd finished her tasks, she went to the cabin to look for her friend, since they'd arranged to go ashore together. Minnie's things had disappeared from the cabin. Esmé wondered if she'd moved cabins. Her friend had been tense since their argument.

The ship was a hive of activity as cabins were cleaned and the ship provisioned. Perhaps Minnie had slipped ashore with some of the staff, she thought. She must stop worrying about her friend. She would probably turn up at the last minute.

Then she learned that Wally had left the ship in Melbourne, and Minnie had gone with him.

There was a note left for her with Eric Blair.

She was in the salon with the small dance floor, going over the programme for the journey home when Eric handed it to her. He was apologetic. 'Sorry, Esmé, Minnie asked me to wait until we sailed.'

'Did you know about this?' she asked Liam.

The two men exchanged a glance, then he shook his head. She wondered if he was lying.

Her hands were shaking when she tore the envelope open.

Dear Esmé,

By the time you get this Wally and I will be married. I didn't tell you because I know you don't approve of him. I borrowed one of your dresses to get married in, and a couple of other items . . . and I didn't have the courage to tell you I was leaving the ship, because you would have tried to stop me.

Esmé, I did something stupid . . . you'll know what that is, I imagine. To be honest, Wally wouldn't have been my choice for a husband, but at least he was willing to shoulder his responsibility. Don't think too badly of me, Es; you're the only friend I've ever had and I love you dearly.

I didn't mean what I said about Liam. I hope you're happy together, and I hope he proves to be worthy of you.

When the ship next docks in Melbourne look me up.

Minnie

There was an address scribbled in pencil on the bottom of the note.

Tears in her eyes, she handed the letter to Liam, who grimaced when he read it. 'At least she'll have a ring on her finger. That's better than nothing for a girl in her position, I suppose.'

She rushed to her friend's defence. 'You seem to forget it was a man who put her in that position.'

'But it's up to the woman to say no, and . . . he didn't have to marry her.' Liam handed her a handkerchief, then when she'd dried her tears, he said, 'I'm sorry, love. Here . . . perhaps this will make up for it.' He slid a ring on her finger. It was a small square diamond with a garnet either side.

Anxiety filled his eyes when she gazed speechlessly at him. 'You haven't changed your mind, have you?'

'No . . . it's a sweet ring. Thank you, Liam.'

'I'd rather you told me you loved me.'

She avoided his eyes, unable to utter the lie he wanted to hear from her. 'I'm a bit worried about Minnie.'

Tipping up her chin, he kissed her, and then smiled. It all seemed so passionless, as if her senses hadn't been engaged beyond the surface. 'Don't fret about Minnie, she's a survivor, and old enough to look after herself.'

It wasn't until they'd sailed from Wellington that Esmé discovered that the money she'd hidden in her stocking had gone. She'd never have thought Minnie would steal from her.

She cried – not for the stolen money, because she would have given it to Minnie if she'd needed it – but because Minnie had not felt able to trust her. Despite their bickering of late, she already missed her friend's company.

An hour after Minnie married Wally Prichard she met his parents. The hotel they owned turned out to be a grimy public house in an overcrowded area. The ceiling was mustard-coloured squares, like old nibbled biscuits, and the place smelled of stale cigarettes and beer. Flypaper swung in the breeze, black corpses trapped on its sticky surface.

She rounded on him. 'I thought you said it was a hotel.'

'This *is* a hotel. What did you expect, The Ritz?'

A man came out from behind the counter wearing a stained shirt with a waistcoat over the top. Wally resembled him. He wiped a smelly grey cloth over the bar. 'Oh, it's you, is it, Wally? Who's the sheila with you?'

Wally grinned. 'Hello, Dad, long time no see. This is Min.'

Minnie lowered her case, prepared to do battle. 'My name is Minnie James, and I'm Wally's wife.'

'You're Minnie Prichard now,' Wally reminded her, giving a bit of a smirk.

She threw him a look, knowing she'd made the biggest mistake of her life by getting involved with him. 'I'd be obliged if you'd ask your parents not to call me names.'

'Ask them yourself, they're not deaf. Look, Minnie, they didn't mean anything by it, you'll have to get used to Aussie ways.'

A heavy-looking woman joined her mate. 'Here, who's she to be issuing orders round here?'

'I'm not issuing orders; I'm trying to introduce myself. I'm Wally's wife.'

'Wally's wife, is it?' She put her fists on her hips and looked her up and down, her eyes lingering on her stomach. Minnie blushed. The women smiled and took a stab in the dark. 'Got one in the oven, have you? I told you to keep your snake inside your trousers, didn't I, Wally boy? Now look where it's got you; hitched up to some flighty British bit. Serves you right.'

'Give it a rest, Ma,' her husband said and held out a hand to her. 'I didn't mean nothing by that, Minnie, love. It's just the way we say things round here. My name's Harry, and Wally's ma there is called Marlene . . . Ma for short.' His palm was as moist and as cold as a slug, and he gave a bit of a chuckle. 'While we're talking about snakes, I had a parrot called Minnie when I was a lad. It used to swear like a trooper. Then along came this hungry python. The bugger climbed the tree Minnie's cage was hanging from, and it slithered through the bars in the cage. It swallowed the bird whole. The snake's stomach was so big it got stuck trying to get out of the cage. My pa took up an axe and chopped its head clean off. Damned me if my Minnie didn't come walking out swearing her head off.'

It had the sound of an often-repeated story, and Minnie dutifully cued in on the punchline and produced the expected laugh.

What had she got herself into? Unobtrusively wiping the sweaty residue from Harry's palm against her skirt, she shuddered as Ma gave a squawk of laughter more raucous than any parrot could produce.

Wally opened the flap in the bar and they passed through. 'We'll use my room, all right, Ma?'

'It's all right as long as you can help out with the expenses. This place is only just paying its way, and I can't afford to keep the pair of you, not the way things are. You can help out in the bar, and teach Minnie how to draw a pint. A pretty face behind the bar will bring the customers in. Oh yes . . . and we don't have a slate, any more, otherwise the customers will swill like hogs and won't be able to settle up at the end of the week.'

'Minnie's going to try and get a job as a nurse. She has the name of an agency. As soon as we've got a few quid behind us we'll be going up country to Saltshaker Lake. I thought we could live off the land for a while if I can't get another job.'

'Good luck to you then. The last time I saw the place it wouldn't support a row of rats, let alone a mob of sheep.'

If anything, upstairs, the hotel was worse. A narrow corridor with hanging cobwebs had living quarters at one end, consisting of a living room and two bedrooms.

'The pump is in the yard outside the kitchen door. If you want hot water you'll have to boil a kettle.'

'What's in those two rooms at the end of the corridor?'

'Guest bedrooms. We get the odd salesman or two stopping by.'

Dust flew when Minnie opened the windows, and yellowing curtains billowed under the flow of unaccustomed air. She sneezed.

'I wouldn't do that too often.' Wally laughed, and then looked around him as though he was seeing it for the first time. 'I'd forgotten what a bloody awful dump this place is. Mum and Dad only come up here to sleep. Our bedroom's this way.'

It looked out over a back lane with a little shed at the end. 'What's in there?'

'It's the dunny.'

'The what?'

'The dunny . . . the lavatory, old girl.' His words were a mockery of British upper crust. 'The cart comes along every night to empty the pan.'

Gorge rose up in her at the thought. 'It's a bit primitive isn't it?'

'Yeah, well, I suppose it is. You'll just have to put up with it, won't you . . . the same as we all do. It will be better when we go to Saltshaker Lake. You can use the nearest bush as a throne, and there's nobody to see.'

The bed was unmade, but at least there was room for two in it. 'Where's the clean linen kept?'

'It's in the cupboard at the end of the hall. Leave it for now,' he said pulling her down on to the mattress with him. 'Let's celebrate our marriage, Mrs Prichard. You haven't let me touch you since that night.' He placed his hand over her stomach.

She shook him off. 'You only got to touch me then because you got me too drunk to realize what I was doing. Isn't the coming baby celebration enough?'

His eyes were hard as they met hers. 'That was a mistake, and I did my part by putting a ring on your finger. After all, I have no proof the brat's mine, except your word. It could be any joker's kid and I want more than a mistake for my trouble.' He slid a hand under her skirt and jerked her knickers down to her knees. 'Let's get rid of these passion killers for a start. There's not much use having a blue-eyed blonde in my bed if I can't make use of her.'

Wally was too strong for her, and soon overcame her initial resistance. A few minutes later the bedhead banged against the wall and the springs creaked in unison. Wally began to pant. Eventually he collapsed on top of her with a little shudder. Lighting a cigarette he lay back in a cloud of stinking smoke and watched her retrieve her knickers and step into them, his eyes half closed. 'You've got a nice arse, Min.'

She fetched some well-patched sheets, which were clean,

and stared down at him. 'Are you going to move so I can make the bed?'

After a moment of childish resistance at being told what to do, he rose and adjusted his clothing. 'I'll be going off to see my mates, then,' he said, avoiding her eyes, and he checked his wallet.

The folded wad of notes looked familiar, as did the string tied round it. 'Where did you get all the money from, Wally?'

'What's it to you?'

'That's Esmé's money, and she's my friend.'

'So what? I just borrowed it, that night we got drunk. You owed me the money that you'd lost, and you told me you'd borrow it from your friend, and she kept it in her case under the bunk. I saved you the bother of getting it yourself, since you were too drunk to stand up. We can pay her back the next time we see her.'

'You can go and pay her back now, before the ship leaves for Wellington. How could you, Wally?'

'It's already gone. Stop telling me what to do.'

'I've only just started. And don't smoke your fags in the bedroom, when you can use the living room. I have to sleep in here too, and a smoky atmosphere is bad for a growing baby.'

'Don't nag, Minnie; I'm not in the mood. Make yourself useful; you can tidy this place up a bit while I'm gone.'

She was angry that he'd stolen Esmé's money, and furious at herself for drinking so much that night. What would Esmé think of her when she discovered the money was missing?

Wally didn't return in time for dinner, but came back during the night, his breath smelling of whisky. She tried to fight him off but he pushed her nightgown up, spread her legs apart and rolled on top of her, naked. After a few minutes he grunted in satisfaction then rolled off and went to sleep. He was a pig, she thought.

A month later Minnie had washed the curtains and scrubbed the place clean, and was coming to terms with her in-laws. They were rough, but straightforward. She was beginning to like the thought of having a baby to love, even if it was Wally's. One morning cramps woke her, only to discover that her body had begun to abort the tiny foetus. Tears pricked her eyelids. It was obviously not meant to be.

Wally blanched at the sight of the blood, though it was only a little heavier than a normal period. She would douche herself with vinegar in water when it was over.

'Do you need a doctor?'

'I can manage without.' She hadn't thought losing her infant would hurt so much.

'Good; because they cost money.'

'You always seem to find some for gambling. Don't you care that I've lost our baby?'

There was something insincere about him when he said, 'Of course I do, but it's no good worrying about it now. We can always have another baby sometime.'

Minnie registered with the nursing agency and was offered a post at a small town called Pepperpot Creek. The agent showed her its location on the map, one hundred and twenty miles from Melbourne. She saw Saltshaker Lake a little further along. That must be where Wally's farm was.

'What happens at Pepperpot Creek?'

'Gold mining, mostly . . . there's a general store and a bar, and a few houses where families have joined their menfolk and thrown up a bush shack. There are a couple of smallholdings like your husband's that run a few sheep and cattle, mostly in the Pepperpot Creek area.'

'How did it get that name?'

He grinned. 'The place was salted with fool's gold back in the gold rush days. The owner made a fortune selling off the claims.'

'And Saltshaker Lake?'

'The miners diverted the stream in the early days and the salt levels rose. There's also a mission, so having a nursing post there is convenient. Think it over and let me know, Mrs Prichard. There's no rush, the current nurse doesn't leave for a month or so.'

'What if there was an emergency . . . something I couldn't handle?'

'You'd have back up. There's a pedal wireless, so you'd be able to get advice from a doctor.'

A pedal wireless? She couldn't even imagine what that was.

The day after that Wally had a sizeable win. 'On the horses,' he'd said.

Jubilant, he'd arrived home driving a battered Ford. 'You'll be able to take that job now, Minnie. The money will help see us over the first year while I'm setting the farm up, and I'll teach you how to drive the car so you can get yourself to work and back.'

'We'll be off in a day or two,' he told his parents.

'Don't forget you owe your pa and me for board.'

'With all the work that Minnie put in on the place, you should be paying us.' He took out his wallet, and, reluctantly extracting two pounds from the several notes it contained, laid them on the bar. 'Will that do?'

Ma's podgy hand beat Harry's to the prize and she slid it into her pocket, laughing. 'You're getting a bit slow, darls, I'll have to swap you for something faster.'

Harry gazed at his son, his expression dubious. 'You're a bit flash with your money, aren't you son? You've been getting up to your old tricks and running a book, I reckon. You'd better be careful that John Teagan doesn't come looking for you.'

'I've heard that he's inside.'

Horrified, Minnie stared at him. 'You shouldn't associate with criminals.'

Ma shook with laughter. 'You haven't told her, then.'

Staring from one to the other, Minnie asked him, 'Told me what?'

'Shut up, Ma. It's none of her business.'

'She's your wife and she's got a right to know what she's let herself in for. Wally's been inside a couple of times . . . mostly for illegal bookkeeping, but also for taking part in a robbery. Mind you, he was young then, and easily led. John Teagan and his thugs used him as a lookout.'

Minnie gasped. The next moment she remembered the money he'd taken from Esmé, and knew her own behaviour had been just as bad as Wally's in the eyes of the law. She should have insisted on him giving it back to her friend. Had Esmé reported her loss, the police would be looking for her, and would probably have caught up with her by now. Minnie intended to repay Esmé when she could, but it was still theft.

'I haven't done any of that stuff for years.' Wally gazed at the floor and dug the toe of his shoe into the beer-stained linoleum, a sign that said he was lying.

'So where did all that money come from?'

Without looking up, he shrugged. 'Not that it's any of your business, Ma.'

Ma made no bones about who was in charge of the conversation. 'It will be if the cops come knocking on my door.'

Wally's face was red when he finally looked at his mother and said a trifle aggressively. 'Oh, all right . . . so I ran a book. I only did it to give Minnie and me a good start. My luck was in, so I went on to a poker game and put all we had on it, and I won a heap.'

'Where did you get your stake from?' Minnie asked.

His eyes flickered towards her and her heart sank. She didn't have to ask to know where from.

'Somebody on the ship . . . it was only a loan. Never mind, I'll pay it back the next time the ship's in port. Besides, it will be the last time.'

Ma's eyes mirrored her scepticism. 'Make sure it is then. You've got a wife to support, and I don't want any trouble brought to my doorstep.'

It would be her own wage supporting them until they got established, Minnie thought, but she'd put something aside in a safe place each week, so eventually she'd have enough money to pay Esmé back.

They left early the next morning, a crate of fluffy yellow chicks tweeting in the back seat, a gift from Harry and Ma for Christmas.

Ma gave her a hug. 'Goodbye, Minnie love. You're more than our Wally deserves, and if you ever need help, you know where we are. I'm sorry about the baby, truly I am.'

'Best of luck,' Harry called out as they moved off. 'Watch out for the snake, especially the trouser snake.'

Minnie turned to grin at them, and waved.

The pair was still cackling with laughter when they turned the corner.

'They liked you,' Wally said, his hand going to her knee and squeezing it.

She moved her knee away. 'I liked them too. What's the house at Saltshaker Lake like?'

'It's nothing fancy as I recall, but I haven't been there since I was a kid . . . Well, for some time, anyway. My uncle had lots of plans for the place. Let's see. Inside, there were two bedrooms and a living room. The kitchen is tacked on the back. There's a tub and a pump. Oh yes . . . and a veranda. It's a bit on the primitive side.'

The understatement of the decade, Minnie thought later, when she set eyes on it. The place was crude, a hovel built of wood, and with a brick chimney at one end. Half the roof was missing.

'It probably blew off in a storm. I can see it over there.' Wally pointed.

'Where?'

'That piece of corrugated iron hanging from the tree.'

'But it's rusty and full of holes.' Minnie didn't know whether to laugh or cry, so she did both.

He patted her on the head as though she was his pet dog. 'It's all right, love, the holes will give us some fresh air. The roof timbers and ceilings are still intact. I'll fix it up for you with some tar paper and nails, and we'll soon be as snug as bugs in a rug. I wonder where Uncle Jim kept his tools.' He gazed around him, scratching his head as though they'd suddenly appear.

Her uncertain emotional state changed her ire into a definite giggle, and then uncontrollable laughter ripped from her.

He gazed at her, raised one eyebrow and grinned. 'She'll be right, Blondie, you'll see.'

There was something totally irresistible about that grin of his, and for a moment Minnie forgot he was a con man, and that she disliked him.

Seven

Soon after they'd auditioned in London, Esmé and Liam were on the train to Dorset.

'What did your friend say?' Esmé asked, for the auditioning agent had taken Liam to one side and they'd spoken together, their backs turned towards her.

Liam hesitated, then said, 'I'm to contact him in a few days.' He'd been preoccupied on the train, gazing out of the window as though he had something on his mind.

She sympathized with him because she knew how badly he wanted to dance, certainly more passionately than she did. The thought of dancing back and forth across the North Atlantic wasn't all that appealing to her, now she'd been confronted with the constant closeness of perspiration, aching muscles and blistered feet, and the dictate that she be perfectly groomed at all times when she was on the passenger decks.

She'd rather stay on firm ground. Even the thought of Hollywood held very little appeal. That was Liam's dream, one he'd had since before she'd come on the scene. He was certainly good-looking and talented enough. But then, Rosemary Mortimer, who'd been married to Major Henry, had also been good-looking and talented, and had possessed a wonderful singing voice. She'd gone to Hollywood with dreams of fame and fortune, and now her name was hardly ever mentioned.

March winds buffeted them as they stepped on to the crude wooden platform at Creekmore Halt. Liam gazed at her as the engine puffed off, asking for the second time, 'Are you sure your family won't mind me coming home with you?'

Head to one side she slanted a smile at him, hiding her own uneasiness. 'If we're to be married you've got to meet them sometime, Liam. My sister will probably be relieved because I haven't been carried off by pirates or eaten by cannibals.'

'We could run away and get married . . . tell them afterwards.'

'It would hurt their feelings terribly. They're my family, Liam. I love them, and I want them to be at my wedding. You've been gloomy ever since the audition. What's wrong?'

'Nothing . . . I'm nervous, that's all. I've never contemplated marriage before.' He slid his arm around her waist and held her against him as they walked. A few minutes later he began to sing his own lyrics to the latest routine they'd used in the audition.

'*Dance . . . dance . . . dance, Lady Esmé, dance with me . . .*'

Out of habit they skipped together in the right place, dropped their bags and went into the routine. Soon they were doing the foxtrot in the middle of the road and singing at the top of their voices. When he lifted her by the waist, twirled her round and set her down, they were breathless. They collapsed on to a fallen log and gazed at each other, laughing.

'I love dancing with you, and I love you,' she said, surprising herself, because she didn't really know if she did, or not. Instantly, she wished she could take the words back, for the statement seemed to make things more permanent. *It would be permanent!*

His smile widened, and then faded. 'You mean that, don't you, Es? It sounded as though you were trying to convince yourself.'

'Would I have said so if I didn't?'

'No . . . I suppose not. We haven't known each other very long, and for that reason alone I don't think your family will approve of me.'

The reluctance in his voice was marked; as if he was as uncertain as she was now that their union was close.

She touched his face. 'They don't have to approve of you, but it would be nice if they did. They won't, unless they're given the chance to get to know you. Are you getting cold feet?'

'I don't want to alienate you from those you love. Family is important to you.' The small touch of yearning in his voice reminded her that he had no family to welcome him home.

'Yes they are. They'll grow to love you when you become one of us. Our children will have cousins and aunts and uncles.'

Doubt filled his eyes. 'I don't know how I'll function in such an environment. I've always been a bit solitary, and thought you would become my family, not the other way round. As for children . . . I hadn't given them much thought at all.'

Neither had she given any thought to children, just took it for granted that there would be one or two.

'Except for a short time with my brother, I can't remember ever being part of a proper family.'

They should have discussed all this in advance, and Esmé didn't quite know how to handle it. 'Then it's about time you were. Wait till you meet my niece, Meggie. She'll want you to teach her all the dances. I showed her how to dance the Charleston before I left. She couldn't figure out how to coordinate her hands and knees without knocking them together.'

There was something strained about his laughter. 'She got herself in a tangle, did she?'

'My nephews are typical boys, and my brother-in-law is a well-respected surgeon. He loses his doctorly dignity when he's home. He eggs the boys on, usually when it's their bedtime. My sister pretends to get cross with him, and Denton pretends not to notice. He adores Livia.'

Taking her face between his hands, he gazed into her eyes. 'And I adore you, my darling Esmé. You're my best friend, and I've never thought of any woman as that before.'

Mindful they were on a public road, however remote, potholed and stony it was, his kiss was light against her lips, and without much passion . . . but then, she only had Leo Thornton's kiss to compare it to, and Leo had an unfair advantage. But then again, she'd probably never see the Australian again . . . and there was probably more to him than just being good at kissing.

They'd just moved apart when a car came rumbling towards them. It skidded to a halt in a cloud of dust. A heap of people tumbled out and swept Esmé into their midst.

Livia said straight away. 'Before you say anything, I'm sorry I was such a bad-tempered wretch the last time I saw you. Forgive me or I'll never speak to you again.'

Esmé's laughter was carried off by the wind. 'Is that a promise? Of course I forgive you, Livia, as long as it's reciprocated. I've missed you so much.'

'Now you're home I'm never letting you escape again.'

Esmé flicked Liam a glance, but he was gazing warily at Livia, as if he thought she might set about him.

Her glance moved on to Meggie next. 'Hallo Meggie Moo. You must have grown three and a half inches taller since I last saw you.'

Meggie cast a doleful look at her budding breasts, then folded her arms over them and hunched her shoulders. 'I loathe growing up.'

'It's better than growing down.'

'You might grow roots if you did,' Luke said.

'Or have branches growing out of your head with a bird's nest on top,' Adam added.

The boys howled with gales of laughter at the stale joke, which was borrowed from their father, and was one of his less impressive efforts.

Dropping a kiss on Meggie's head Esmé exchanged a sympathetic smile with her sister. 'I don't suppose males can help being like that, can they?'

Meggie giggled. 'Who wants brothers. They're dire creatures . . . honest.'

Nevertheless Esmé loved them to pieces. She gave them a quick hug and kiss before they realized her intention.

'Disgusting . . . germs!' Adam said, and Luke grabbed at his own throat and made strangling noises.

'I've missed you, Meggie, come and give me a hug.' Her glance went to Livia's flat stomach. 'Have you had the baby then?'

'I lost it . . . him . . . It was shortly after you left.'

A small surge of guilt stabbed at Esmé. 'Oh Livia, I'm so sorry.'

'I'm over it now. It wasn't anyone's fault . . . something to do with the placenta being in the wrong place and becoming detached.'

Meggie's gaze wandered to Liam and she whispered. 'Who's that man with you?'

Esmé had almost forgotten about Liam in the pleasure of being home again. 'His name is Liam Denison. Liam's my dancing partner, and . . .' Her eyes met his and she smiled to reassure him of his worthiness. 'He's also my fiancé.' Holding out her hand she drew him into the circle. 'Come and meet everyone, Liam.'

'Goodness . . . that's a surprise.' Livia gazed at him, a frown wrinkling her forehead. 'You seem familiar, Mr Denison. Are you from these parts?'

'I grew up in London.'

'How long have you and Esmé known each other?'

Esmé experienced a withdrawal in Liam, as though he'd closed a door on himself.

'We've known each other for a few weeks,' she said. 'Now, can we get home. I take it you're going to offer us a bed each for the night.'

'Yes . . . yes, of course.' There was something cool about her sister's manner now. 'We might be a bit crowded because Chas and his friend will be home for the weekend. You remember Leo Thornton don't you, Esmé? You met him at the New Year's Eve weekend party. He's heading home to Australia next week. A pity. I rather liked him, and he fitted in so well.'

Esmé absently touched her fingertips against her mouth and tried not to grin. How that man kept popping into her thoughts! Leo wasn't the type to go unnoticed, even when he wasn't present. 'Yes, of course, I remember Leo.'

'Aunt Es can sleep in my room with me,' Meggie said. 'I can use the truckle bed. Liam can sleep in her room, and Leo can bunk in with Chad.'

'They're grown men, Meggie, and grown men take up a great deal of room.'

Liam was apologetic. 'We should have telephoned you first. If it's inconvenient I can stay at a local hotel.'

'There isn't a local hotel. I imagine we can fit you in somewhere though. The couch in the small sitting room might have to do, but I daresay you've slept on worse.'

'Haven't we all, Mrs Elliot,' Liam murmured, diverting what seemed to be a deliberate slight by her sister with a light laugh, though there was something unsure about it.

'Right then, let's all get in the car. Grab the handle and give it a turn, please, Billy.'

'It's Liam . . . not Billy,' Esmé reminded her.

Her sister's gaze engaged Liam's directly. 'William . . . Liam . . . Billy . . . what's the difference?'

Liam appeared embarrassed by her sister's challenge, for

colour appeared in his cheeks. He held his ground though. 'It's simply a matter of preference on my part.'

Livia was immediately contrite. 'I'm sorry, that was rude of me.'

'Yes . . . it was, and apologizing doesn't make it any less rude.'

It was Livia's turn to squirm while Liam bent to his task, but Livia had deserved it. Goodness, this wasn't going anything like Esmé had expected.

When the engine fired into life, he said, 'There's not much room left in the car. I'll walk, I need the exercise.'

Livia said stiffly, 'As you wish. We'll see you later, I imagine.'

Meggie flung herself from the car, bristling with defiance. 'He might take the wrong turn, so I'm walking with him.'

Livia was brusque. 'Suit yourself, you usually do.'

Esmé, with Luke and Adam flanking her, didn't have time to join them because Livia immediately put the car into gear and they were off.

What had happened to her loving closely-knit family? Esmé wondered in dismay. That had been instant antagonism. When they got to the house Esmé waited until the children had gone inside, then said, 'You froze him out, Livia. Why?'

'Yes . . . I suppose I did. What do you know of his background?'

'Liam is all alone in the world. I'm going to marry him, that's all I need to know.'

'Do you remember Billy Bastard from the orphanage?'

Unease made muddy inroads into her stomach. 'Not clearly. I try not to think of our time in the orphanage.'

'I think Liam Denison is one and the same.'

'What if he is? It's not his fault he was orphaned. His parents died during the war.'

Livia gave an impatient cluck of her tongue. 'He's lying if he told you that. He was called Billy Bastard? His mother was a prostitute and had two children out of wedlock. Apparently the woman didn't even know who the boys' fathers were. He has a brother, I recall. Timmy, I think his name was.'

'Liam did have a brother. Tommy died in the Spanish flu outbreak.'

'There . . . what does that tell you?'

'That he had a brother who died in the Spanish flu pandemic. How very sad. I'm glad I didn't lose my brother, and pleased I managed to stay alive at the time when so many didn't.'

'You're being deliberately provocative. That man comes from bad stock . . . you can't marry someone from that background? He's a dancer. How will he support you when he's too old to dance? I'm ashamed of you, Esmé.'

Esmé had wondered that herself on occasion. She was ashamed too – ashamed that her sister thought like that. She understood too well where it came from. Despite being middle class their own parents had lived beyond their means and had left them destitute. At fourteen, Livia had been sent from the orphanage to work as a maid in Foxglove House, where she'd married the doomed and disabled Richard Sangster – a move that had ensured a future for them all. Meggie had been produced from that short marriage.

But she couldn't dance to Livia's tune any more. Her sister had gained everything she'd ever wanted from life . . . a loving husband, a family, and some standing in the local community. Granted, Livia had been like a mother to her and Esmé didn't want to hurt her sister. But Livia lived in a small world within her own boundaries, and Esmé had stepped outside it now.

'Perhaps you'd prefer it if we postponed the wedding until I can sort things out with Liam. You might be mistaken, you know, and does it matter? I'm sure you'll like him once you get to know him properly.'

Livia's sigh held relief. 'I knew you'd see sense, Esmé.'

Just then Meggie came bounding down the road. She came to a halt, panting for breath. 'He's gone, Aunt Es.'

'Liam's gone . . . gone where?'

'Back to the station. He said he didn't want to be the cause of any trouble.'

Livia gazed at her. 'I told you he didn't fit in.'

'You never gave him the chance to find out.' She started back towards the station at a run, for the up train was due before too long. Meggie began to follow her.

'Go home, there's a love, Meggie Moo,' she shouted over her shoulder. 'This is private, and it's between myself and Liam.'

Liam was sitting on his bag. Her own bag was next to him, as though he'd expected her to return and join him. Gazing up at her, he smiled. 'Well, let's be having the inquisition.'

Anger rippled through her. 'Why didn't you tell me?'

'It's not something I wanted to remember.' He shrugged. 'Your sister knew me right away. I could see the disdain in her eyes, as though she thought me beneath her.'

'Did you recognize her right away?'

He nodded. 'She brought some food to the orphanage a couple of times. Once, you were having a birthday. She hugged you and your brother. I asked her to hug my brother, as well . . . and she did. Tommy never forgot it. When he was delirious with fever from the flu he asked if she'd been our mother. I lied to him, and said she was, and she'd be coming back for us. Our own mother promised to come for us when she left us there, but she never did.'

Tears filled her eyes. 'Livia was in the orphanage too for a while. We had a different background than most, and she remembered it. The change affected her badly. Chad and I were young, and the orphanage is all we knew. It was easier for us because we always knew she'd come for us one day.'

Liam drew in a deep breath. 'I ran away from the place when I was thirteen, and lived by my wits for a year or so. Then I found a job cleaning a theatre. Eric was in the chorus line. He taught me the routines and I was taken on as a dancer.'

'What did living on your wits entail?'

'Nothing a nice girl like you should know about.'

'By running away now you're forcing me to choose between you and my family, Liam.'

'That's not really a choice, Esmé. If you loved me there would be no choice to make. I can't be slotted in as part of your family, my love. You're different to me. We want different things. Come what may I'm sailing on the *Aquitania*. That's what I want.'

Bewildered, she gazed at him. 'But you said you had to contact them—'

'I lied. They offered me a job, and I'm taking it. I want to make something of myself.'

Her smile came, and just as quickly fled as his words sunk in. 'They didn't want me, did they. Why didn't you say so?' The train whistle blew in the distance. He shrugged. 'I didn't know how to tell you.'

'Ah . . . I see. It seems as though lying is a habit with you. You're very good at it, Liam.'

He was curt. 'Then I'll try not to sugar coat it. They didn't want a couple, and you'd have been out of your depth, anyway. You would have looked like the amateur you are, and would never have managed the routines.' After a short pause, he whispered, 'I was undecided, wondering if my wage would support us both, and whether to take the job or turn it down. I didn't want to hurt you. Meeting your family decided me.'

'But it's all right to hurt me now. You're saying it was Livia's fault?'

'Nothing is her fault, and you wanted the truth. She's watching out for your interests, as she's always done. I've got nothing to fall back on in the way of fortune or skills and she knows it. But then, it's not something I've tried to acquire because I've just drifted from job to job before, and without being answerable to anyone. I don't need you, Esmé.'

The brutal cut wounded her deeply. 'Am I to take it you were going to end our engagement, and all the talk about being in love with me was lies?'

'No . . . oh, God . . . I do love you, Es. I love you with everything that's in me, which isn't much I might add, because I'm sort of hollow. All this domestic stuff isn't for me. I never wanted marriage until I met you, and at the moment I certainly don't want the responsibility of raising children, or wrestling with the politics of brothers and sisters. I've been struggling about accepting this job on the *Aquitania*. If I turn it down we can stay on the *Horizon Queen*. But this opportunity only comes once in a lifetime. At the moment I can only offer you the life of a gypsy. Take it or leave it.'

'You could settle down if you put your mind to it. You could learn to be anything you wanted. You can't dance forever, your body won't let you, and having children would ground you. You're using that as an excuse. You want me to be the one to choose, because you know what my answer will be. I care for you too much to tie you down, but d'you know something? I don't really love you . . . not yet. I was hoping it would grow. You're a coward, Liam.'

He flinched as though she'd struck him. 'If that's what you want to think.'

If she stayed she'd become a millstone around his neck, so she did what he expected. She took off the ring and held it out to him. He closed her hand over it. 'Keep it. It isn't worth much.'

'It isn't worth anything. I thought you were better than that.'

He withdrew into himself, into his hurt. 'So did I, but there's obviously some truth in the saying that a leopard never changes its spots.' He gently kissed her when the train came into view, then picked up his bag. 'Thanks for everything, Esmé. Come if you like but you'll have a better life without me in it.'

Gazing into his eyes she said deliberately, wounding him as best she could, 'I know I will. Goodbye, Billy Bastard.'

She got through to him with that, and immediately felt guilty when he flinched, as though she'd struck him. 'I guess I deserved that. Try not to hate me, love. I'm hurting as it is.'

A healthy dollop of anger surged into her. *He* was hurting! How did he think she was feeling?

Getting into the carriage he gazed at her through the window. She could see the reflection in the glass of her bag at her feet. All she had to do was pick it up and join him. But she couldn't spend her life being consumed by Liam's search for self-worth. She'd struggled too hard to hang on to her own.

She should leave, walk away from him. They stared at each other through the grimy glass, and Liam looked as miserable as she felt.

When the whistle blew he placed his palm against the window. She wanted to go with him, but her feet wouldn't move, and she shoved her own hands in her pocket. Get off the train, she silently implored, but he didn't. Two seconds later the train lurched forward, taking Liam and the remains of her pride with him. Picking up her bag, she turned and walked away.

It had been a messy end to her first real love affair, if one could call it that, certainly nothing like the movies. It had left her feeling soiled.

Meggie was waiting for her, her eyes wide with worry. Esmé was wrapped in her hug. 'I thought you might get on the train with him. Then I thought you might need me if you didn't.'

'I nearly did . . . and I do need you Meggie, love. Thank you for waiting.'

'Don't you love Liam any more?'

'I'll always love him a little, but perhaps what's happened is for the best.' She felt too hollow to cry.

'Will you be staying home now?'

'It isn't really my home, Meggie Moo. It belongs to your family. I'm grateful for being included as part of it all these years.'

'Where will you go?'

'I'm going to telephone the shipping company I work for and ask them to re-engage me as a nurse for the cruise to Australia. I need to know that my friend Minnie is all right. We'd made plans, you know, and she might need me. I'll write to you when I get there.'

Her sister would argue, but it was about time Livia learned that Esmé's world didn't revolve about her sun, but had an orbit all of its own to complete. 'Hold out your hand.' When Meggie did, Esmé dropped her discarded engagement ring in the palm. There was a twinge of remorse when she realized it had probably cost Liam more than he could afford. 'You can have this if you'd like it.'

Meggie slid it on to her finger and admired it. 'It's lovely . . . so shiny. The rubies are pretty.'

Although she felt like kicking the nearest tree, Esmé managed a smile. 'Don't be fooled by its glitter, they're garnets. I have it on good authority that the ring is not worth much.'

'You're wrong, Aunt Es . . . everyone and everything has got a value, it's just that some people place a lesser price on their own worth than it deserves.'

Meggie constantly surprised her with her insights, and she was probably right, Esmé thought.

Eight

If that noisy kookaburra didn't keep its beak shut she'd wring its stupid neck. 'We'll see if you laugh then,' Minnie muttered. And if Wally didn't stop snoring she'd do the same to him.

But at least the roof was now repaired, and the holes were more or less patched.

She went to the room that served as a kitchen and stoked the stove up with the dead sticks she'd collected from those that littered the ground outside. The fire began to crack and snap.

The mine shop had provided her with eggs. The chicks were long gone so the promised chicken coop had never been needed.

'Snakes would have eaten them,' Wally had said, laughing when she'd cried over the fate of the sweet fluffy creatures that had disappeared one by one. She cursed when she noticed that the goat had gnawed through its rope. There would be no milk until it was found.

Wally had eaten the last of the bread and she didn't have time to make any now. It would have to be pancakes. She made a pan of porridge, as well, and ate hers with honey. That would have to do for breakfast.

She could have lived in the small flat attached to the nurse's post at the mine site, with meals thrown in, but there wasn't room for two people to live comfortably inside it for any length of time, and Wally had scorned the job he was offered there at the time, in favour of self-sufficiency.

They'd been here for two months, and she was coming to the conclusion that she couldn't keep this up. Wally wasn't pulling his weight. Apart from fixing the roof, a temporary effort by the looks of it, he'd cleared some of the debris away from the house, and had dug over and planted a vegetable patch. Seedlings had been planted, and the tender little shoots had disappeared by morning.

They'd laughed about it, but as a forerunner of things to come, it hadn't really been funny. Wally hadn't bothered to replant them. She didn't know what he did all day when she was at work. The whitewash she'd bought to brighten up the place was still untouched, except for a slap or two on the bedroom wall.

She took his mug of tea through and gave him a nudge. 'Wake up, Wally. Breakfast's ready, and I want to talk to you before I go to work.'

He came to the table a couple of minutes later, unshaven and bleary-eyed, and scratching his stomach. 'You forgot to put milk in my tea.'

'There isn't any; the goat's run away. You'll have to find her before you do anything else. And I haven't got time to make any bread. Drop me off at the nursing post then you can go to the store and buy some to tide us over.'

'I haven't got any money.'

'Take it from the pot.'

'I used that for fuel for the generator.'

'For God's sake Wally, you can spend money faster than I can earn it. I'm running myself ragged while you're sitting around on your backside, and I'm still trying to save up enough to pay Esmé back that money you stole from her. Why don't you take that job they offered you at the mine site?'

'I didn't steal that money, I borrowed it, so don't start nagging me about that, again. I've got plenty to do around here.'

'Then why don't you get on with it? This place is a disgrace. The whitewash has been sitting there for a month, and the windows need cleaning.'

'Lay off it, Minnie. They'll only get dusty again. Besides, it will rain soon. I'll run a cloth over them, then.'

She rummaged in her bag and came out with a florin. 'That's all I've got until pay day. If it's not enough they'll have to put it on the slate.'

She was glad to get to work. The nursing post at Pepperpot Creek had been built, and was maintained, by the mining company. The area was gently hilly, the lower slopes thickly wooded. As it got higher the peaks steepled and the trees thinned out. Bald patches appeared where trees had been felled, signalling the workings of the mines. Tunnels were bored into the hills like giant wormholes. Carts on rails came and went all day. The creek trickled off downhill, thick with tailings and sludge, and past various private claims that had been bought up by the company.

As well as the nursing post, there was an assay office, a general store, a mine office and a canteen.

The nursing post consisted of a small waiting room with a bench on the veranda for the overflow of patients. At the back was a consulting room with an examination table and a cupboard filled with lotions, potions and pills. Beyond that was a small office where the files were kept and the pedal radio housed. It was similar to the one the company had installed in a small corner of her living room, and it didn't take long to learn how to use it.

The premises were as clean as a building in a mining town could get, and were kept that way by one of the miner's wives, a thin-faced woman called Sally Bowers. Sally had some previous nursing experience, though she had never qualified. Minnie had started coaching her, so she could qualify as a practical nurse at some later date if she got the opportunity. Her assistance was available whenever it was needed.

'Good morning, Sally,' she said, and nodded to another, younger, woman, who followed her in with a baby in her arms. 'You're a bit early for Charlie's check-up?'

'Yes, Nurse Prichard, but I've heard there's an outbreak of chicken pox up at the mission, and those nuns might take it into their heads to bring those kids in. I don't want my Charlie to be exposed to it.'

'The sisters aren't daft,' Sally told her, scoffing at the young mother's fear. 'It wouldn't do him any harm. It's a mild disease, and once he's been exposed to it he would be immune.'

'That's usually the case, Sally. But there can be complications, like high fever, which might cause convulsions. It's highly contagious because it's passed on through the air when people who have the disease cough.' She tickled the child's stomach. 'You've picked yourself a good mum, Charlie, boy. Well done. In you come, then.'

Mother and child smiled at the compliment.

Wally honked the horn and waved as he drove off. The baby jerked and gave a yelp of fright.

'The bloody idiot,' Sally Bowers said, not bothering that she'd been overheard by the bloody idiot's wife.

Minnie agreed. Wally had forgotten to stop off at the store for bread.

After checking Charlie over, she logged in with the mining company, informing them she was open for business. She then contacted the mission.

'Good morning, Sister Bernadine,' she tapped out. 'I'm given to understand you have a chicken pox outbreak. Over.'

The mission sister answered her immediately. The woman was more qualified than Minnie in experience, and it must have been irksome for her to take orders. But it was part of Minnie's job to make sure the mission sisters were doing the right thing, since the government paid her wages.

'You know the treatment, Sister. Keep the children as cool as possible and use plenty of soothing lotion. Report any high fevers or complications to me and I'll get the mine manager to bring me out . . . over and out.'

The small waiting room filled up quickly. There were various ailments, mostly minor; a festering splinter embedded in a thumb, a cut that needed a couple of stitches, a foreign object to be removed from an eye . . . two newly expectant mothers to be advised. Her job was interesting, and she enjoyed the responsibility that came with it, though she hoped she didn't get anything too big to handle. She was glad that the matron in charge of her training had been thorough. That busy, but sheltered life on the wards seemed remote to her now.

She wondered what Esmé was doing, and felt bad about Wally stealing from her friend. She'd lost her own money to him too, in a card game. She shouldn't have told him that Esmé had that money, and couldn't imagine how she'd ever been attracted to him. She wished he'd deserted her. He'd turned out to be a lazy so-and-so.

The morning went by quickly. Waiting until dusk was falling she made her way through to the mine office to cadge a lift home.

Ben Smith, the grizzled mine foreman smiled at her. 'I'll take you.'

'Thanks, Ben. I don't know where Wally is. Perhaps the car's broken down.'

'I reckon it must have, at that. You should move into the nurse's quarters.'

'It would be more convenient, but it's too small for both of us.' The flat consisted of one bedroom, and one living room and kitchen combined. There was a cold shower on the veranda with canvas surrounds for privacy, and the usual facilities situated a discreet distance to the house.

'We'd be tripping over each other all the time, and Wally said he wants to get the property up to scratch.'

'Wanting to and doing it is two different things. That land has had it, and the next strong blow will probably take the house off its stumps. His uncle should have sold it to the mining company when he had the chance.'

The house was in darkness when they got there and the car was missing. The goat was chained to a veranda post with her kid suckling at her teat. She offered Minnie a plaintive bleat.

'I'll see you safely indoors, love.'

The generator wouldn't start, and she didn't know where Wally kept the fuel. He said he'd bought fuel for it. A hand over the stove told her it was cold too. There was a note on the kitchen table.

> *I've gone to the city for a few days, and I might go back to sea if I can get a berth. I'll come back and fetch a few things in a couple of days. But don't count on it. See you Blondie.*
> *Love Wally*

Feeling only relief, she checked her small store of money, which she kept in the toe of one of her shoes. There was ten pounds. It looked pathetically small, and it would take her ages to save up a hundred.

A moment of self-pity thickened in Minnie's throat and she drew in a long breath to calm herself before doing what felt more appropriate, which was throwing Wally's note at the wall.

Ben smiled at the gesture. 'It saves you chucking him out, aye, lass.'

'You're right about that, Ben. I only wish I could, but I'm married to him.'

How had she managed to get herself into such a situation? She wished Esmé were here to lean on. Her friend was always so calm and rational. 'How does he think I'm going to get to work and back?'

The reply was blunt. 'The man's a fool, just like his uncle was. Look love, I can't leave you all alone out here. Fetch everything you need for the next few days. You can stay at the nurse's quarters till he comes back.'

'What about the goat?'

'Set her free. She won't wander far, and she and the kid can forage for themselves for a while, though she'll probably join one of the wild herds eventually.'

When Wally hadn't put in an appearance after several days, Minnie began to worry.

'I'm going to the city on business,' Ben Smith told her. 'Didn't his folks have a hotel? Give me the address and I'll drop in and see what he's up to.'

Ben was back a couple of days later. 'Wally's old man upped and died, and he's helping his mother out until she decides whether to sell the hotel or not.'

'Did he send a message?'

'He said he might go back to sea once he sees his mum settled, so don't worry if you don't hear from him for several weeks.'

Good riddance, she thought uncharitably, because never seeing Wally again would be soon enough. 'I won't do that, but I can't have you running me back and forth when you have your own work to do. I'm not living at the homestead by myself. The place is too isolated. What's more, it isn't fit to house pigs. Will you take me there and wait while I gather a few things together? I'll try and be quick.'

'I've seen pigs housed in worse. I'll take the radio back while I'm here. I wouldn't put it past the bugger to collect it and sell it.'

'Wally said his uncle had some gold hidden somewhere. He

said it's down a snake hole, so not to put my arm down one looking for it, else I might get a nasty surprise. As if I would. Snakes scare me to pieces. They ate all my poor little chicks when we first came here.'

Ben shook with laughter. 'His Uncle Jim's gold is a legend. Wally would have torn the place apart looking for it if he'd believed it. As for snakes, they won't bother you if you don't bother them. They'll move into the scrub when they hear you coming, so tread heavily. They keep the mice down, if nothing else.'

'I'd prefer the mice.'

Ben shuffled from one foot to the other and he couldn't quite meet her eye. 'There's something else, love.'

'Let's be having it then.'

'Word is that Wally is into stuff that's not quite legit, and he's treading on a few toes.'

'I'm not sure what you mean. He plays cards, but I don't know any of the crowd he mixes with. We haven't been married very long, you see.'

His face mottled. 'There's that, too.'

'My marriage . . . what of it? It's quite legal.'

'He's . . . well, he's got another woman on the go. Lillian, her name is.'

Minnie wasn't surprised that Wally had turned out to be unfaithful. She tried not to be hard on him. He wasn't all that bad, and had a good-natured but shallow sort of charm about him. He seemed to lack a sense of responsibility and wasn't really much of a man at all.

'Word is that she's the sister of a man called John Teagan. Wally has known her a long time and has always fancied her. He's heading for trouble with that one. She's young and flighty, you see.'

'Oh, my God,' she whispered as it sank in. Ma had said John Teagan was a right villain, and he'd been in jail. 'I wonder if Ma knows?'

'Ma didn't, by all accounts, but when she found out she kicked up merry hell and won't let her in the hotel. My woman said I should tell you, lessen you took it into your head to go to the city to pay him a visit. At least you'd know what to expect.'

Minnie might know what to expect, but that didn't mean she knew what to do. She told herself that Wally wasn't her responsibility. But he was, since she was married to him. She had no intention of becoming his proper wife again though, and was going to try to get a divorce.

The first thing she intended to do was go through the homestead and see if there was anything of value she could pawn, to recoup the money he'd taken from Esmé.

'Do you think the mine would still buy the place? Perhaps I could persuade Wally—'

'Not a chance, your man was too greedy. Besides, it's Wally's name on the deeds. You might as well know why I went to the city; it was to see the mine owner. Between you and me, he intends to close down operations by the end of the year. The amount of gold we're getting out of the mine isn't worth the cost of the labour and things are going to get worse. The wife and I will be all right, since I'll be staying on as a caretaker. I reckon the nursing post will close down, though. The mission can get in touch with the medical services direct.'

Minnie was tempted to hand in her notice and go back to England, but she'd signed a contract for a year. Besides, she'd become aware that this other woman thing might just be empty gossip. If she were to divorce Wally, it would be more difficult to do that from England.

She gathered everything together that was hers – not that it was much – and threw her cases into the truck. She found a couple of shillings in small change.

Ben dismantled the radio and said, 'Flippin' wonderful these things are. You wonder what the world's going to come up with next.'

Two days later Minnie was ensconced in the nurse's quarters and had just finished hanging out her washing when the pedal radio alerted her to a call.

She typed in the keys that operated the Morse signal. *Pepperpot Creek. Nurse Prichard here. Over.* She must remember to change her name back to Nurse James when she left here.

It was the agency. *I've got someone here who wants to speak to you, Nurse.*

She hoped it wasn't Wally. *Go ahead.*

Minnie . . . it's me, it's Esmé. Are you all right?

I thought you went back to England.

I did . . . then I came back . . . alone. I was worried about you.

A warm feeling, like a smile lit up inside her. So, Esmé hadn't married Liam after all. And Esmé had come all this way to check up on her. Minnie wondered what had gone wrong between them, and suspected it was her fault, since she'd made a mess of just about everything. *We'll have a good chat when we see each other. How long are you here for? I can't take time off to come to Melbourne, but you could get a lift to Pepperpot Creek. Ask the agency to find someone coming this way. I think the supplies are due to be renewed.*

The agency man took over. *I'll send the little lady up the day after tomorrow. Any problems?*

Not if she didn't count Wally's deceit. *Everything's fine. The chicken pox outbreak seems to be over, and the Stephens' baby is due this week. Can you look after my friend, tonight?*

Miss Carr can stay with my family tonight. Over and out.

Esmé arrived towards the end of the afternoon consultations. 'Help stack the delivery away, Es. The drugs go into the locked cabinet . . . the key is in the drawer.'

She examined Connie Stephens. The mound of her stomach was striated where the skin had stretched. Her baby's head was well down in the pelvis and its heart was beating strongly. 'The baby's as snug as a cork in a bottle,' she told Connie, 'but your blood pressure is up a bit. What have you been up to?'

A small movement pushed against Minnie's palm. It could be the infant stretching, or settling in . . . or . . .? She smiled down at her patient. 'Are you having any contractions, by any chance?'

The woman shook her head. 'I don't think so.'

'Have you had a show?'

'What's that?'

'It's trace of blood and mucus in your drawers.'

The woman shrugged. 'There was something a couple of days ago. It wasn't much. I keep peeing, that's all. It's a nuisance. I'm wearing a path to the outhouse, running back and forth.'

Minnie hid her grin. 'I hope you won't mind if I call my friend in to examine you. She's a midwife, too.'

'All right, but I'll be happy to get out of this position. My back hurts like crazy. I think I must have bent the wrong way this morning because the pain in my back keeps coming and going.'

Minnie exchanged a grin with Esmé after the examination. 'Well?'

'She's your mother. You tell her.'

Minnie beamed a smile at Connie. 'I'd say that you're well and truly in labour, and have been all day, Connie, and just when my friend is paying a visit. It looks as though you'll have two midwives helping with the birth now. I'll do an internal to see how far you've dilated. I'll just give my hands a scrub.'

The examination didn't take long. 'It will be a few hours yet. We'd best get you home to rest before the birth.'

'My Pete's waiting for me outside. Can you help me off the couch, please? I feel like a stranded turtle.'

'We'll drop in on you in an hour or so and see how you're going.'

They ate in the small canteen, along with the miners, filling themselves with a hearty stew with dumplings. Bets were being taken on whether the baby would be a boy or a girl, proceeds to go to the mission.

Minnie had bet on a girl . . . so Esmé put her sixpence on a boy.

They were called at ten by the child's father banging on the door. 'Connie said to come now.'

They'd often delivered babies together, previously. It had been when they were training . . . but that had also been in a hospital with a safety net of experienced medical help at hand.

'Fingers crossed,' Minnie whispered. 'It's been ages since we did this.'

'It's your baby. I'm just doing the dirty work. Remember what Matron told us?' She assumed the tone of voice the women had used. 'Always appear confident, nurses. The mother will be relying on you for guidance.'

The baby came easily, slipping from the mother with little

fuss. He was a strong lad, his cry lusty, and loud enough to momentarily silence the crows that squabbled in the gum trees outside the bedroom window.

Minnie tidied up the mother while Esmé, who was seeing to the needs of the infant, called out, 'Heavens, what a whopper. He weighs nine pounds and two ounces! How on earth did you manage it?'

'That's a big boy, and with no stitches needed,' Minnie said in admiration, and with a small twinge when she remembered her own lost infant. She began to fill out the birth details to record for the certificate. 'What are you going to call him?'

'Donald, Peter.'

'Nice names.'

She remembered what the mine manager had told her about the mine closing, and wondered how Donald's parents would look after the child when his father was out of work.

There would be many like them.

When Connie got her infant back, clean and tidy and wrapped in a cotton rug, she placed him at her breast. It was as though she'd handled babies a dozen times before.

'She'll be a good mother,' Minnie said, as they made their way back to the flat, their arms around each other's waists. 'Shall we talk for a while. I've got something I need to say to you.'

'I know what it is and I'll take it as said, Min. I wish you'd asked me first though.'

'Wally took your money, not me. I feel responsible because I told him where you kept it, that night when he got me drunk.'

'What's happened to Wally? Where is he?'

'He's gone back to Melbourne, and he might even have gone to sea again. The marriage was a mistake, and I lost the baby.'

'I'm sorry.'

'I'm not . . . well, I'm sorry about losing the baby, though perhaps it's just as well, considering what happened. What about Liam?'

'He put his career first. It was odd really. I took him down to meet my family, and he and Livia were at each other's throats right away, while we were still at the railway station. We'd been in the same children's home, and she recognized him, though I hadn't.'

'How strange that he didn't tell you, when you were both in the place at the same time.'

'I think he was ashamed of being in there. I can understand that. He wouldn't go any further and wouldn't let me sort it out. He said he didn't want to be part of a family, and he'd been offered a job on the *Aquitania*. They didn't want me because my dancing wasn't good enough. So much for my dancing career.' The wry smile she gave hid the gut-wrenching twist of pain she felt when she thought of Liam.

'So he turned out to be a rat, as well.'

'No . . . he's not a rat. He was terribly mixed-up. I could have gone with him. He wanted it so much, and I didn't want it enough.'

'But you said he put his career first. So why didn't you go?'

'I've had time to think it over and it's a bit complicated. I didn't want to be the one who got in his way. Whether he knew it or not, he was using emotional blackmail. I'd always thought he was so sure of himself, but he wasn't. He wanted me to lean on, to have someone to blame if he didn't make it. I would have felt guilty if I'd tried to stop him from going after what he craved. Besides . . . I couldn't bring myself to turn my back on my family.'

'Yet, you're here.'

'Not for good. Because of our past, Livia is insecure. We all are . . . and we need each other. Liam saw that right away. The trouble is, he needs the same thing. Because he knew me in the orphanage he'd begun to think of me as his family. Livia soon put paid to that notion. She saw him as a threat and made it clear to him that he was an outsider. I still feel affection towards him, you know . . . at least, I think I do. It all feels like a bad dream sometimes.'

'I know the feeling. You'll get over it.'

'Yes . . . I imagine I will in time. I'll have to.'

'He had a nice body. You should have gone to bed with him.' She laughed when Esmé blushed at the thought. 'Have you got a new dance partner?'

'I'm employed as the ship's medical officer. We're sailing without a doctor on board this time.'

'So we're doing the same sort of job, me at a mine site and you on a liner. I wish we could work together again. It was so much fun. I don't particularly like this sort of responsibility. I'm worried I might do something wrong and the isolation scares me.'

'At least you've got back up?'

'Yes, there's that . . . and the new doctor has a plane so he can fly himself in if he's needed in an emergency. I've only had to call him out once. He's really something. The mining company has built an airstrip now. If only I was single,' she said with a sigh.

'You're incorrigible, Minnie. I missed having you around, even though we were fighting like a couple of cats before we parted company.'

The two women gazed at each other, and Esmé smiled wryly when Minnie said, 'We both made a mess of our love lives, didn't we?'

'I don't think I'll bother with men again for quite a while. It hurts when things go wrong.'

'Wait until you see the doctor, Es . . . he's a sweetheart. Your heart will do a backflip.'

'I'm especially resistant to doctors. I've been surrounded by them since I was a teenager, so you can have him.'

'I don't want him. Not only has Wally cured me of men, he's cured me of Australian men in particular.'

Esmé began to laugh. 'You can't blame all Australian men for the actions of one.'

'Allow me to enjoy my woman scorned moment, I'm sure I'll soon get over it. How long can you stay, Es?'

'For a couple of days . . . but I'll be back at intervals, as long as the ship keeps sailing to Australia and back.'

'My contract is for a year at the mine site. But between you and me, with the way things are going I expect to be out of work before it runs out. We can keep in touch through the agency, though. So much for our Australian adventure – all those plans we made, and I ended up here while you ended up bobbing about on the ocean like a cork.'

'But look how different it is for both of us. It's awe inspiring here. I've never seen such a flaming sunset before.'

'They become commonplace after a while.'

Minnie let them into the flat and gazed doubtfully at the small couch. 'I hope you can fit on that. If not, you can have the examination couch. It's as hard as a plank though.'

'The couch will do, it's about the same size as my bunk on the ship, and at least the floor won't be moving under me.'

Even so, Esmé couldn't sleep. Wrapping her blanket around her she let herself out on to the veranda. The night was velvety soft and she gazed with awe at the stars, appearing so low in the sky that she felt she could reach out and pluck one, like a diamond from a branch.

Faintly, the sound of the radio came to her ears. A woman was singing to an orchestra playing an Irving Berlin song. Her voice had a low, throbbing quality to it. '*The song is ended but the melody lingers on.*'

Esmé was overcome by melancholy. Obviously, another person out there couldn't sleep either.

The music ended, leaving her with nothing but an occasional sigh of wind that rustled the trees. She was alone in a vast darkness, and she could hear its spirits whisper as it cradled her. The breeze was a humid kiss against her skin and she was comforted by it. The sky moved, taking the stars with it, as if it had moved on, taking her problems with it. She came to the conclusion that they were little more than hurt pride.

Gradually, her pain and anger was absorbed by the peace of the night, and she allowed it to drain away. Talking things over with Minnie had helped her to come to terms with herself.

There came a time when her sense of aloneness scared her. It was as if she was the only person left alive on earth, and she craved companionship.

Meggie would love this place, she thought, yawning as she headed for the uncomfortable couch.

Nine

A couple of days later Esmé did meet the doctor.

It was late afternoon and the day had been quiet. They were sitting on the veranda, a glass of lemonade cradled in their hands.

There was a commotion and a woman came running, a child in her arms. 'Quick, help! I can't stop the bleeding.'

'Mrs Tomlinson . . . what's happened?' Minnie paled and sprang to her feet when she saw the screaming child carried in by his frantic mother.

'He fell over with a glass in his hand, and hit his head on a bucket. He's gashed his hand and has got glass sticking out of his face. He also has a big lump on his head.'

She eyed the chunk of glass sticking out of his face, not far from his eye socket. Immediately, Minnie said, 'I'm going to have to call out the doc. Would you see to Brian, please, Esmé.'

'I'll try and stop the bleeding.'

Brian screamed louder when Esmé began to examine him. His mother tried, with some success, to soothe him. Esmé managed to pick a couple of large pieces of glass from his hand then applied a pressure bandage and immobilized the injured arm with a sling that kept his hand above heart level. The blood loss slowed.

She felt for his pulse, which was a little fast, but that was hardly surprising after such a fright. 'How old are you, Brian?'

'Five . . . nearly six, Miss. I'm bleeding, and it tastes nasty. Am I going to die?'

'No, you won't die. It's quite all right, Brian. You have plenty more blood left inside you.' Except for the occasional sob, his fright seemed to abate a little at her words. Esmé smiled encouragingly at him. 'You're being a brave boy. I'm going to look at that eye next.' She rinsed the blood off and gently probed the area. The glass shard was stuck firmly into his cheekbone. 'Best to wait for the doctor to see to that, I think. Does it hurt very much?'

He nodded and gave a snuffle.

'I'm not surprised, since you landed on it. You've got a whacking great lump on your head, as big as an emu's egg. You look like a frightful monster with that blood all over you. Would you like to see yourself in the mirror?'

When she held a mirror up so he could see himself his eyes widened and he gave an admiring, 'Crumbs . . . wait till my friends see it.'

She exchanged a glance with his mother, who shook her head despairingly and muttered, 'Sometimes you wonder what boys have got for brains.'

Esmé put the mirror away. 'Can you count, Brian?'

'Yes.'

'How many fingers am I holding up?'

'Three.'

'Now?'

'Six . . . no it's five . . . no . . . six, it's a bit burred.'

'Keep your head still and follow my finger with your eyes.' He had a job keeping them focused. 'Are you tired?'

'It hurts when I try to look at things, so I want to close them and go to sleep.'

'I need you to try to stay awake, Brian. I'm going to wash some of that blood off you now. I've got nephews of about your age, you know. They have a big black dog called Shadow. Have you got any pets?'

'I've got a pet cockatoo, and my Dad had taught him to say swear words. You talk funny, miss.'

'Do I?'

'All posh. Like Nurse Prichard. Dad said she's from England, and they all talk like that, there.'

She grinned as she thought of the many different accents and dialects in England, and checked the bandage. A little blood had seeped through the fabric, but not enough to be alarmed about. The boy was trembling. He was able to move his fingers, and she reassured the mother. 'He'll be all right, I imagine, but I'm leaving most of the glass for the doctor to see to. How did the accident happen?'

'I was only gone for a couple of minutes. He fell off his chair and hit his head on the log bucket. The glass was still in his hands and it smashed when he fell. The little bugger won't sit still for five minutes.'

'Be thankful he missed his eye. Was he unconscious for any length of time?'

'I don't think so, but he was a bit dazed. Why are you asking all these questions?'

'Routine. It will help the doctor to have a detailed account of the accident.'

'But Brian will be all right, won't he?'

'We'll know for sure as soon as the doctor has examined him, but I don't think your boy is in any danger. Why don't you go and clean yourself up, Mrs Tomlinson. The sink's through there.'

Fetching a bowl of water, Esmé began to wash the child's face. Immediately his face screwed up in protest, like those of her nephews always did.

Homesickness hit her with some force. Liam had been right. She didn't like being apart from her family.

Minnie came in. 'What luck, we've just caught the doctor. He's over at one of the stations and will be here in three-quarters of an hour, probably less. How's Brian?'

Esmé lowered her voice. 'I can't see any lasting damage, though shock is beginning to set in. Pulse is a bit fast and his head hurts. He's also sleepy so I think he has a mild concussion. His responses aren't too bad though and the blood loss has been arrested. His fingers are pink and flexible, so I'd say the nerves have been spared. I've made notes, but you might like to check him over for yourself, Min, in case I've missed anything. After all . . . I have no authority here.'

'You're a better nurse than I'll ever be. You're always so calm.'

'Nonsense. I've just got more confidence. That's what comes of growing up surrounded by doctors and would be doctors. I'll go and make a cup of tea, I expect Mrs Tomlinson could do with one after the fright she's had, don't you?'

Esmé took hers out on to the veranda. It was almost twilight, and the air was tinted with a dusky purple haze.

It wasn't long before she heard a plane fly over. A short time later the mine manager's truck arrived in a cloud of dust. A lanky figure unfolded from the front seat, and then reached inside for his bag. He straightened up and turned. For a moment he stared at her, then a smile widened across his face as he drawled, 'As I live and breathe; you're the last person I expected to see in this neck of the woods. G'day . . . Esmé Carr. Aren't you a sight for sore eyes.'

'Leo Thornton?' The first thing that came into her mind was his mouth on hers, and several seconds of intense pleasure. Colour rose to her cheeks. She shouldn't have remembered that when she was still getting over Liam.

He laughed, obviously remembering it too, and said under his breath, 'Shame on you, Esmé Carr.' Then louder, 'Where's your patient?'

'Inside . . . actually, he's not my patient. I'm just visiting my friend Minnie, and will be leaving in the morning.'

'Esmé did the initial assessment while I did the peddling,' Minnie said from the doorway.

'Hello, Nurse Prichard. We meet again.' His bluer than blue eyes engaged Esmé's. 'Since you did the initial examination, perhaps you'd tell me about the patient, Nurse Carr?'

'It's a male, aged nearly six. His name is Brian Tomlinson. His palm is badly lacerated and needs several stitches. I removed two small pieces of glass and washed out the wound, but I suspect there might be more at a deeper level. He's lost a small amount of blood, but that's stabilized. Shock is apparent, but it's under control. He has movement in the fingers, but I haven't worked them too hard. The boy has a sizeable haematoma and, as you can see, a biggish chunk of glass stuck in his cheekbone. His head aches and his vision is blurred a little. He mentioned he felt sleepy when he tried to focus. Mildly concussed, I'd say.' She smiled at the boy. 'Brian also has a parrot that swears.'

'Very thorough.' Leo's smile was turned Minnie's way, easy and relaxed. 'Do you agree with those observations, Nurse Prichard?'

'I'm not sure about the swearing parrot, but I did a secondary examination of the patient and reached the same conclusions,' Minnie said.

They barely fit around the examination couch, and Mrs Tomlinson was shunted into the waiting room. Esmé stood on one side of the table, while Leo took over the other. Minnie busied herself preparing iodine, lint and fresh bandages.

'Nice work, Es,' he said, giving her a quick smile as he unwrapped the dressing and examined it.

There was a grumble of a man's voice in the waiting room outside, and Esmé guessed that the boy's father had turned up.

Leo quickly examined the wounds and gave Brian a smile. 'I'm going to give you an injection to deaden the area, old chap. It will sting a bit, but I expect you've felt worse. You're not scared of needles, are you?'

'I'm not scared of nuthin.' A statement that ran out of bravado when Brian gave a yelp or two as the needle went in.

'Good,' Leo said a couple of moments later. He examined Brian's palm through a magnifying glass, and pulled several tiny chips of glass from the wound with tweezers. Then he began to pull the jagged edges of flesh together with swift, neat stitches. 'I understand you have a parrot that swears. What's his name?'

'Cusser.'

'Very apt.' Leo chuckled. 'What does he cuss?'

Minnie aimed a mock frown at him. 'Never you mind, Dr Thornton. Shame on you for encouraging him. Don't you dare say one cuss word, Brian Tomlinson, else I'll stitch your tongue to your big toe, then we'll see how many chairs you can climb on.'

Leo and Brian exchanged a grin.

'I'm going to remove that glass now. It might hurt a little.' Leo removed it easily, then swabbed the wound with iodine, and because it was deep, he closed the wound with one suture.

The boy was handed over to his parents with, 'He should rest until morning. The lump will go down in a few days and the bruise will fade in its own time. That hand will hurt a bit when the injection wears off, though, and he'll have a tiny scar on his face.' Leo handed over a bottle with a few pills in it. 'Give him half an Aspro every four hours if he needs it. Call me if he starts to vomit or if his headache worsens over-night. I'll be at the mine manager's house. Bring Brian to Nurse Prichard in ten days, and she'll remove the stitches.' He gently ruffled the boy's hair. 'Don't fall off chairs with a glass in your hand, any more. All right?'

Brian nodded. 'Reckon I won't, then.'

Leo took a barley-sugar twist from his pocket and handed it to Brian. 'That's for being a good lad.'

'Cor . . . thanks, Doc,' he said.

After they'd gone, Leo turned to them, his smile expansive. 'I hope you ladies will join me for dinner in the canteen? It's not often I get the opportunity to dine with two English roses at the same time.'

They dressed for the occasion. Esmé, who had nothing to change into except fresh underwear, a pair of brown slacks and a cream blouse, borrowed her own dress – the one Minnie had taken to get married in.

'Have it back if you like, I've looked after it,' Minnie told her, shamefaced. 'I'll never wear it again. And I've got ten pounds saved from that money Wally stole from you. I know it's not much, but take that as well. At least I've paid something back.'

'It's not your responsibility. It's Wally's.'

Minnie nearly choked on her laughter. 'You'll never get it out of him. Take it, Es. I'm responsible, and it's the one thing that will make me feel better about what happened.'

Outside, the cicadas were a noisy, high-pitched orchestra. The screech stopped momentarily when they closed the door, and then started up again.

'Noisy critters,' Esmé said.

'You get used to them after a while. I like your Leo Thornton,' Minnie remarked as they walked through a soft, warm twilight towards the canteen. 'Where did you get to meet him?'

'My brother brought him to the house a couple of times.' Esmé pressed her hand against her stomach to slow down the carousel of horses galloping around it. 'And he's not my Doc Thornton . . . he's yours, really.'

'If he were mine I'd keep him under lock and key.' Minnie's scoff of laughter warmed her ears. 'He could barely take his eyes off you, and you blushed every time he looked at you. It felt as though I was invisible. He was good with the boy, wasn't he? There was barely a squawk out of Brian.'

But Esmé's mind had already wandered off course. To that New Year's Eve party.

'Why the sigh?' Minnie said, and Esmé's blush rose to the surface when she answered absently, 'Leo kissed me under the mistletoe once. It was a long time ago.'

'It must have been some kiss, you're almost comatose from the effect that thinking about it produces. Tell me more.'

She laughed. 'It was the first time I'd been kissed. I can't remember it clearly. It was New Year's Eve. The caterers had been late and my sister Livia was in a froth over them not arriving on time. She looked pretty and was wearing a dark red dress—'

'Leave out the domestic details, just get to the important bit.'

'Important bit?'

'The kiss, you dope!'

They both jumped as a figure loomed out of the darkness, and Leo said smoothly, 'Ah, there you are, ladies. I'm sorry if I scared you, I was just coming to collect the pair of you.'

There was a whiff of hospital disinfectant about him as he inserted himself between them, offering an arm apiece.

She had a flicker of homesickness for the comfortable den that was Eavesham House, life on the wards, and Denton coming home to her sister, smelling of carbolic soap. There was a lot of love in her sister's home, despite the silly squabble they'd had.

'I believe we have the choice of rabbit stew and dumplings, or dumplings with rabbit stew, for dinner.'

'And there will be canned fruit with Ideal milk for dessert,' Minnie said.

'Apparently there will be tapioca pudding as well, in honour of my visit.'

The three of them groaned and Minnie said, 'I should have known I'd have to pay a penalty in calling you out.'

'I'm glad you did, Nurse. It gave me the chance to catch up with Esmé again. Ben has suggested that you fly out with me in the morning, Es. It will save him having to drive you to Melbourne.'

'I don't have to be back on board until evening.'

'Good, because I have a day off tomorrow. We can drop in on my parents, and you can spend the day with me if you like, so I can repay the hospitality I enjoyed in your sister's home.'

Put like that she could hardly refuse. She resolved that she wasn't going to get involved with Leo, however charming he was. After her failed engagement to Liam, she doubted if she'd ever trust a man again.

But when she hesitated, because she had come here to visit Minnie, it was Minnie who answered for her by saying, 'Of course she will. I have a stocktake to do tomorrow.'

The aeroplane was a Moth biplane, with a single engine. They posed in front of it while Minnie manoeuvred them into position to capture them in the viewing window of her Box Brownie. Her hand batted them this way and that until she had them posed with Leo's arm around Esmé. 'Don't move,' she called out.

They aimed cheesy smiles at the camera and then at each other.

'Another one for luck. Try and look casual, Es.'

She pulled on her best casual face and gazed up at him. 'Is this your usual job?'

'No . . . I'm filling in time before I go back to England, and I'm gaining experience by acting as a locum, since I've got my own plane and a pilot's licence. They give me the patients who are unlikely to need ambulance services.'

'Have you had your licence long?'

His grin filled with mischief. 'Not very long; are you scared?'

'A little . . . I've never been in an aircraft.'

'You'll be fine once you get over your nerves.' He handed her a leather flying helmet and jacket. 'Put those on, it can be cold upstairs. Make sure your straps are nice and tight. I don't want to see you trying to fly by yourself if we hit an air pocket.'

'That's not very reassuring, Leo.'

'Don't worry, Es, you're going to love flying, and I'll check the straps for you.'

When he was doing that task, he gazed into her eyes. 'The pilot usually gets a kiss from the passenger for luck.'

'You fly this plane on luck instead of fuel?'

'Stop being a wise guy and kindly purse your lips,' he said from the side of his mouth in gangster style. It was a tender, lingering kiss, one to add to her growing mental index of Leo Thornton kisses. She sighed when it ended. 'That was nice, Leo.'

'Can't you do better than that, Es my darling?'

'Sensational then.'

His smile illuminated her world. 'Yes . . . it was. Thanks for not being a shrinking violet. I must do it again some time.'

'Yes, please.'

Soon they were trundling along the runway, and her stomach was left behind as they lifted off. They circled the tiny airport, the noise of the engine almost deafening and the smell of hot oil in her nostrils. She waved goodbye to Minnie and Ben with some regret. The mine area seemed tiny from the air, a small scar hiding its golden riches in the midst of forest. Soon, the currents were lifting them gently over the hills and the engine had settled down to a steady thrum.

'All right, Es?' Leo shouted from behind her and she waved her hand.

After a while they entered an expanse of cleared land.

She had not expected that they'd drop in on the family sheep station for lunch. A truck headed out from the homestead with two dogs chasing after it. A man who looked a lot like Leo, but who was shorter and slightly older, hopped out, just when Leo was lifting her down from the plane.

The two men exchanged big smiles, punched each other on the shoulder, and then had a short, friendly wrestling match. Boys never grew up, she thought, smiling to herself as she remembered Adam and Luke often doing the same thing.

'Meet Nurse Esmé Carr. Es, this is my brother, Alex.'

Alex folded her hands between his, which were calloused. 'Where did you find such an exquisite creature?'

'At the mine.' Leo gazed down at her, not bothering to hide the admiration in his expression. 'She's something special, isn't she?'

'Yours?'

'Yes . . . but she hasn't realized it yet.'

Esmé couldn't help but laugh. 'Leo Thornton, behave yourself.'

The dogs arrived, tongues hanging out and milling around them with flaying tails and yips and yaps as they competed for a pat. There was a chaotic but friendly feel to the scene, a bit like when Denton arrived home from work and became the centre of attention of his wife and children, as if they were stars revolving about his moon.

The three of them squeezed into the cabin of the truck and with the dogs on the tray, headed back to the homestead.

There, she was introduced to Gwen and Bob Thornton, the parents of the brothers. Esmé was eyed with a certain amount of friendly interest by the couple, and questioned about her background.

Nevertheless, it was a pleasant two hours, and as they were about to depart for Melbourne, Gwen whispered, 'Leo's never brought a lady friend to meet us before. I despair of either of our sons getting married and providing us with grandchildren.'

Esmé didn't know quite what to say, except, 'My brother met Leo at medical school in England and they became good friends.' And in case they had matchmaking on their minds, she added, 'We're just acquaintances.'

When Leo took her back to the ship he gazed down at her. 'Will you be my girl, Es?'

It was tempting because she liked him a lot.

But it wouldn't be fair to him. 'Leo, I don't think it's a good idea when you live in Australia and I'm in England. Besides, your mother has practically proposed to me on your behalf already.'

He chuckled. 'Yeah, well, I reckon she must've liked you as much as I do. We could work the distance thing. One of us would have to move. I'm willing. Right . . . what's your next excuse.'

'I'm still getting over a broken engagement.'

'Good . . . I'm glad you're getting over it because there will be room for me in your life, now.' He gazed down at her, smiling. 'Think about it.'

He was incorrigible. He was delicious. She was about to

laugh when he kissed her. It was a fiery little scorcher of a kiss . . . every bit as delectable as she remembered, and leaving all her bits glowing. It didn't take much of his flame to light a bonfire under her. Lord . . . she hadn't expected this, not so soon after Liam. In fact it was different altogether than what she'd felt towards Liam.

'Now, what do you think?' he said.

'I think you'd better not kiss me again, Leo Thornton. I don't want any complications.'

'There's nothing complicated about love. Me . . . Leo the jungle boy. You, Essy the tabby cat.' He beat at his chest, and when he was about to yodel she kissed him to put a stop to it and it faded off into an ecstatic growl.

She fled up the gangplank, past the grinning officer on watch. Leo waved and went dancing off, executing a sideways heel click in the air without mishap.

He turned and blew a kiss towards the ship, shouting, 'I'll see you in ten weeks, my lovely.'

Ten

Meggie couldn't understand why she felt so guilty, when Foxglove House belonged to her.

A year had flown past since her grandfather had handed her the key. She'd got to know him well in the time they'd spent together, and enjoyed his company as well as the secret they shared.

It was hard to be not quite grown-up. Her breasts had grown large enough to be noticeable. One day her liberty bodices disappeared, and two white cotton brassieres occupied the space instead. She'd also found a packet of sanitary napkins with a belt folded up on top, to attach them to. 'When will I need these, and why does this unpleasant thing have to happen?' she asked her mother.

'It would be best if you asked your Auntie Es to explain when she next comes home. She's a nurse.'

Esmé had laughed at that. 'Ah . . . so your mother has left it to me to deliver the coming-of-age message. Do you want the detailed version complete with ovarian function, or the standard version with hygiene included?'

'I'd prefer to know everything, as long as it's not too *medical*. My friend Susan has told me something about how babies are made . . . and it sounds so ridiculous that I don't know whether to believe her or not. It's embarrassing, and all the girls at school snigger about it.'

Sex, Esmé imagined. What did she know about it? Her own experience was nil, though her emotions were telling her it was better if love was involved. She supposed she could manage the anatomical. 'Fetch your coat then, we'll go for a walk. Shadow will come with us, no doubt.' And a little later . . .

'It's like this, Meggie Moo . . .'

Meggie had never felt so embarrassed in her life. Becoming a woman seemed a rather untidy transition. 'It sounds rather a bore,' she said, when her aunt finished, pretending indifference.

'Oh, you learn to cope with it . . . you have to, I'm afraid.'

She asked Aunt Es the question she was burning to know the answer to. 'How do babies get inside a woman? Susan said you have to be married first. Did my mother do it with Richard Sangster.'

'It's quite possible to have a baby before you're married. Morally, it's not the done thing because people will no longer respect you. So, yes, being married is a rather sensible idea if one wants a baby. I do think it would be better if we didn't talk about the personal relationships of your mother.'

'She hardly ever talks about him to me, and there are things I want to know. Mother always brushes me off. I mean . . . I'm Richard Sangster's daughter, and nearly everyone in the house knew him, and they know more about him than I do.'

Her aunt's eyes widened at that. 'At your age one tends to see everything from the viewpoint of only how it affects you. Believe me, things tend to fall together as you get older.'

'You mean I'm self-centred.'

'Not exactly, but girls of your age have a tendency to drama-tize things and read more into them than there is. Your mother loved Richard Sangster. We all did. It was sad that he died without him getting to know you, or you to know him. But your mother has married again and has Dr Denton and the boys to care for, as well. She's had to put the past behind her and move on, for their sakes.'

'Do I sound horribly selfish?'

'No, you're fast becoming a woman, and I'm sure your mother will tell you what you need to know regarding your place in the family when she's good and ready. It's not for me to interfere.'

It wasn't until they reached home that Meggie realized that her aunt hadn't given her the information she'd wanted. But then, her aunt wasn't married, so perhaps she didn't know much about the act of procreation, either.

'We could always ask the vicar,' she suggested to Susan, the thought of which kept them laughing for the rest of the week.

The subject became a bit of a passion with them. Meggie

and Susan enjoyed endless whispered conversations about what took place between men and women, and they giggled a lot, especially when Susan found some postcards of almost naked women in her brother's coat pocket and they tried out the poses, though with their clothes intact.

It was a pity her mother didn't recognize the onset of her womanly attributes as a signal that she'd grown up, Meggie thought, because she was still treated as if she were a child, despite the brassieres.

And even though she'd passed one hurdle it seemed to Meggie that there was another. She wouldn't be regarded as a proper woman until she'd married, and had gone through the experience of losing her virginity. As if she would do such a thing after seeing that diagram of a naked man and woman together. It all seemed so ridiculous, and she wouldn't be able to stop laughing if it happened to her. Why couldn't women just lay eggs and go about their business until they hatched?

But what if she never married, like poor Aunty Es, who although very pretty, must be at least twenty-four?

She started looking at boys in a different way, and found some grown men to be a little uncomfortable with their furtive glances . . . even her grandfather, who often patted her on the knee or on the bottom, and put his arms around her shoulders sometimes, as if he wanted to kiss her. She instinctively shrank away from any attempt at grandfatherly affection from him. Could she dare ask her mother the truth about doing It?

No . . . her mother was bound to think she was precocious. She'd give her that look, the one that said she was wondering what on earth she'd given birth to. Then she'd send her scurrying to do some task rather than give her an answer.

Meggie did the next best thing. She waited until she was alone in the house, and then fetched one of the medical books down from the bookcase. There were diagrams, and her eyes widened. She'd seen her brothers in the bath when they were babies, of course, and they had floppy little appendages to indicate they were male . . . but heavens! This drawing wasn't in miniature, but man-sized. And she hadn't known that they could point upwards like that. It was exactly how Susan had told her. Meggie knew, of course, that men and women were different, but hadn't known why . . . now she did. How utterly hilarious!

Meggie couldn't look at either her stepfather or her mother for a while after the talk without having to stifle the urge to giggle. They must have done it at least three times to produce the boys, and her mother had done it once with Richard Sangster as well.

Armed with this knowledge, she felt more grown-up and important, and, when her menstrual period finally arrived, rather dignified, so she walked rather than ran, and kept her knees together in a ladylike manner when she was seated.

On one occasion she affected the mannerisms of the vicar's wife when the woman came for tea. Her mother had sent her to fetch the cake, and then followed her out.

'What on earth do you think you're doing, Meggie?'

'I'm practising to be a lady for when I grow up. Mrs Avery is awfully pretty and smart, isn't she? They're nicer than the last vicar and his wife. What a pity her front teeth are a bit crooked, though. I'm glad mine are even.'

Her mother bit down on her lip as though she wanted to laugh. 'If she saw you crooking your little finger like that she'd be horribly embarrassed, and so would I.' Her mother's sigh was one of pure exasperation. 'Honestly, Meggie . . . I could shake you. I sometimes wonder what you'll do for a living when you grow-up.'

'Oh . . . I might become an actress, like Rosemary Mortimer. Being a family member, she might invite me to Hollywood and I'll have four husbands, fur coat, lots of glittery diamond rings to flash, and I'll become the famous star of the silver screen. I'll call myself Eloise Elliot. It's a much better name for a film star than Margaret, since practically every woman in the world is called that.' She pouted her lips and fluttered her eyelashes at her mother.

Her mother looked stunned for a moment, then said quietly, 'Who told you about Rosemary Mortimer?'

Oops! Meggie scrambled for a credible answer, and then decided to brave it out. 'Oh . . . everyone in the district seems to know about her. Wasn't her name Sangster, and wasn't she married to—'

'Rosemary Mortimer was only a Sangster by marriage.' Meggie refused to be put off. 'To Major Henry, my Sangster grandfather,' she finished. There, it was out, and the subject now dangled like the sword of Damocles over her head. She hoped the horse's hair it was suspended from was a strong one, because now she'd named the unnamed she was attacked by a sense of overwhelming doom. Her brain seemed to shrivel in the long, cool assessment her outspokenness attracted. Her mother's eyes were glazed over and almost icy. Under it lurked a sense of vulnerability, as though Meggie had mortally wounded her.

Voice even, though in a tightly controlled sort of way, her mother said, 'Enough! Bring that cake in, please. After that you may make your excuses to Mrs Avery. No doubt you can think of an excuse that's convincing. Then you can go off and practise being a lady elsewhere . . . preferably in your room.'

How cold she sounded. Meggie mentally flinched, and, overcome by guilt, whispered, 'Sorry, Mother.'

'I'll talk to you later.' Her mother then turned and walked away, and Meggie decided that being ignored was worse than a lecture, because waiting for the latter was fraught with tension.

But that aside . . . what was it about Major Henry that brought such a response from her mother? What had he done? Perhaps she would ask him.

Feeling penned inside her natural need to rebel, she ignored her mother's suggestion to retire to her room, pulled on her coat and the cheerful red gloves and scarf Aunt Esmé had knitted for her, and then went out into the cold November afternoon.

Dr Andrew Elliot's car was parked outside Nutting Cottage. She hoped her grandfather wasn't sick. But no . . . old Dr Elliot often called in on him, the major had told her. So did her father, and the district nurse, and the lady who came to clean and do his shopping. But rarely in the afternoon, so it would be best if she visited then.

She went past, deciding to look in on him on the way home, and a little while later she let herself into Foxglove House. Usually, she enjoyed the solitude of the place, but today she was unsettled and upset by the argument with her mother . . .

and all over a stupid crooked finger. It seemed that she could never do anything right. Soon she wouldn't be allowed to breathe without a lecture.

Her throat ached with the tension of unshed tears. She picked up a photograph of her father and absorbed his smile, her mind reaching out for any trace of him that might still reside in the house. He looked jolly, dashing and nice. She wished he were still alive so she could talk to him.

She went upstairs to the room where he used to sleep. Misty afternoon light came in through the grimy window that gave her enough illumination to see clearly. There was a safe in the room next door. She knew where the key was kept; in a secret compartment in the dresser. The door swung open easily when she turned it in the lock.

A bulging brown leather document case took up most of the room inside. Tipping the contents on to the bed she shuffled through it. There, she found the details of the Sinclair side of the family, including a couple of Richard Sangster's diaries. But they were old ones, and shed no light on events that occupied her mind. But there was a record of his war service, birth, marriage and death. And there was a family tree. The last person who was recorded on it, in her mother's hand, herself. Margaret Eloise Sinclair Sangster. She giggled when she realized that the initials spelled MESS.

She'd been born . . .? She stared thoughtfully at the date, and at the date of her parents' marriage. So that was it! Her mother had been expecting her when she'd married Richard Sangster. He hadn't lived long enough to see his own daughter born.

But what had that to do with not being allowed to see her grandfather? She wished her mother would tell her. It must have been something really bad . . . or perhaps it was because the marriage had been one of convenience.

The light was failing fast, and the temperature plummeted with it. She hurried home through the gloaming light, leaving the diaries where they were, but taking the family tree to study. It was too late to see her grandfather.

Her mother was waiting for her, annoyance painted on her face. 'Where have you been, Meggie? I was worried.'

Her chest felt bulky where the document was flattened against her body. She kept an arm over it in case it slipped to the floor. She thought fast and uttered the first plausible lie that entered her head. 'Aunt Es is due home soon. I went to see if she was on the train.'

'She usually rings us when she's on her way. You're very dusty, go and tidy yourself up, then come down to the sitting room, I want to talk to you while the boys are out.'

She presented herself, and said before her mother could get the first word in, 'I'm sorry I was rude to Mrs Avery, and to you. I don't know what comes over me sometimes, and I have this horrible sense of humour that makes me want to giggle at times, when everyone else wants to be serious.'

'You should try to control it. I don't like my guests to be embarrassed.'

'Remember, Mr Pike's funeral? When the hearse went past and everyone closed their curtains, I peeked out, and I wondered how the undertaker had managed to fit such a large man into such a slim box.'

Her mother chuckled. 'I wondered exactly the same thing. Listen now. Meggie. What happened was my fault, and it's me who should apologize. Being a teenager is not easy, and I think I expect too much of you.'

'Were you really worried . . . why? I won't become an actress, I promise.'

'Because my father-in-law saw you walking past Nutting Cottage.'

She found a plausible connection. 'Well, you have to walk past it to go to the station.' She hesitated. Her mother seemed to be in an approachable mood. 'Will you tell me why you don't like me mentioning my grandfather?'

The blank look appeared in her mother's eyes, then she sighed. 'I suppose you're old enough to know. He had a mental breakdown after his wife left him and was in hospital for a while. He's on pills to stop it happening again. I've always been worried in case his mental condition deteriorates. Denton said it's unlikely.'

Meggie remembered her grandfather telling her that he was mad – and she'd thought he was making it up! Even so, the confirmation from her mother's lips was not what Meggie had expected to hear. 'I thought . . . I thought it was something to do with you being pregnant to my father before you married. I don't mind about that . . . honestly.'

'*You* don't mind *what!*' Her mother's eyes flew open. 'Who told you such a wicked lie, Meggie? You were born early, that's all. You were lucky to survive.'

'Nobody told me . . . I just guessed.'

'Guessed?'

'I think I saw the date of your marriage on a form you filled out. It was seven months before my birth.'

Her mother's eyes impaled her, so she felt like an insect pinned inside a specimen cabinet. She wriggled but couldn't escape.

'What form was that?'

'I can't remember now . . . it was ages ago though. Does it matter?'

'It does if you go around blurting such things out to all and sundry. And am I to take it that you've been snooping into matters that don't concern you?' Thank goodness her mother didn't require an answer, for she went on, 'If I ever hear you repeat what you just said, or indeed, find out that you've discussed family business with anyone, I'll . . . well, I'll probably slap you. Do you understand?'

Meggie was sure her mother wouldn't perform such an aggressive act, but she certainly could have predicted that their conversation would end up in its usual manner – with them at loggerheads.

Her mother just didn't understand her.

She sighed. 'Yes, Mother.'

Eleven

1935

It seemed to Esmé that dates always managed to conspire so she spent Christmas in England.

It had been a wet year, the ticket inspector on the train had told her morosely, and she'd need her umbrella.

She arrived at the station on Christmas Eve, pleased to see that they'd left the rain behind. She hadn't telephoned to tell the family she was coming, else she would have missed the train. But they usually checked with the shipping company, and somebody came to meet her. This year there was nobody.

She left her suitcase with the stationmaster, with a promise to get someone to pick it up. It was a long walk to Eavesham House in court shoes, and she was laden down with parcels she'd decorated with festive green, red and gold ribbons.

It was nearly dark when she passed Foxglove House. It looked cold and unwelcoming against the grey expanse of sky. Grass grew in tall yellow fronds under the shuttered windows. It was hard to believe she'd spent part of her childhood there. She remembered the summer when Richard Sangster had left them . . . remembered his brilliant smile, his laughter and vitality and the way his spirit shone through his pain.

They had been in the garden. Richard had been under the oak tree in his invalid chair, watching them play. Denton had been part of their game. It seemed as though Livia had known, for she'd turned and given a little cry. It was if, at that moment, the world had stopped turning for her sister. She could see them all, standing like a frozen tableau. It was hard to believe Richard no longer existed on earth, but she liked to think he was looking down on them, especially his daughter, Meggie, who'd been born after he'd died.

She lit a golden candle in her heart for him. 'Have a joyous Christmas with the angels, Richard,' she murmured.

Nutting Cottage wasn't far away. The major would be spending another lonely Christmas, she imagined, and wished Livia would unbend towards him.

Placing her shopping bags down, because the biggest one in particular was getting heavier by the minute, she stretched.

She heard a car coming up behind her and turned. Thank goodness. It was Chad driving an Austin Morris Seven. Bringing the car to a halt he beamed a smile at her.

'You haven't driven all the way from Edinburgh in that tin can, have you?'

'No. I've been here a week . . . it belongs to Livia. She said that it's more her size than the old one. I've been into Blandford for some last minute shopping, and was going to see if you were on the train. Only I was a bit late. The stationmaster told me you'd arrived, and I've got your case. Hop in; you can throw your parcels in the back seat. I hope there's one for me . . . that big one looks exciting.'

'That's a joint one for Denton and the boys, but they might allow you to play with it while you're home.'

'Will you be staying for New Year?'

'No . . . I'll be on board the ship for that. We'll have a terrific party, I imagine. It's hard to believe that 1936 is just around the corner.'

Exchanging a hug with her twin, she said, before he set the car rolling forward, 'How is the studying going?'

'It seems endless. But I'm keeping up with it. What about life on the ocean wave?'

'Relaxing. Most of the passengers are brimming with good health, and the novelty has worn off.'

'Bored, are you?'

She slid him a glance. How well he knew her. 'A bit . . . but the ship's only got one journey left in her. I believe the immigration department has scraped up a load of migrants to make another trip to Australia worthwhile, though they won't find the streets paved with gold . . . the Depression is beginning to bite hard there. We'll drop off passengers in Australia then the ship will go to Singapore to become scrap.'

'How will you get home?'

'I don't know yet. I hope the company will offer us a return fare, or I can work my passage on another ship.'

He gave her a quick glance. 'If you get stuck, I can probably manage a return fare.'

'Thanks, Chad, but I hope I won't need it. I thought I might stay with Minnie for a while. She expects to lose her position soon, too, due to a mine closure. By the way . . . I ran into that friend of yours . . . Leo Thornton. He sends his best.'

'Leo? Good Lord . . . what a coincidence!'

'Yes . . . it certainly was. He was doing some locum work and was called to attend an accident at the mine site, where Minnie runs the nursing post.'

'How is Minnie; is she still a flirt?'

Esmé didn't want to discuss Minnie's hurried, but already failing marriage, or the reason behind it. That was Minnie's business. So she just said, 'Minnie has married an Australian.'

'And Leo?'

Her smile was spontaneous. 'He's just as confident as the last time I met him. He took me to meet his parents and brother. They have a sheep station, and it's huge. His brother runs it with his parents.'

'Leo took rather a fancy to you when he was here.'

'He took every opportunity to remind me of that. He asked me to be his girl before I left Australia.'

'And . . .?'

'He hadn't considered the difficulty of courtship when there are thirteen thousand miles between us. That was the principal reason Liam and I decided to part.'

Chad laughed, and then offered her an amused, 'I thought it was because Livia froze him out. You're not still dreamy-eyed about Billy Bastard are you, Es?'

'Don't call him that, Chad. He's doing his best to manage his life, and without the privileges we enjoyed. We're no longer children, and it tends to diminish you, rather than him.'

Colour touched his cheeks. 'Yes, I suppose it does. You might as well know that I checked his background. He'd been an inmate of Borstal a couple of times?'

She hadn't known, but he'd said he'd done things he was ashamed of and wanted to forget. 'That's the boys' prison, isn't it?' Although she dreaded the answer, she had to ask it. 'What did he do?'

'Housebreaking the first time. The second time he broke into a shop. Then he was caught dancing in the street outside a theatre, and passing the hat round.'

'That's not much of a crime.'

'He had no fixed address and was sleeping in an empty house he'd broken into. He was eighteen at the time. When he came out, the theatre gave him a job.'

He'd met his best friend Eric then, she recalled. Eric had obviously been a good influence on Liam. Although he was pleasant, he kept his distance, and she'd formed the impression that he disapproved of her engagement to Liam.

'Thank goodness we didn't have to sing in the street to feed ourselves.' She felt a niggle of resentment because Chad had felt it his duty to check into Liam's background. He couldn't help his background or upbringing. 'Liam has grown up with quite a few good qualities, Chad. You tend to overlook that. He used to defend you from the bigger boys.'

'Yes . . . I suppose he has.'

'Let the matter drop, please, Chad. Liam's past is his own business, and one he regrets. He's grown up since then, and you can afford to be charitable.'

'Yes, I know . . . sorry . . . I thought you'd want to know, and it's only because I care for you, and don't want you to be hurt.'

'Liam wouldn't hurt me. He always treated me with the utmost courtesy and respect. In fact, I always got the impression he liked his best friend, Eric Blair, more than he did me.'

'Did you ever think . . . no, perhaps not.'

'Stop trying to be enigmatic. Tell me.'

'Well . . . some men are *different*.'

'In what way?'

The look he flicked her had an awkward edge to it. 'You know, Es. They prefer the um, friendship of close men friends.'

Her cheeks heated. 'Enough, Chad, you're embarrassing me.

I'm sure Liam was nothing like that. Besides, you have no reason to suggest such a thing.'

'Did he ever take any liberties with you?'

'No, never! He kissed me when he proposed, that's all. Liam has always been a perfect gentleman. What are you reading into that?'

'That some men marry to prove themselves to themselves. You're a lovely-looking woman. It would be natural for a man with marriage on his mind to drool over you. I'm glad he walked out on you else your marriage might have ended up as one of convenience.'

'Ugh . . . how perfectly horrid of you to say so. In return for your advice, I promise to mind my own business, and not to interfere when you find yourself a girlfriend. You can make your own mistakes your own way.'

'Touché, Sis,' he said, and laughed as he brought the car to a halt. 'I'd be lucky to find a girl who'd want me, I think?'

Chad was of medium height and handsome in a quiet sort of way. Some would call him ordinary, but his brown eyes held warmth in their depths, and they resembled hers, reminding her that their mother had nourished them both at the same time.

Overwhelmed with love for him, despite her anger, she kissed his cheek. 'I'm sure some girl will take pity on you eventually . . . and Chad,' she said, before she got out of the car, 'I think *she* will be the lucky one.'

The Christmas tree in the window welcomed Esmé home, and as she walked inside the house the fruity aroma of Christmas puddings brought the past rushing into the present.

She thought of Minnie celebrating it at the nursing post at Pepperpot Creek, and wished she could have stayed longer to keep her company.

There was a clatter of feet on the stairs, followed by a surge of hugs, kisses and the din of family talking over each other. She couldn't tell who was doing or saying what in the mixture of bodies.

'Look at that suntan. I'm envious.'

'Did you see any crocodiles, Aunt Es?'

Grinning, Chad headed for the kitchen with a box of groceries in his arms.

'Hello, Aunt Es. We thought you were never coming.'

'Who is that big parcel for?'

'Wait and see.'

'There's some mail in your room, Aunt Es.'

She set the box down. 'Boys, you can put these parcels under the tree, and no peeking, or else.'

Livia came scurrying through to collect a kiss, her hands covered in breadcrumbs. She smelled of sage and onion. 'I'm just stuffing the turkey. Won't be long, Es darling. I'm glad you got here in time for Christmas.'

His tail wagging, Shadow brought her his leash, and went through the ritual of stretching his muscles, just in case.

Esmé patted his head. 'Not a chance, Shadow. Try me again tomorrow.'

The boys returned and Luke adopted a solemn expression. 'Whiskers died, and we buried him under the apple tree.' There was a moment of combined sadness, followed by, 'He went to sleep and didn't wake up. Daddy took Whisker's pram up to the attic.'

'We didn't notice until Whiskers didn't come down for dinner,' Meggie said. 'He was still curled up in his pram and I thought he was asleep. But he was cold and stiff.'

'I said a prayer.' Adam's voice wobbled a bit. 'We sang a hymn and Meggie cried like billy-o.'

'I did not. I had something in my eye.'

Tears pricked Esmé's eyes, but Whiskers had lived a long life. All the same, it felt as though another part of her child-hood had gone.

'Thank you all for looking after him; I'm pleased he went peacefully.'

Denton arrived, and the welcoming party gravitated towards him. There was a moment when everything faded and nostalgia overwhelmed, so her eyes became blurred.

Whatever happened in the future, she'd always remember her family like this – a combined hug, a babble of voices and love revolving around each another. No matter where they went or what they did, they would always have each other.

She greeted Denton with a hug, and then escaped upstairs. There was a card from Liam that read: 'Thinking of you, have a wonderful Christmas, Esmé. Sorry things didn't work out for us, but perhaps it was for the best. Love always, Liam.' A photograph slid into her lap. It was a publicity shot. Liam wore a tuxedo and top hat, and was surrounded by long-legged girls dressed in wide smiles, satin tunics and lots of feathers. He looked neat and muscular. His autograph was scrawled across the bottom.

Esmé wished she'd sent him a card. She'd thought to make a clean break, but now knew it was impossible. She couldn't throw the affection she felt towards him aside like rubbish, or forget it easily. It lingered, like an infection that never quite went away. But the wound of his abrupt departure resurfaced at odd moments, leaving her feeling inadequate.

She wondered if what Chad had indicated held any truth. Was Liam a man trying to convince himself he was someone else? Her love for him had always been tenuous and she'd been more chagrined than broken-hearted by his abrupt departure from her life. He'd stood on the outside of her family circle, but hadn't possessed the courage to step inside it.

'Do you still love Liam?' Meggie said from the doorway, and Esmé looked up and smiled at her.

'A little . . . people you've known and loved become memories, and you can't help thinking about them. There was something vulnerable about Liam. It doesn't hurt so much now.'

Meggie held out the ring she'd given her. 'Mother said I should give this back. She said you'd probably regret giving it to me because it was a spur of the moment decision. She feels guilty about the break-up.'

'No . . . you keep it, Meggie. It wasn't Livia's fault. I made the decision myself. I could have gone with him.'

'I'm being horribly selfish, but I'm glad you didn't.'

'So am I. We both needed someone, but instinct told me it was not each other.'

Picking up the photo Meggie gazed at it, and giggled. 'He looks terribly suave and handsome, doesn't he? Mother would have a fit if she saw you dressed up like those dancing girls. Don't they look glamorous?'

'You're underestimating your mother. As for the dancing

girls, they probably ache from head to toe, and have blisters as big as hens' eggs on their feet. I know I did.'

'I wonder how many ostriches it took to provide the feathers, the poor creatures. Do you suppose there are bald ostriches running around in the African desert, or do they kill them and pluck them, like we do the Christmas turkey? They'd need a big plate to carve it on. I say . . . I wonder if ostrich feathers grow again?'

That was more like the Meggie she knew. Esmé chuckled, and her niece giggled . . . and then the pair of them started to laugh, just for the fun of being together, and couldn't stop for a long time.

The clockwork train she'd bought for the boys was a great success. 'It's not very big, but it's a Hornby, and there's a catalogue. If you like it you can add to it. Perhaps have pieces as gifts for birthdays and Christmas. They have electrical powered trains as well, but I remembered you were still on gas.'

'Not for much longer, thank goodness,' Livia said with a smile. 'We're converting to electricity next year.'

Esmé had added an engine driver's hat and a whistle in a package for Denton. Denton blew her a kiss. There was an enquiry in Livia's eyes at she gazed at her husband.

He grinned at her. 'I told Es of my secret yearning to be a train driver. I have fond memories of trains, because that's where I first met you,' and he leaned forward and kissed her, making her blush.

'It's super,' Meggie exclaimed when she saw the green leather journal Esmé had bought her. It came complete with brass lock and key. Eyes shining, she went upstairs with it.

The boys headed up to the attic with the train set, with Chad offering to help them set it up. The older Dr Elliot fell asleep in his chair despite the thumping from above as the attic was converted into Waterloo station without the trimmings.

Helen Elliot began to tidy up the kitchen.

Shadow appeared with his leash, and Esmé fetched her hat and coat. 'Come on then. I need to walk off the Christmas pudding. Leave that for me to do,' she told Helen when they went through to the kitchen.

'No . . . I can do it, dear. I was going to ask that niece of yours, but no . . . she went rushing past and said she was going to try out the bicycle Denton had bought her for Christmas. I don't see why she couldn't have been given your brother's old bike. A lick of paint would have made it look like new.'

Esmé could have given her plenty of reasons why not, the chief amongst them being that Chad's bike had seen some rough usage over the years, and was too old and rusty, and the wheels were warped. But she didn't want to upset the woman.

'You should relax after dinner, like everyone else is. Why don't you leave this. I'll do it when I come back.'

'I like to keep busy.'

'Yes . . . I know, but there's really no need to do everything at once. Livia invites you for Christmas because she wants your company, not your skills as a pot cleaner. Leave it. I'll catch Meggie up, and when we come back we'll do it, like we intended to do in the first place.'

Helen dried her hands on the tea towel and smiled. 'Very well, you're a thoughtful girl, Esmé. Thank you.'

There was no sign of Meggie on the road ahead. Esmé picked up speed, with Shadow trotting beside her. Now she was home it seemed as though she'd never been away. But she would go away again. She'd decided to go back to Australia on the *Horizon Queen*. This time she'd stay longer and keep Minnie company, like they'd intended at the beginning.

Her friend had put on a brave face the last time she'd seen her, but apart from the unreliable Wally, she had nobody close she could turn to.

Deep in thought she nearly missed seeing Meggie's bicycle hidden behind a shrub outside Nutting Cottage. As she stopped to gaze at it, the door opened and Meggie came out.

Esmé ducked behind the privet hedge when Meggie called out, 'Goodbye, Grandfather. I hope you enjoy the book, and you like Agatha Christie. It's called *The Hound of Death*.'

'Thank you, dear. It sounds very exciting so I'm sure I shall. Happy Christmas. I've left a small gift for you at the house.'

'Don't forget to listen to the King George's speech on the radio.'

The major shuffled forward into the light. 'I won't forget.'

Esmé hadn't seen Major Henry for a long time, and she was

appalled. He was very thin and there was a telltale bluish tinge to his lips.

Shadow had gone on ahead, and Esmé quickly followed him. She drew him into a hedge, one hand over his snout and the other holding his collar. As Meggie peddled past them at speed he strained to escape and run after her.

Meggie had dropped her bicycle in the grass, and had run around to the back of Foxglove House, leaving the long grass flattened where she'd trod. Following her niece Esmé discovered the back door unlocked, and went in.

It was dark inside, but the faint glow of a torch lit Esmé's way through to the drawing room.

Meggie was in the process of unwrapping a small parcel. She gasped at what it contained, and breathed, 'How pretty.'

'Does your mother know you come here?' Esmé asked quietly.

A frightened yelp came her way, but Meggie recovered quickly. 'No, she doesn't. Why are you spying on me?'

'I'm not. I'm taking Shadow for a walk, and I saw you come out of Nutting Cottage.'

'Please don't tell Mother. She'll be furious.'

'It's not like you to be deceitful, Meggie.'

'My mother said he's mentally ill, but I don't believe her.' She smiled and held out a silver locket. 'My grandfather gave me this. It has his photograph inside it. Promise you won't tell mother.'

She nodded. 'What are you doing in Foxglove House?'

'Why shouldn't I be here, when it's my house? I come here and practise the piano. It's always so quiet and peaceful . . . and sometimes I want to be alone. Besides . . . there are reminders of my father here. Sometimes I can feel his presence. He'd already died when I was born, you know. I like to think that his spirit is still here, and this is the only place where he can see me. I know it sounds stupid, but sometimes I talk to him. I do wish I'd known him.'

'Richard was a sweet man; you would have adored him. You'd better hide that locket else your mother will want to know where you got it. You can keep it in my jewellery box if you like. I'll show you how to open the secret drawer.

Come on . . . let's go now. We have the washing-up to do between us.'

Meggie groaned. 'You won't tell on me, will you?'

'I promise.'

As they headed home Esmé wondered what to do. She couldn't encourage Meggie to deceive her mother. Then again, she'd promised her niece she wouldn't tell Livia.

'Why don't you ride the bike and I'll sit on the rack at the back,' Meggie said. 'It will get us there quicker.'

They wobbled all over the road to start with, but soon got the hang of it and began to sing Christmas carols with Shadow dodging from one side to the other and barking.

The day before Esmé was due back on board, and when they were waiting in the hall for the others to join them to walk to church, Esmé managed to catch Denton alone.

It was unfair to ruin his Sunday with this, she thought, especially since she'd been told in no uncertain fashion that the relationship between Livia and her headstrong daughter was not her business.

There was trepidation in her when she said cautiously, 'If you were the recipient of an unwanted confidence that could affect the relationship of two people you love, and you didn't have enough information to make a wise decision of how to handle it, what would you do, Denton?'

His eyes sharpened. 'It would depend on the two people concerned. Define the problem a little, please.'

'I'm damned if I do and damned if I don't, would cover the situation adequately.'

'I can sense Meggie's hand in this, and Livia. You're the meat in the sandwich . . . yes?'

'Potted tongue would be a better description.'

He laughed. 'Then leave it potted. There's very little that goes on that we don't get to hear about, and where Livia and Meggie are concerned, things usually end up sorting themselves out without any help. Meggie has been listening to idle gossip, I suppose.'

He was making it obvious he didn't welcome her advice. 'May I ask you something, Denton?'

He gave a wary nod.

'Why isn't Meggie allowed to visit her grandfather? You've said yourself that he's harmless?'

The sigh he gave was heavy. 'You must know by now that I won't answer that particular question.'

The conversation broke off as the boys came clattering down the stairs. Luke grimaced as he said, 'Do we have to go to church?'

'Yes, I'm afraid you do.' Livia came down after them, looking pretty in a blue, ankle-length skirt with a long, edge-to-edge cardigan over a ruffled blouse. Her glance ran over the heads and discovered one missing. 'Where's Meggie? That girl can never be found when you want her.'

'She went out on her bike, but she'll turn up . . . she always does.' Denton held her coat out for his wife, and kissed her ear when she slid her arms into the sleeves. Livia smiled up at him when she turned, her eyes joining his in an unbridled exchange of love.

Their togetherness was so apparent that Esmé couldn't imagine her sister being in love with somebody else . . . not even Richard Sangster. She hoped she'd meet someone who would love her as much as Denton loved Livia.

She thought of Liam then and felt a moment of regret that she'd let him go. She knew now that they hadn't loved each other enough. They'd been attracted to one another certainly, but romance between them had been a myth that the reality of settling down and sharing a future together would have probably exposed, especially after what Chad had said.

She suspected that Liam was scared of commitment, and it was nothing more than that, coupled with his personal ambition.

And then there was Leo Thornton, as friendly and boisterous as an overgrown puppy, who'd said he wanted her to be his girl. She remembered his fingers, long, tanned and deft, as with great delicacy he'd stitched the lacerated edges of Brian Tomlinson's hand together.

Esmé was about to flirt with danger by remembering every minute detail of Leo's kiss when a clatter announced the arrival of Meggie. She burst through the front door, her cheeks flushed from the cold and her hair untidy. Her socks had slid down to her ankles.

Her brilliant smile as she gazed round at her family made Esmé feel guilty.

'Oops . . . am I late for church? I'm sorry, I forgot to wind my watch.'

Twelve

February, 1936

This time the rumour had been true. The *Horizon Queen* unloaded her passengers in Melbourne and paid off most of the staff.

With a skeleton crew aboard she'd be heading out of the harbour for her first and last voyage to Singapore. There, she'd be stripped of her furnishings and dismantled.

Esmé's heart gave a bit of a wrench at the thought, and then she laughed. She hadn't expected to find herself being sentimental over a ship. To her relief she was given a bonus, an amount that should cover her passage back to England. With it she intended to open a bank account. That would allow her enough money to get her home if she couldn't pick up a job, and with a little left over. She'd learned the hard way that having cash lying around was too much of a temptation for some.

It was late February, the hottest time of year in Australia, and the day was uncomfortably humid.

Clearing customs, she was about to head for the agency when she saw Leo in the crowd milling about on the wharf. A big grin came her way when he set eyes on her. Taking a grey trilby from his head he waved it at her. He had the type of hair the wind liked to ruffle, curls that sprang here and there.

She resisted the urge to run towards him and ruffle it herself, but she couldn't have done so anyway as she was weighed down with an overstuffed suitcase. Her heart soared when she reached him, and she felt shy. 'I didn't expect to see you.'

'I told you I'd be here.' Leo took the case from her and lifted an eyebrow. 'You're staying, if the weight of this is anything to go by. Did you remember the kitchen sink?'

'I'm afraid it wouldn't fit in.'

'Good. The car's this way. Where are we going?'

'To the nursing agency first, I must register for employment. Then I need to open a bank account. After that I must contact Minnie, and I'll need to find somewhere to stay.'

'You were going to do all that? It's already four o'clock, and the banks are shut.' He placed her suitcase alongside his doctor's bag in the back seat of his car.

'Oh, are they? What a nuisance.' No wonder her stomach rattled like a train over the tracks. She remembered Minnie telling her that her mother-in-law had guest rooms at her hotel. She had the address in her diary. And if Wally Prichard happened to be there she'd ask him for the money he'd stolen from her. It wasn't right that Minnie should have to pay his debt, and he was lucky she hadn't reported the theft of it to the police.

The hotel was a shabby building on a street corner. It had a smell lingering about it, as though the lamp post outside served as a territory marker for every dog that wandered by. It probably did.

Leo looked dubious. 'This isn't a very good area. Let me find you somewhere decent to stay.'

'I can't afford anything else. And before you offer . . . no, I will not borrow the money from you.'

'I was going to offer you a room in the flat I rent.'

'Not a good idea, Leo.'

He grinned. 'But worth a try.' The door was locked, so Leo rattled it. 'Obviously it's not opening time yet.'

Peering through the window, Esmé was rewarded by the sight of Wally's head emerging cautiously from behind the door. Rapping on the window she called out. 'It's me, Wally . . . Minnie's friend . . . Esmé Carr.'

He opened the door a chink. 'Well, if it isn't Lady Esmé in person. The *Horizon Queen* is still on the run then . . . I'm surprised.'

'I've just been paid off. She's heading for the scrap yard in Singapore first thing.'

His expression became speculative. 'What do you want, Esmé? Minnie's not here, she's still up at the mine site.'

'I want a room for the night.'

'You can't have one . . . my mother's sick.'

'Very well, then perhaps you'd repay the money you *borrowed* from me on the ship. I'll be able to stay somewhere else then.'

'I don't know what you're talking about, and in case you don't know, there's a depression going on. I haven't got any money. If I had I'd fetch a doctor for my poor old Ma.'

Leo placed a well-shod foot in the door when Wally went to close it. 'There's a doctor right here.'

From the back room a voice croaked, 'Who is it Wally?'

'Nobody, Ma.'

Esmé wasn't about to be put off and she raised her voice a fraction. 'It certainly is somebody, Mrs Prichard. I'm Minnie's best friend.'

Footsteps shuffled across the floor, and through the crack in the door Esmé saw a woman leaning on the bar. She was breathing heavily. 'Minnie's friend, did you say? In that case you can call me Ma. Wally, open that door at once, else I'll fetch you a good clout.'

She didn't look as though she had enough energy to clout a fly – a thought that took Esmé's glance to a curl of sticky paper that served as a fly trap.

'Quickly,' Wally said, and after they'd slid through the door he gazed cautiously up and down the road. 'Did anyone see you?'

Leo didn't seem to notice the smoke-stained ceilings, gritty windows and the grimy interior. 'Everybody in the street, I imagine.'

'If anyone asks for me I'm not here.'

Leo smiled pleasantly at him. 'What about the money you owe the lady?'

'I gave it to Minnie to look after the last time I was up the mine site. I even paid some interest on the loan . . . a fiver.'

'It wasn't a loan. You removed the money from my suitcase when I was asleep. I know it. You know it, and Minnie knows it.'

'Now I know it too,' Leo said. 'Neither of us was born yesterday, so cut out the crap.'

Esmé's eyes flew open and she stifled a laugh when Leo gave her a contrite look and murmured, 'Sorry, Es.'

Wally shrugged. 'I haven't got any money on me, but I

could probably get some if I tried. I know where there's a game . . . all I need is a stake.' His expression was assessing as he eyed Leo up and down. 'Ten quid would do it, I reckon.'

Leo tossed him a pitying look.

'A fiver then?' Wally said. 'I haven't got any cash on me, and the bank's closed.'

'Don't you give it to him. If he loses it you'll never get it back.' Ma's laughter became a paroxysm of coughing and Esmé stepped forward. Sweat beaded the woman's body, yet her teeth were chattering. 'How long have you been like this, Ma?'

'Three weeks, give or take. It's suddenly got worse.'

'You have a fever . . . you should be in bed.'

Wally said, 'She can't get up the stairs, and I can't carry her by myself. She's been sleeping on the couch in the back room since my dad died.'

Leo stepped forward. 'I'll help you to get her up there.'

'That's right kind of you, Mr . . .?'

'Dr Thornton,' Leo said briefly. 'Will you allow me to examine you, Mrs Prichard? I'll go and fetch my bag from the car.'

'I can't afford to pay, mind,' she wheezed. 'I haven't been able to run the bar by myself since my old man died, and Wally is as much use as a ship in a desert.'

Wally shrugged. 'You said you had a cold. You should've called the doctor out at the beginning.' He turned to Leo. 'If you've got anything moveable in the car you'd better bring it in, else someone will help themselves to it. They're a load of thieves around here.'

'Yes . . . we've noticed,' Esmé said, and had the momentary satisfaction of watching Wally turn a dull shade of red.

Leo went outside, returning with her suitcase as well as his bag. Between them, he and Wally got Ma upstairs.

'I'll see to her.' Esmé undressed the woman and got her into her nightgown.

Wally suddenly became helpful. 'I'll fetch your suitcase up and put you in the guest room at the end of the corridor, while the Doc takes a look at her. I'll get some clean sheets, too.'

While Wally was doing that, Leo examined Ma. 'Acute

bronchitis . . . you'll have to stay in bed for at least two weeks. No going into the bar with its smoky atmosphere.' When Wally appeared Leo asked him, 'Have you got any Aspro?'

Wally shook his head. 'I can go to the chemist and buy some before they close.'

'Do that . . . give her one Aspro four times a day, it will help bring her fever down . . . and I'll leave you a bottle of cough syrup. A couple of drops of eucalyptus oil in hot water used as an inhalant will help loosen the phlegm.'

'Where do you keep your purse, Ma?'

'In my black . . .' She hesitated, obviously debating the wisdom of telling Wally. 'There's some change in a glass behind the bar . . . that should be enough for Aspro. And make sure you're home in time to open up.'

When he'd gone Ma turned to Esmé. 'I can't take you in as a paying guest, love but seeing as you're being so good to me you're welcome to stay for nothing. Like as not you can take a spell in the bar, like young Minnie did. A nice girl, she is. No nonsense about her, and a hard worker. She's far too good for the likes of my Wally. A pity about the baby . . . it would have been the making of him, and I'd have liked a grandchild.'

'Yes, it was a pity Minnie lost the infant. Perhaps it was for the best because it must be hard for a woman on her own to work, as well as look after a baby.' Esmé dished it up with a smile, because the woman was Wally's mother, after all. 'I'm going down to boil a kettle so we can give you a wash and make you comfortable.'

'Sorry to be so much trouble, Doc, though worth it to have a good-looking man in my bedroom, at long last.'

Leo smiled at his unexpected patient. 'Behave yourself, Ma. I want you to get better so I can have my girl back. I'll be back in a day or two to check on you both. Es . . . can I see you a minute.'

She followed him out the room, and his eyes reflected on her for a moment. 'I don't like leaving you here.'

'I'll be all right. She will recover, won't she?'

He lowered his voice. 'She should get over it, as long as she rests. You're a nurse; you know the routine.' He gently moved a strand of her hair to one side and smiled, the creases in his face white threads against his tan. 'We're like ships that pass in the night, you and I . . . yet I feel a strong connection, as though we're meant to be.'

She felt exactly the same. She liked him . . . she more than liked him. She tried to ignore the oddly pleasant churning in her stomach. 'You're not going to go all romantic on me are you, Leo? Doctors and nurses know too much about human bodies to be truly romantic about them.'

'My guess is that you'll forget that anatomical nonsense when we make love and discover each other's tickly bits.'

'Don't be so presumptuous.' She covered her blush with her hands, but couldn't help laughing. 'I thought we were going to consult about the patient.'

'I'd rather consult about us. I suppose you're going to go all prissy on me and tell me you're not that sort of girl.'

'Why should you suppose that I'm prissy?'

He was grinning when he pulled her hands down. He kissed her with unhurried pleasure, his mouth engaging hers with some heat. Then said, 'Hello, Esmé Carr. It's lovely to see you again, more than that . . . it's wonderful. You're wonderful.'

'You can stop grinning like a Cheshire cat, because you're right. I'm not that sort of girl, so behave, Leo Thornton. Go away . . . I've got work to do. I'll see you in a couple of days.'

He leaned forward and was about to kiss her again when Ma had a coughing fit.

The look she gave him was filled with laughter. 'Oh dear . . . you'll just have to wait for that one.'

'I think I'm in love,' he said before he left.

Esmé went back upstairs and Ma croaked, 'I've had a hard time of it since my Harry upped and died on me. I'll be glad to have some company.'

Wally didn't get back in time to open the bar, and Esmé went up to consult with Ma.

'The price list is under the counter. Most of the customers will drink schooners. We no longer have a slate. It's cash or nothing.'

'Schooner . . . that's a sailing ship, isn't it?'

'I'd forgotten you're from the old country. It's the second

biggest glass. The biggest is a pint, followed by the schooner, a pot, a glass and a pony. They all go down in size. You'll soon get the hang of it. When Reg comes in he'll show you how to pull a beer, and explain which glass is which. You can't miss him; he's got a white beard that hangs to his chest. Likely he'll jump behind the bar and give you a hand if you get busy. He's a nice bloke. Give him a schooner if he does . . . but only one.'

Esmé pulled her first beer to the good-natured teasing of several of the regulars.

She grinned as the customer cautiously sipped at it. His upper lip was coated with foam as he announced the verdict. 'You could do with a bit more beer and a bit less froth, love.'

'Aw . . . shuddup,' Reg told him. 'That's not bad for a first try. You're lucky you're getting a drink at all, what with Ma laid up in bed and Wally lying low. Esmé is a nurse not a bloody barmaid.'

'She can look after me any time she likes.'

'Watch your lip, Bluey. That girl behind the bar is a little lady, and she's not used to dirty talk.'

'I hear John Teagan will be out of the clink as soon as he gets his parole, and Wally's been doing the dirty with his sister.'

'You don't say . . . and him with that nice little wife of his working up country. He doesn't know which side his bread is buttered on, doesn't Wally. He deserves a good thumping.'

'He'll probably get one when Teagan catches up with him.'

Esmé enjoyed her time behind the bar. It was a far cry from England, where she'd spent a sheltered country life after she'd left the orphanage. Livia would be horrified if she knew what her present occupation was. Although she and Livia were alike, Esmé knew she had the edge when it came to toughness. She'd acquired it over several years of surviving in a children's home.

Besides being able to tell a schooner from a pony by the end of the evening, Esmé had also gathered up some interesting snippets of gossip. Walter, it seemed, was not very well liked. She couldn't imagine what Minnie had seen in him in the first place.

She washed the glasses and bar, and tipped the stools upside down on the tables. She wasn't about to wash the floor. Wally could do that in the morning. He hadn't pulled his weight. In fact, he'd been noticeable by his absence, and she intended to have words with him.

Counting the money, she placed it into a bag and, not knowing what else to do with it, decided to take it up to bed with her, along with a bottle of ginger beer. Switching off the one light she went up, looking in on Ma on the way past. The woman was asleep, but restless, and her breathing was noisy.

Her own room smelled of dust and trapped heat. The sheets were folded up on the bed, and although clean, they had the smell of long residence in the linen cupboard. Opening the window she breathed deeply to get some air into her lungs. It was wonderful after the stale, smoky atmosphere of the bar.

Wally hadn't come back with the Aspro, and she remembered she had some in her handbag.

Her bag was on the chair. Inside, her purse gaped open. She silently cursed when she checked the contents and found two pounds missing. She should have remembered not to let Wally near her bag, she thought, and angrily snatched up the pill bottle. No wonder he'd made himself scarce.

Ma began to cough. Pouring some ginger beer into the glass she took two of the pills through to her. 'Here, take these. And you can have another dose of the cough syrup to see you through the night.'

'It makes me cough.'

'It's supposed to. It helps to loosen the muck from your chest.'

'Better out than in, aye love.' Ma swallowed everything down with a bit of a shudder, then asked, 'Did you find everything?'

'Yes . . . I managed. I've got the takings in my bedroom.' She told Ma the amount.

'That's not bad . . . it's nearly double what we've been taking recently. Word must've got round that there was a new barmaid and they came to size you up.'

Or Wally's hand had been in the till, Esmé thought uncharitably.

'Wally helped you out, I suppose?'

'No . . . but Reg did. Wally went out somewhere.'

'I expect there's a game on the go. Let's hope he's lucky. He'll pay you that money back then. He's not a bad lad, just weak. He can't help himself when there's a game going. He means well.'

Wally was an expert at helping himself in her book, but she kept her mouth shut. She didn't want to distress the woman by saying her purse had been raided. 'Let's hope you're right. Is there anything you need before I go to bed.'

A work-worn hand clutched at her sleeve and tears gathered in her eyes. 'You won't go off and leave me like this, will you. I feel so fatigued, what with my man dying suddenly like that, and now this on top of it. Wally's not much good. I'd thought he'd settled on a career on the ships, but back he comes with young Minnie in tow, and her with a ring on her finger, and a bun in the oven, as well, though the poor little tyke wasn't meant to be. Harry and me thought she'd be the making of him, but I reckon she's thrown him out, and I reckon he deserves it.'

Esmé murmured something non-committal.

'He said he loves Minnie . . . and the other woman was nothing.'

'Hush now, Ma.' The last thing Esmé wanted to hear was the excuses and confessions Wally had made to his mother. The man was a liar, a confidence trickster and a thief, and she could find half a dozen more labels to stick on him if need be. If he loved Minnie he'd be with her now, working to provide a future for them together, not skulking about down here with another woman. 'Don't upset yourself . . . what's done is done and you can't change it.'

'You're right, lass. Wally might not be back for a while, and I was worried you might go off with that doctor chap of yours. Now there's a catch. He's got a nice backside on him.'

Esmé giggled. 'I haven't had time to inspect Leo's finer points, but I'll make it my business to the next time I see him.'

'You do that.' Ma heaved a sigh. 'I wish I had a bit more energy. If I can't keep the bar open my livelihood has gone, then what will happen to me? I can't afford to hire anyone and they don't give women a helping hand here.'

'Don't worry, Ma. I'll do my best to help while I can . . . but if you don't allow me to go to bed I'll be too worn out to do anything tomorrow.'

Reg dropped in next morning. He made sure the floor was kept clean, and polished the wooden bar. A toffee-coloured surface emerged from under the stains and Reg ran his hand over it. 'A nice piece of oak, is that, it must have come from the old country.' He served the customers and chased off the beggar boys looking for a handout.

Several women came looking for work. Esmé voiced what was obvious. 'These men don't work during the day, so where do they get money to drink with? Women are looking for work, and there are hungry kids begging on the streets?'

Reg shrugged. 'That's the way it is. The men get the money, but fair goes . . . I dare say they hand most of it over to their wives, since the man is the breadwinner. You don't begrudge a man a drink, do you?'

'Of course not. What if it's a single woman? What do they get in the way of relief?'

He shrugged again. 'Don't ask me, love. Women tend to help each other out and there's schemes going. But anyway, employers won't give a women work if it's a job a man can fill, and neither will the unions. That's the way it should be.'

Esmé was appalled that they'd spend their dole money on beer. 'That's unfair. Isn't relief money meant to help feed their families?'

'Be that as it may, it ain't none of my business how a man spends his cash.' He sighed, and said, 'Leave the bar area to me, Miss. I'll hold the fort till Ma's well. Best not to meddle in men's business, less they take it personally and go elsewhere. Where would Ma be then? You should just go about doing what you're trained to do. Nursing isn't it?'

Uncertain whether it was a reprimand or not, but knowing emotional blackmail when she heard it, Esmé bit down on a reply. 'That's kind of you to help out, Reg.'

'I'm doing it for Ma. She's had a bad time of it lately. I reckon she needs a hand, and it keeps me busy.'

'As you keep reminding me. You don't work yourself, then?'

'I'm a carpenter. Nobody is building houses these days, but if you hear of a job going I'm cheap. And if you want time off, let me know.'

She raised an eyebrow and grinned. 'Funny, but I could have sworn that Ma placed me in charge of her business. Until she says otherwise, I'm the foreman here, not you. On that basis, if you want to help out, fine. If you don't want to help out, that's fine too.'

He laughed. 'You certainly know when to apply the stick. All right. You win. You know what I meant, though. I'm willing to keep my eye on the place if you want to go off somewhere and I can keep Ma company at the same time. She likes being in the thick of things and having a good old natter.'

Ma also seemed to enjoy the company of Reg, though Esmé had the feeling he was keeping Ma informed on everything she did.

Leo turned up the day after he said he would. He pushed his way through the smoky atmosphere, his smile a mile wide. 'Sorry I'm a day late; I had to go up country.'

'I was raised by, and worked with doctors. They rarely run on time . . . it's the nature of the job. Come on in, Leo.' She raised the flap, allowing him access behind the bar.

A cheer went up when he gave her a smacking kiss.

'Can I have one?' someone called out.

'Find your own girl,' Leo told him.

'Will you stop calling me your girl, please. I'm no such thing.'

'I'm warning off potential husbands.'

She giggled, then gazed around the bar and whispered, 'Really . . . which one of them do you consider to be of husband potential?'

His dark lashes feathered the intense blue of his eyes as he said gently, 'How are you coping, sweetheart?'

'I can't say I'm cut out to be a barmaid. I'm managing, with Reg's help, though.'

Leaving Reg in charge she followed Leo up the narrow staircase, taking care to inspect the taut rear moving under the grey, pinstriped trousers. Ma was right . . . he had a nice back-side – and her observation had nothing to do with the anatomical, but the perfection of the physical form. She gave a little growl, which was quickly changed into a cough when he turned to gaze suspiciously at her. All the same, she grinned at him.

He returned the grin, murmuring. 'I fancy you like crazy, Es, my darling. It's only a matter of time, but why wait? Marry me.'

'No.'

'Why not?'

'Because we haven't known each other long enough.' She hadn't known Liam very long either . . . she'd just let herself be carried along. It would have been the biggest mistake she'd ever made if she'd married Liam. She wasn't going to allow that to happen a second time.

His head slanted to one side and he offered her a winsome smile that was beguiling. 'Tell me when we've known each other long enough and I'll ask you again. In the meantime I'll give you a few flying lessons, which will give me an excuse to keep seeing you.'

'You really don't need an excuse, I like seeing you.' Laughter bubbled up in her. She felt happy when she was with Leo. 'I'll give you top marks for persistence. Now, go up and see Ma.'

Ma's condition had improved a little.

'Temperature is down so you can go off the Aspro,' Leo grunted, and applied his stethoscope to her chest. 'You're rattling like a tram with a wheel missing.' His eyes engaged hers. 'I don't suppose it's any good telling you that the smoky atmosphere downstairs is doing you more harm than good.'

'I've got to earn a living, and I don't know how to do anything else.'

'Yes . . . I suppose you must. How old are you fifty . . . fifty-five?

Ma snorted. 'I'm forty-nine.'

'Do you get any tightness in your chest.'

'Sometimes, but it soon goes. When can I get up and go about my business?'

'When I say you can. If you intend to waste my time by not listening to, or not taking my advice, say so now. I have more deserving cases to deal with.'

Ma opened her mouth, and then closed it again.

'Now . . . I'll prescribe you some pills. Keep them on you, and place one under your tongue if you have chest pain. Be careful with them, and use strictly as advised. See your own doctor when you run out.'

His firmness surprised Esmé and she gazed at him through new eyes. Despite his easy-going nature, Leo Thornton was no fool. Ma wouldn't spend money on a doctor when she didn't have to, and he knew it.

'How bad is her heart?' she asked him when they went downstairs.

'A bit erratic, but she's been under a lot of stress. Get me the name of her doctor if you would, and I'll write him a letter.'

'I've let Minnie know you've arrived and where you are,' Leo told her, straightening up. 'I'll call in to check on Ma in about a week, and a few days after that I'll be flying you out to Pepperpot Creek. I'll give you a flying lesson on the way, if you like.'

The thought robbed her of breath. 'I don't know about that, Leo.'

'It won't be much of one, so don't panic. I'll remove the rudder pedals in case you forget what your feet are doing.'

The time moved swiftly, and soon Ma was up and about. March came in a little cooler, especially at night. It was difficult to get used to the swift change of seasons.

It seemed to Esmé that she'd worked her fingers to the bone at the hotel, and she felt sorry for Ma having to do everything by herself. But she was glad to be moving on, she was looking forward to seeing Minnie.

'Come any time,' Ma said, giving her a hug. 'I've got those guest rooms going begging.'

Soon they were at the airfield, which was little more than a paddock with a windsock. A large hanger sheltered several small aircraft.

Leo spoke briefly to a man in an office. 'We'll be following the road out to Pepperpot.'

'She's all fuelled up, and a message has come through for you.' A piece of paper was handed over to him. After perusing the contents Leo slid it into his pocket. 'Radio them back. Tell them I'll be two hours at the most.'

Leo's mouth grazed gently across hers as he strapped her into the harness. 'When we get upstairs if you keep your hands lightly on the controls you'll soon get the feel of her.' Reaching under the instrument coaming he brought out a rubber tube with a cone on the end. 'If you need to talk to me, use this. I can talk to you via that tube attached to your helmet. All right?'

I love you, she thought, and smiled with the pleasure of being with him.

'Good,' he said, as though he'd read her thoughts.

They were soon in the air and following the road beneath them. The air was fresh, the day bright. The control stick hardly moved against her palm as Leo kept the plane in trim, and she was acutely aware of the connection between herself and him, via the control stick.

She felt for the cone and brought it to her mouth. 'Leo, what are those dials with numbers on the control panel?'

'Altimeter tachometer speedometer . . . to name a few. Don't worry about those today. Can you bring the nose up a little?'

She moved the stick back the fraction required to perform the required manoeuvre. 'Now . . . gently go left by moving the control to the right.

She moved the stick to the right and the aircraft obliged by heading left.

'Now go to the right.'

That done, he said, 'We'll need to lose height before we land. Push the stick forward, but very gradually.'

A thought occurred. 'Leo . . .'

His chuckle warmed her ear and he purred, 'Yes . . . you are flying the Moth mostly by yourself, and have been for the last five minutes. But not completely, since I have the rudder controls. See if you can circle the airport as we go down. We land into the wind.'

As the land got closer she began to panic. 'Leo . . . I don't know what to do.'

His voice came, calm against her ear. 'The same as you've been doing. We'll be landing her after this sweep . . . straighten up the wings. The airstrip is up ahead. If you look over the side you'll see it. We always take off and land into the wind.'

'How will I know which way the wind is blowing?'

'The windsock will tell us which direction it's coming from. There's a bit of a crosswind today.'

All she could see was a blur of land passing under them, and a kangaroo bounding off towards the trees. It looked very close, and she said, 'I can't see anything that looks like a sock. Help!'

He laughed. 'I've got you, Es . . . you're quite safe and we're doing it together.'

She tried not to panic as she saw the ground wheeling below, though her heart beat at a thousand miles a minute. Then the plane straightened up and they were down, bouncing erratically along the airstrip. Esmé laughed with relief and shouted her elation exuberantly out loud as she punched the air. 'That was the absolute aces.'

Minnie was already on her way, looking forward to seeing Esmé again, though goodness only knew where they'd find work, and they would both need to. She loved Australia and the Australians for their openness and big hearts. Her only regret was that if she'd stayed in England she wouldn't have met Wally, and she'd be securely employed in the profession she'd been trained for.

But then . . . she'd wanted adventure in her life, so she mustn't complain.

When she'd seen the plane fly over she'd left the nursing station in the hands of Sally Bowers and headed for the manager's office. 'Can I borrow the truck, Ben. I'm expecting my friend.'

He nodded. 'Don't forget to bring the mail back with you.'

It was a short dash through a dusty track that had been chopped by a bulldozer through the eucalypts and thick undergrowth. It turned to mud when it rained.

Minnie had watched from the truck's cabin as the Moth circled the airfield several time, its wings not quite level. She'd wondered . . . what was the doctor up to . . . was he drunk? Perhaps something was wrong with the plane. Her mouth dried. Not that. Dr Thornton was too nice a man. Besides, she didn't think she'd be able to handle that sort of emergency by herself. She wouldn't know which one to treat first. Es, or the Doc.

While she'd been casting off that scenario, the plane had eased lower. The wings suddenly levelled out. It landed on its two front wheels then bounced a couple of times before it slowed down. The tail had dropped, its wheel settling on the ground, and the aircraft had run the length of the runway, losing speed. It turned at the end and slowly trundled back to where she stood.

Esmé punched the air, and her shriek of laughter made Minnie smile. Her hand went to her mouth. Surely that hadn't been her friend at the controls?

The lanky form of Leo Thornton slid out from the cockpit, and when Esmé emerged, he took her by the waist and swung her down and around. They were laughing together as she slid from the cabin and waved.

The plane was still ticking over.

'I didn't really fly the plane, did I?' Esmé said, her eyes shining with the delight of it. 'Look, there's Min. She'll be green with envy when I tell her.'

Leo nodded, and they wandered over to where she stood, arms casually around each other's waists. 'I thought you might land us on one wing with the crosswind, so took over then. Actually, it wasn't bad for a first go. You'll make a good pilot.'

Eyes bright, Esmé was still laughing. 'It was such fun, Leo, I enjoyed it.'

Leo's glance came Minnie's way, and he handed over a packet of envelopes. 'Is everything all right, Minnie . . . anything to report?'

'Nothing I can't handle.' She gazed at the envelopes and shuffled through them. They were uniform in size, obviously sent from the same source. 'Hmmm . . . this looks as though my job's about to disappear. I've been expecting it. Are you staying for a while?'

'I've got to get over to Tunbridge Downs station. The Dunston governess has broken her arm.'

'So that's the way the wind blows,' Esmé said, the laughter still colouring her voice.

He looked at the windsock, then down at Esmé and grinned before kissing her gently on the mouth. Then he hauled himself on to the wing walk and climbed into the aircraft. He blew Esmé a kiss, then as an afterthought blew one Minnie's way. 'I'll be seeing you, ladies.'

'I wish I could attract a man like that,' Minnie murmured.

Taxiing down the runway Leo turned the aircraft into the wind and picked up speed, the plane lifted gracefully into the sky. They watched it bank in an arc to change direction and gain height, then it moved into the distance, swiftly becoming a small speck in the sky.

Esmé sighed, already missing Leo's company. 'He looks like a small bird in such a large sky,' she whispered, and wondered if he was lonely up there all by himself.

'I can see that you're well over Liam,' Minnie said, grinning at her.

'Yes . . . I'm over Liam.' She gave her friend a hug. 'I'm definitely over Liam.'

Thirteen

Minnie handed the mail to Ben, who frowned. 'These look like the ones I've been dreading.'

'Is there one for me?'

Shuffling through them he drew out the one with her name on. 'Sorry, love.'

Minnie tore it open. 'I've got to vacate the nursing post by the end of the month. They're going to put everything in mothballs until finances improve. The mission sisters will collect what's left of the medical supplies. They've included a reference for me. Oh well, I can't complain . . . I can always move into Wally's place if need be, though it's a bit of a hovel.'

'You shouldn't stay there by yourself, love.'

'I'll have Esmé to keep me company.'

'If you do move in there and need to pick up anything from town let me know . . . though we can raid the company store of what's left. Are you sure you want to stay there?'

'I'll see what state the place is in first. I left some canned food and milk in the cupboard, and there's flour in a tin. We might stay for a few days then move back to Melbourne and sign on with the agency again. At least Esmé can have the experience of living in the bush.'

'Take the truck over tomorrow so you can give the place the once-over. Make sure the pump's working and you've got everything you need. I'll lend you the pedal radio from the nursing post in case you need to get in touch urgently.'

'Thanks, Ben, you're a brick.'

When they were on their way to the nursing post, Esmé told her, 'Ma said we can both stay with her in Melbourne, if we like . . . help her out a bit. It won't interfere with us looking for work.'

Minnie made a face at her. 'You're forgetting one thing . . . Wally might turn up and remember he's my husband.'

'Oh, of course . . . I'd forgotten about him. Then again,

he may have gone to Singapore on the *Horizon Queen*. He was scared of his own shadow when I saw him, and expecting a visit from John Teagan, I believe.'

'No wonder . . . he's been seeing Teagan's younger sister.'

'Don't you mind?'

'I'd pay her to take him off my hands if I had any money. I just wish he'd left me the car. He's probably sold it.'

'Still, it's nice to know we have somewhere to stay in Melbourne while we're waiting for work,' Esmé told her. 'Wally told his mother that he loves you, and the other woman means nothing to him.'

'Wally tells people what he thinks they like to hear. He knows that his mother and I get on together, and telling her I have his undying love will stop her nagging him. He's a cheat and a liar, Es. I can't understand how Ma keeps getting taken in by him.'

'He's her son, Min . . . he's all she's got left and she loves him.' Saying that made Esmé think of Livia. She'd filled the role of a mother figure, and love for her sister came as a strong surge.

'I suppose, but what if he turns up at Ma's while we're there?'

'We'll sleep in the room with the twin beds and the bolt on the inside of the door.'

'A good idea.'

Over the next couple of weeks it was sad watching the remainder of the workers depart, some on foot with their children in tow, their carts or vehicles piled high with household goods they were unwilling to leave behind.

Minnie hugged them all and wished them luck.

Ben put the sides up on the truck, and those with only themselves to think about piled into the back, quiet and thoughtful, already looking worried at the thought of what lay ahead.

Then it was their turn. Ben left them at the gate to Wally's homestead. 'I don't like leaving you here by yourselves, so I'll drop in every day to see how you're going. If you need anything you must let me know.'

The state of Victoria had impressed Esmé with its lush

vegetation and soaring mountains, but nothing could have prepared her for the ramshackle building in front of her. 'Wally bought this?'

'He inherited it from his uncle.'

The thought was too awesome for words, and a giggle tore from Esmé's mouth. 'That husband of yours must be the world's biggest loser.'

Minnie grinned. 'He said he was going to settle down and grow vegetables, but the first lot of seedlings he planted disappeared overnight and he lost heart. I think the rabbits ate them.'

Their grins became laughter as they gazed at each other, and soon they were doubled up. From somewhere in the scrub a kookaburra joined in.

'I can't remember the last time I had a good laugh,' Minnie said, holding her aching stomach. 'Here's something else funny. Wally is convinced his uncle stashed a fortune in gold down a snake-hole under the veranda.'

That started them laughing all over again.

Minnie fetched the key from the ledge over the door, which opened with a creak. Something scuttled in the shadows.

The hair on the back of Esmé's neck prickled as she stared at it. 'I hope that wasn't a spider.'

'So do I. I'd hate to meet one that size.'

'It's got scales. It might be a snake.'

Minnie peered at it, her eyes growing accustomed to the gloom. 'It's got legs, so it's a stumpy-tailed lizard. It's not venomous, but make sure you don't get bitten because its mouth is full of bacteria.' Minnie picked it up, and, ignoring its warning hisses, placed it outside. 'Off you go; you're more bark than bite.'

'You're brave.'

'Living here has taught me what's safe to handle and what's not, and that most things run away if they hear you coming. If you'd rather, we could go straight to Melbourne.'

'It would be nice to have a bit of a rest from Ma. Let's stay. We might be able to find the gold.'

'If you think I'm sticking my hand down a snake hole you can think again. Wally can keep his secret stash.'

The romance of communing with nature wore thin after

the first week. They began to run out of food, and they lived on pancakes, porridge and eggs for two days before Ben delivered some canned goods to see them through. Tinned peas had never tasted so good, and they feasted on preserved fruit.

'I'm going into Melbourne in a week or so. Let me know if you want a lift,' Ben said.

Minnie gave him a relieved smile. 'I'll let you know now. We most definitely will.'

To keep themselves busy they cleared the undergrowth away from the house and whitewashed the inside walls. They generally tidied the place up, though there wasn't much they could do in the way of repairs.

When they had a rainy day the roof leaked and they put buckets and bowls around to catch the drips. A windy day nearly ripped off the sheet of corrugated iron and it flapped up and down, making a horrific screeching noise that put their teeth on edge, and kept them awake all night. But the rain filled the water barrel, so the water lost its brackish taste.

The next morning dawned fresh and bright, with a stiff breeze rattling everything. 'I'd better try and repair the roof while we can,' Minnie said, the doubt in her voice all too evident. 'Make sure you hold the ladder steady, because I'm scared of heights.'

Esmé took the hammer and nails from her. 'You hold the ladder and I'll do the repairs. I don't mind heights, and besides, I'm wearing slacks. I helped build a chicken house and Chad allowed me to hammer in a nail, so I'm experienced.'

When Minnie started to laugh, Esmé grinned. 'It happened to be a very superior chicken house, fit for a royal rooster.'

The roof wasn't all that high, but the beams creaked when she put her weight on them, and she didn't feel very safe.

'Be careful, Es,' Minnie called, her worried voice contributing to her uneasiness.

The sheet of iron was so flaked with rust and full of holes it was hardly worth the cost of a nail, let alone several. Still, it was all they had. Esmé set to work, banging nails in where she could. They went in easily. The beams underneath were spongy, and offered no resistance. The wind would soon loosen them again, but it might last until they left. After that it was Wally's problem.

She gazed down at Minnie. 'It might be better if we put weights on the roof. Could you pass up those flat stones from the path?'

'I'll try, but they're heavy and I'll need two hands, so I won't be able to get up the ladder.'

'If you take the washing line down we can use that. Hand me up one end, then tie a stone to the other one and stand back. We'll only need about four, So I'll try and haul them up one by one.'

The wind brought a faint droning sound, but when Esmé turned her ear upwards towards the sound it had gone, lost in the noisy thrash of the foliage flaying in the wind. It was probably a bee flying past her ear. Her hammering had disturbed all sorts of small creatures, lizards, beetles, and spiders, swooped on by birds taking advantage of the unexpected snacks on offer.

Minnie's hand appeared over the gutter with its rope offering. Esmé grabbed it, and a couple of minutes later she began to haul on the rope. The stone was heavier than she expected, but it came smoothly. Just as she was about to heave a sigh of relief it caught on the gutter and stayed there.

She needed to put some weight into this operation. Crawling up the beam she stood upright, and with her legs apart, braced herself and tugged. The stone moved, but didn't quite make it over the lip of the gutter. It fell back, knocking a plank from the wall, and nearly jerking her arms out of their sockets.

When she swore, Minnie giggled. 'I didn't know you were familiar with such language, Lady Es.'

'Stand well back, Min, I'm going to have to drop it if I don't manage it this time.'

Using all her weight she dug in her heels and gave a prolonged heave on the rope. The stone slipped over the gutter and on to the edge of the roof. Strength spent, Esmé stopped for breath. Before she had time to congratulate herself there came an ominous crack from the beam, and it fell, still attached to the roofing sheet, bent and buckled beyond repair. She slid down the corrugated iron gathering splinters of rust and fell through the attic into the house space below, accompanied by a dozen decades of debris and dirt.

She bounced off a bed, automatically flinging out an arm

to save herself. A sharp crack sent pain ratcheting into her arm, neck and shoulder and she screamed out with the agony of it. Bombarded by falling bits and pieces, she reached out with her usable hand and managed to grab up a pillow. She held it over her head until everything stopped dropping on her. The iron sheet tipped sideways on to her, and something heavy landed on it and pinned it there.

There was a scrabbling sound nearby, and a scream from Minnie. 'Es, are you all right? I'll never forgive myself if you're dead.'

'I'll never forgive you either.' Esmé's laughter bordered on hysterical, but she couldn't stop herself. At the same time, tears trickled down her face. 'I managed to get the stone up.'

Minnie gave a hiccup. 'Congratulations. I wouldn't have suggested we whitewash the walls if I'd known you were going to demolish the place.'

'Whatever you do, don't pull on that rope if you see it. And if you can get to the pedal radio to call for help, I'd be grateful. If not, you'll have to go to the mine and ask Ben. Don't try and move me from under this pile of junk by yourself. You might bring the rest of it down.'

'Do you have any injuries, Es?'

She was beginning to feel a bit shaky, and the pain was making itself known to her. 'Quite a few, I'd say. I think my left arm is broken, and possibly my collarbone, and a rib or two. I don't know about the rest, though I can wriggle my toes. The bed took the brunt of it, but everything hurts.' Her teeth began to chatter. 'I'm beginning to suffer from shock, so don't be too long.'

Minnie bit back a sob. 'All right, Es, just lie there and take it easy. I'm sorry I made a joke out of it.'

'Be thankful for small mercies. That sheet of iron could have cut my head off.'

Minnie was back in a few minutes. 'The radio is useless. Hold tight, love. I'll be as quick as I can.'

Esmé felt alone after her friend had gone. Her heart pounded and her mood went from despair, to hysteria, then back to despair again. Above her the beam supporting the stone creaked. The pile of splintered planks, iron sheets and broken glass gave an occasional creak as it settled. Dust rose in the air and was either whipped away by the wind, or threatened to choke her.

Part of the pillowcase had been ripped off, and the rag was hanging on a nail not far from her face. With one arm trapped and the other one useless, she managed to grab it with her teeth when it was blown in her direction. After a short tug of war it loosened from the nail and she was able to draw it down through the small opening above her. It settled on her face, where, clenched between her teeth, it would act as a makeshift filter.

Her chest ached, but she couldn't move. Just as well really, because she felt broken into pieces. She seemed to be wedged in, though she could see daylight and clouds racing across the sky through a tiny gap. Under her was something soft . . . the mattress off the bed, she thought, and was thankful for small mercies. Now and again her body began to shake and her teeth chatter. Coldness crept into her limbs and weariness crept through her body. She closed her eyes, and then jerked them open again. She mustn't go to sleep. She drifted off again, then jumped when she heard the truck.

There was a crunch of footsteps, then, 'Stone the crows! That's a work of art. How did she manage to bring that lot down on her?'

It wasn't Leo's voice, it was his brother's.

Leo's voice came next, laconic, but with an unmistakable fear in it. 'Beats me.' She smiled when he said, 'Esmé, love . . . if you're still conscious, talk to me.'

Nobody else could say her name like that. Opening her dust-encrusted eyes she spat out the rag and croaked, 'Leo . . . how did you get here so quickly?'

'Alex and I came to pay you both a surprise visit. We bought lunch with us, and were on our way out here in Ben's truck. We nearly ran over Minnie, who was running so fast in the opposite direction she overtook a kangaroo. She said you've done yourself a bit of damage. Is there any neck trauma, d'you think?'

It wasn't as casual a question as it sounded. 'I don't think so, Leo. My toes and fingers still work. At a guess my left arm is broken and my collarbone and ribs are damaged. There's a bit of shock thrown in, and splinters and bruises, I expect. It's all so heavy, and there's hardly any space to expand my chest, so I can only take shallow breaths.'

'It could be worse. We'll soon have you out of there my brave girl.' His voice was kind and concerned. It made her want to cry.

'Don't encourage me to snivel, Leo, because I'm not far from a fully-fledged bout of hysterical self-pity. And be careful of any rope that's hanging down. It's tied to a paving stone that's still balanced on the edge of what's left of the roof.'

'Yeah, we know about it, sweetheart. I've stood Alex under it, so if it falls and lands on his head it will simply bounce off.'

Alex said something rude, to which Leo laughed. 'Your language is usually more colourful than that, brother.' He addressed her again. 'What position are you lying in, Es?'

'On my back, but I don't know what direction.'

'North, by north east, judging by your voice,' and she giggled, despite the pain she was in. 'Now . . . Alex and I are going to lift this stuff off of you. We'll be as careful as we can.'

She heard the rumble of the truck engine. 'Is Minnie going somewhere?'

'To get my bag from the plane, and to let Ben know what's happened.'

The load became fractionally lighter when they lifted the first beam. 'How are you doing, Es?'

'I don't know. I'm all right, I think.' But it hurt like hell when she breathed, and her broken arm was an agony. She couldn't even move her good arm across to support it, because something prevented it.

'We're going to remove an iron roofing sheet next. You might like to close your eyes against dust and rust flakes.'

'My back is already full of rusty splinters.'

With the iron sheet gone her world lightened a little bit more. Cautiously, she opened her eyes a chink and caught a glimpse of sky through a gap. Leo's face blotted it out, and one blue eye gazed through the hole at her. 'Hello, sweetheart.'

She sniffed, and her eyes swam with tears, so she didn't trust herself to speak in case she started to howl and couldn't stop.

'It won't take too long now. We'll remove the small stuff next. Everything is balanced, like a house of cards and seems to support everything else. There is a beam pinning you to the ground. Once we can get access to it, Alex is going to support the beam with the Jack from the truck, while I pull you out. The bad news is . . . it will hurt like hell. Can you move, at all?'

'Marginally. I seem to be wedged in by the beam, which is pressing on my chest and obstructing my breathing. My good arm is under it, with the forearm sticking out the other side. It's trapped, but I can move it. I just can't bring it through to where the rest of me is.' She was well aware of what would happen if the prop carrying the weight of the beam collapsed. 'I think the beam might be balanced on the remains of the bed, which is supporting it at the high end.'

'All right, love. When the weight of that beam is lifted from you, try and use your good arm as a splint for the injured one. I don't want to damage you any more than you are, but I've got no choice than to pull you out, because you're in too precarious a position, as it is.'

And indeed, there came another warning crack from above, and a shower of debris rained on them.

Her voice wobbled when she said, 'I think I'm lying on a mattress, that might make things easier. Leo . . . please don't put yourself in any danger.'

'This gives me an opportunity to play the hero and impress you,' he said, and his voice moved away. 'Right, let's get on with this, Alex. She's barely hanging on to herself as it is.'

She didn't want him to impress her by putting himself in danger. If anything happened to him she'd never forgive herself for being so stupid.

It seemed ages before the weight was lifted from her chest. She managed to bring her left arm through and cradled her broken arm with it. She'd begun to shake, and with teeth chattering, said, 'I'm ready, Leo.'

Steadily dragged out by her feet, she tried not to scream at the pain of being moved. She groaned, and felt sick when she emerged, shaking uncontrollably. Opening her eyes she panicked. 'I can't see anything.'

'There's a handkerchief over your face.' He removed it. 'Is that better?'

Covered in dust, Leo and Alex smiled at her with the same smile, and she thought inconsequently that they must have been double trouble when they were children, but how wonderful to have such fine sons. Taking up each end of the thin mattress they carried her outside away from the house, just as the truck arrived. The mattress was slid on to the tray.

Minnie said, 'Ben's opening up the nursing post. I've brought a blanket. The mission sisters haven't picked up the equipment yet, so we can use whatever is left. How is she?'

'I'm just examining her, but she's going into shock.' He took Minnie aside and his voice rumbled as he said something to her that Esmé couldn't quite hear. He turned back to her, checked the skin inside her eye socket, pressed her fingernails and took her pulse. 'Tell me if it hurts.' He gently probed her arm and her chest, and she reacted with indrawn breaths and winces. 'Sorry.'

Waiting until he'd finished his examination she asked, 'How much damage is there?'

His eyes engaged hers. 'You escaped lightly, considering that a house fell on you. Apart from multiple bruises and lacerations, at least three ribs are cracked. Your arm is fractured in two places. The good news is that the collarbone seems to be intact, and I think the pain there is associated.'

'Internal bleeding?'

'The signs are mostly good. There is some tenderness around the spleen, but I don't think it's ruptured. You'll be under observation for a while.' He tucked the blanket round her as though she was a child, snuggling it cosily around her neck and ears.

Esmé touched his hand, grateful for the warmth and thankful for his presence. He caressed her arm, then the sharp prick of a needle made her cry out.

'Ouch . . . that was sneaky. What is it?'

'Something to take the edge off your pain.'

The thought worried her. 'Has pain got edges . . . what happens when you remove them? You're not putting me to sleep are you?'

His broad smile said, trust me. 'Would I do that to you?'

She wasn't going to be taken in by that smile of his. 'Would you?'

'No . . . it was a painkiller. It will relax you, so you won't be quite so uncomfortable when we move you.' He sidetracked her adroitly. 'You should have known the roof would have been full of termites.'

She had to think about that for a long time. Termites? They lived in Africa and built mounds out of mud. 'Are you going to tell me off?'

'I think you're old enough to know how stupid you've been by endangering your life in that manner?'

He was right, but she hadn't expected him to be so straightforward. A tear inched down her face. 'Don't be cross, Leo.'

'I'm cross because I happen to love you, and you've scared the living daylights out of me.' He sighed. 'I think you've had enough trouble for one day. Minnie you get in the cab with my brother. Drive like you're on eggshells, Alex.'

Behind them, the stone slipped. Then it plunged to the ground, the rope whipping after it like a long, lashing tail.

'Nice timing,' Leo muttered.

Esmé's ears began to buzz and her muscles relax. Leo was sweet, even when he was being mean . . . she'd be a fool to let him get away. The sky slipped sideways and leaned to one side.

'Try not to move your neck.'

'Tired . . . head is heavy . . . what did you give me?'

Sitting beside her, he grinned. 'Love potion number one.' He placed his hand against her cheek. 'Here, use this as a pillow.'

When his palm took the weight of her head, he stooped and kissed her mouth with such tenderness she had to sniff back her tears.

'Eyes closing,' she whispered, 'Love potion number one . . . you know something, Leo, I think it's working.'

Fourteen

An hour later, Esmé's arm was wrapped in a wad of cotton wool and immobilized by splints, bandages and a sling. 'There, that will have to do.'

Leo stated his intention to bandage Esmé's ribs. 'You know how this should be done, Es. We'll have to remove your garments first, and you must exhale as much air as you can.'

Minnie said, 'It would be best if I did this for her, since we bandaged each other often during training. Take a ten-minute break. I can call you if you're needed.'

Leo nodded, and joined Alex on the veranda outside.

Esmé choked back an assortment of squeaks and groans as the strapping took place. She looked tired now, and her face was ashen from the strain of bearing the pain. Although it was an obvious effort, Esmé was being as brave as she could, and Minnie's heart went out to her. Quickly, she cut the stitches from the sleeve of Esmé's blouse, opened the shoulder seam and took out the sleeve. After arranging the garment around Esmé's body for the sake of modesty, she secured it at the shoulder with safety pins. 'There, that will cover you decently for the time being. I'll keep the sleeve and we can repair it later.'

'Thanks, Min.'

'You can come in now, Leo.'

Leo said, 'I've been talking to Alex. I'll be taking Esmé to Melbourne, where she can be looked after properly. The air ambulance has already been ordered.'

'I feel responsible for her condition, and I'd like to look after her myself.'

'I know, Minnie. But you can't look after her here, and besides, that was quite a fall, and she'll have to spend a few days in hospital so we can make certain that there's no internal bleeding. Have you got somewhere to go?'

'Yes, I'll go and live with Ma. Esmé and I had planned to,

after we'd had a bit of a holiday here.' She shrugged. 'It was my fault. I thought she might like to find out what living in the bush was like.'

'Taking the blame is a waste of time. Anyone with half a brain cell would have known not to have moved into a termite palace.'

'Termite Palace.' Esmé giggled through her tears. 'I feel a bit fuzzy.'

Leo placed a warm hand over hers. 'You look fuzzy too, as though someone has used you as a scrubbing brush.'

'You always say such lovely things, Leo. Do I really look that bad, Minnie?'

'Worse.' Minnie laughed. 'Try not to walk under a magnet else you'll take off like that iron roof did in the wind. Look after her, Doc. As soon as you've gone I must go back and find our bags. I don't know why I didn't think of it before.'

'You had rather a lot to deal with.'

Alex said, 'I'm feeling a bit useless too, Minnie. I'll come with you. Leo, I take it you're going in the air ambulance with Esmé?'

Leo nodded. 'I'll leave Minnie in your hands then. She can't stay here by herself. You can fly her down in the Moth and get her settled.'

'I'll send a message to the folks, too. Tell them what's happened.'

They took Leo and Esmé to the airstrip first, and went back to what remained of the house. Alex cast an assessing eye over it. 'What will your husband say?'

Throwing a sharp look at him, Minnie retorted, 'I no longer live with my husband and I intend to divorce him, when I can find him.'

'Oh . . . I'm sorry.'

'So am I. It was a case of marry in haste and repent at leisure.' She smiled at him, though it felt forced. 'Never mind about my troubles. It was my own fault, and I was stupid.'

'I know a lawyer, if that will help.'

'I can't afford a lawyer. I owe money to Esmé . . . money Wally stole from her when we worked together. Es and I had such plans. Well, I guess it was me who had the plans, and

Esmé fell in with them. We were going to come to Australia and have a working holiday. Then, when her brother finished his medical training, she was going home to work as his nurse. Her family had her future all mapped out for her. I just wanted her to experience something different before she settled down. But it all went horribly wrong for both of us. Poor Esmé. She came back to Australia to make sure I was all right . . . and look what happened to her.'

'It wasn't your fault. It's not as though you made Esmé climb on to the roof.'

'If only I hadn't married Wally.' She drew in a deep, despairing breath. 'It will be a long time before I can afford a divorce. But despite everything that's happened, I like it here. I like the little bit of Australia I've seen; the patterns on the trunk of the eucalypts, the sky at night and the bright colours of day. I like it that the sky goes on forever, and I really, really love having all this space around me. I intend to settle in the country if I can find work, then sort out the legal side of it.'

Alex laughed. 'There isn't much work about, especially in the country . . . though we can usually manage a meal for those who knock at the door. I like your enthusiasm. The government should hire you as an ambassador for Australia. You're a girl after my own heart.'

Her smile faded when she remembered Wally, and it seemed that Alex remembered his existence to, for he said, 'Being married to an Australian might help you with permanent residence.'

'Nothing will induce me to stay married to Wally any longer than necessary . . . not even permanent residence. I'd rather go home, then apply to migrate.' She laughed. 'You and Leo are alike.'

A slightly self-deprecating smile came her way. 'He got most of the brains and I got the brawn. I'm a farmer.'

'You're talking to someone who doesn't know which way up a daffodil bulb is planted.' She waved her arms around. 'This is supposed to be a sheep farm . . . or so I was told. I can't see any sheep. Is your farm about the same size.'

His eyes flew open and laughter came into them. 'Yeah, I guess it's pretty small as farms go . . . about a couple of thousand acres. Dad and his brother had an adjoining farm each, though they worked it together. Leo and I inherited our uncle's between us. Leo leaves it to me to manage his half. His heart isn't in farming, though he helps out now and again. Like I said, he got most of the brains.'

'I imagine it takes quite a few brains to run a farm properly. After all, it is a business.' She gazed around her and laughed. 'Looking at this place you wouldn't think so. Did you want to be a doctor, then?'

'Good Lord, did I give you that impression? I love what I do. Let's talk about something else. Have you noticed that my brother is nuts about Esmé.'

'One can hardly miss it. Esmé is perfect for Leo. She grew up with doctors surrounding her. She knows how to handle them.'

'Doctors need handling?'

'In a hospital environment, they're God . . . especially the specialist surgeons. The man who brought Esmé up is a senior surgeon. They suck humbugs together to see who can make the loudest noise . . . whereas, I hardly dare breath when I'm in his presence. Neither do the doctors under him.'

Alex's laughter rang out. 'He sounds to be quite an imposing man.'

'Esmé took up nursing because medicine is a bit of a family tradition. It was expected of her, you see, and it came easily. I took up nursing so I could move out of home, even though it was only into nurse's quarters. I was all right with the practical stuff, but Esmé spent hours coaching me before a written exam. I wouldn't have passed anything if she hadn't helped me out.'

'Why did you want to move out of home?'

'When Dad died I inherited a wicked stepmother and two ugly stepsons. She made it clear that I wouldn't get anything. My father hadn't made a will, you see. You know when you're no longer wanted, and they made that plain about five minutes after my father died.'

His eyes searched her face. They were a paler shade of blue than Leo's. His smile inched across. 'I wish I'd met you before Wally did.'

Minnie wished the same, but she wasn't about to tell him that, since she wasn't free and she didn't want to encourage him.

He nodded, accepting what he read in her face. 'Too personal was it? Sorry. I've just remembered there's a picnic basket in the truck. It would be a shame to go hungry. How about we have lunch while we're here? It's not a bad spot. You get the picnic basket from the truck and I'll see if I can find us a table and some chairs amongst the rubble.'

He dragged them out and dusted them down, even though they were covered in dust themselves. They lunched under the trees in the soft green light that only sunshine filtered through gum trees could provide. There was chicken and potato salad . . . and a pie his mother had made from bottled apples. And there was home brewed cider and ginger beer.

'Don't drink too much of that cider too quickly. It has quite a kick. Leo and I pinched a couple of bottles and got drunk on it in the shearing shed when I was fourteen. We could hardly think straight for a week.'

She laughed. 'It serves you right.'

'That's what my dad said when he paddled our backsides.' He gazed around him. 'It must have been a pretty spot when the creek ran through the property.'

Alex had turned out to be good company, and he was more intelligent than he'd led her to believe. 'There's supposed to be a secret stash of gold hidden here.'

'It wouldn't surprise me. This is gold bearing country. Do you want to look for it?'

'I don't want anything belonging to Wally, only what he owes Esmé. He can keep his gold.'

'Nobody could call you a gold digger, then.'

Minnie was good at shrugging things off, but the events of the day were beginning to catch up with her. Her nerves were practically in shreds, and tears were not far from the surface. 'Did you think I might be one?'

Silently they gazed at each other. After a while he placed his work-worn hand over hers, saying awkwardly, 'Sorry, that was lame. It was a joke, and not meant to be taken literally.'

Turning over his palm, Minnie ran a finger gently over his calluses. It was an honest hand. 'Farming is hard work.'

'Yes, it is sometimes, but I get a sense of achievement from it. I'd like to see you again sometime if I may, Minnie. No pressure, but after things are sorted out and you can see your way clear, perhaps.'

She nodded, and smiled at him. 'I think I'd like that too, Alex. Thank you for trying to take my mind off Esmé's plight.'

'Despite that, I enjoyed your company. We'd better start work and see what we can rescue.'

After Alex unearthed their suitcases, he found a forked branch to support a beam that looked as though it might drop. Carefully, they sifted through the area where the bedroom had been, collecting clothes from a shattered wardrobe. Some of Minnie's worry left her when she found their handbags. At least they'd have some money for basics. Bits and pieces of jewellery, hairbrushes and the like, were scattered about.

Alex found the pedal radio, the keys full of debris. 'It should clean up all right.' He placed it on the back of the truck, along with the other bits and pieces.

Minnie thought they'd picked the place clean of their belongings, when a shiny reflection caught her gaze. She bent to pull it from under a piece of rubbish. It was Esmé's powder compact and lipstick. Made from sterling silver, the top was enamelled in vivid blue, with a silver bow in the middle.

'That's pretty.'

'Yes, it belongs to Esmé and was a birthday gift from her brother. She comes from a closely knit family and would have been upset by its loss.' Minnie wasn't leaving it for Wally to pocket, and slid it into her friend's bag.

As they drove away she gazed back at the place, hoping she'd never have to set eyes on it again. She grinned as she wondered what Wally would say when he saw what had happened to it.

Despite being nervous, because she didn't like heights, Minnie enjoyed the flight. When they reached Essendon airfield, Alex and another man pushed the plane into a hanger. He got them a taxi, and dropped her off at Ma's hotel. Alex escorted her to the door. He was an imposing figure in his Akubra hat and his best blue visiting shirt, though he was as dirty as she. A suitcase was grasped in each of his tanned hands, as if they weighed nothing.

'Thanks for your help, Alex. I don't know what I'd have done without you. I enjoyed the picnic, too.'

There was an awkward moment when she thought he was about to kiss her goodbye. He didn't, but gave a faint grin as though he was assessing the wisdom of it in his mind. There was a quiet reserve about Alex, one that the more outgoing Leo didn't seem to possess. It was endearing. She doubted if he'd do anything without deliberation.

He brushed a finger down her face and flicked a strand of her hair out of her eyes. 'I like you, Minnie girl. I like you a lot. In case he doesn't get home, tell Leo I'm staying at his flat, and if he wakes me coming in I'll flatten him.'

'I wouldn't put a wager on who would do the flattening, if it came to it.'

When she laughed he chucked her under the chin. 'No, neither would I. Tell him I've got a lift to the turn-off in the mail truck in the morning. I've left the Moth in its usual place in the hanger.' He took the luggage to the door.

Suddenly, she didn't want him to see the inside of the hotel. It was too dreary with its smoke-stained ceiling and the yellow flypaper circling down from the ceiling like a scabby tongue. Besides, Ma would be nosy and ask him personal questions. Minnie realized she was scared he might judge her by it, when she said. 'You needn't come in.'

'Aren't you going to shout a man a beer, then?'

'Well . . . I suppose . . . if you really want one.'

'Not really. Besides, it's not opening time yet.' He nodded, then turned and got back in the taxi, giving her a wave as they drove off.

When she struggled inside with the luggage, Ma welcomed her with a beaming smile, delighted to see her. 'Well, I'll be blowed. Hullo love . . . you're staying, I hope. Where's that nice little friend of yours?'

'Esmé's in hospital, Ma. Wally's homestead fell on her; the beams were full of termites.'

Ma's expression changed to one of worry. 'Is Esmé all right?'

'I think so. Leo was on hand.'

'Thank God for that! I told Wally to get the place looked at, but, oh no, he wouldn't listen. He thought he knew better.

Bloody termites! They'd eat the wooden leg off a cripple before he had time to swallow his beer. Is Esmé all right?'

'She has several broken bones. I'll be going to the hospital later, but I need to wash the dust out of my hair first and sort our clothing out. I think I'll have to wash it all.'

'You know where everything is. Give Es my love, then. Tell her she's welcome to come back here? I got used to having you girls around, you know. It can get a bit lonely now my old man's gone.'

'We were hoping you could put us up.' Minnie didn't want to ask about her absent husband, but thought she should. 'Have you heard anything from Wally?'

'Not a blessed thing.'

'Esmé suggested he might have gone to Singapore on the *Horizon Queen.*'

'I doubt it, since he hasn't got his passport with him. It's still in the dresser.'

'Someone must know where he is.'

Her face took on a bland look. 'If they do, they're not saying.'

'You might as well know, Ma. I intend to divorce him. I'll need to serve the papers on him.'

Ma sighed. 'Well . . . I can't say I blame you. As men go, he's not much of one, and he never could settle to anything. He was always easily led. He hung around with the wrong crowd and landed himself in trouble. He was either flush with money or stony broke, with all the gambling he did. You would have been the making of him, Minnie love.'

'Wally is thirty years old, and he should be made by now. What sort of man leaves his wife in the middle of nowhere and goes off without a word? You shouldn't make excuses for him.'

'He's my son. One day you might have sons of your own . . . then you'll understand. You might as well know. He got Lillian up the duff, and John Teagan is as mad as a cut snake. I don't blame him, what with her being so young, and all.'

That came as a shock. 'The girl is expecting a child?'

'Yeah . . . She came here, all bashed up, and down and out. I gave her a pound to keep her going. I don't know what happened to her after that.'

'You sent her away?'

'Wally's brought enough trouble down on our heads.'

'But she's carrying a child . . . your grandchild.'

'Don't give me the bleeding heart routine, Minnie. You've got to understand that Teagan is a real bad bugger. You stay out of his way, d'you hear?'

Minnie softened her voice. 'I do understand, Ma. I don't want to argue, and I don't want to put you in the position of taking sides. I just want you to know that my marriage to Wally is over. If you don't want me to stay here because of it, then say so.'

'Don't be so daft.' Ma gave her a hug. 'It's not opening time yet. Go and put the kettle on and we'll have a good natter before you go to the hospital to see young Es. You can bring back some fish and chips for tea. And Minnie —' she said, while she was heading towards the stairs — 'my Harry was careful with money. The thing is, he had life insurance, and enough so I don't have worry about my old age. When it comes through I'm going to repay the debt Wally owed young Es. I'll not see her go without . . . or you come to that.'

'Thanks, Ma . . . I appreciate that but it's not your debt, it's mine and Wally's.'

Fifteen

When Esmé woke she was in a green tent. At least, it resembled one, but it quickly became a curtained off space containing her hospital bed. There was a sense of familiarity at the smell of disinfectant, the muted voices of visitors and clang of metal pans and kidney dishes. She ached all over.

Cautiously she moved her head. Her left arm was plastered and in a sling. Her right one was dabbed with iodine, where they'd cleaned up the grazes. Her left rib area was sore. There were two stitches in a small cut, where they'd dug a piece of buried glass from her right arm. Her body, legs and arms had received the same iodine treatment, going by the feel of them.

The bottom half of Leo was on the seat next to her. His top half had fallen forward on to the edge of her bed. Head to one side, he slept peacefully, his mouth slightly squashed, and open on the side where it rested. His hair was a riot of curls and still had dust scattered through it.

She gazed at him for a long time, at the dark lashes that quivered along his eyelids and the shadowed planes of his face. He needed a shave. When she reached out to gently touch his hair it curled around her finger, as if claiming her.

'Leo,' she whispered.

His eyes opened, and he gazed at her through the beautiful bluebell haze of them, disorientated for a moment. Then he focused in on her and smiled. 'I was taking a quick nap.'

'You look sweet when you're asleep,' she said, and he laughed.

'That should be my line. How do you feel?'

'Dare I say, as if a great weight has been lifted from my shoulders?'

'No . . . you dare not.'

'In that case, Leo, I feel battered, but I'm thinking clearly.'

'So if I propose while you are in your right mind, you'll agree to marry me?'

'I imagine so.' She knew she would agree, and so did he,

but couldn't help pushing it a little bit further. 'You could try it and find out, I suppose.'

'Is this what's meant by making me jump through hoops?' He fell to one knee and grinned at her over the edge of the bed.

The curtain was pulled to one side and the ward sister came in. 'Oh good, you're awake.' Her glance fell on Leo and she clicked her tongue. 'What are you doing down there, Dr Thornton?'

'I was about to get into the position to propose marriage to your patient.'

Esmé's snort brought an amused glance from the nurse. 'Dr Sawle said Miss Carr should avoid excitement.'

'Oh . . . I'm not very exciting, I promise. In fact, I think Miss Carr is underwhelmed by the whole idea. Between you and me though, Sister, I'm down here because I dropped my fountain pen.' He made a show of looking under the bed before he stood.

'It's clipped to your pocket.'

Patting his pocket, he stood, his expression one of faked surprise. 'I'll be fuddled, so it is.'

Leo hovered while the nurse went through the rituals of temperature, pulse, pillow plumping and bed tidying. Trying to appear unnoticed made him even more conspicuous. The nurse hung the chart on the end of her bed then gazed from one to the other and grinned. 'There, you can finish your proposal now, Doctor, but make it quick. Miss Carr has a visitor . . . a young lady. She can't stay long, since there's only fifteen minutes left of visiting hour.'

'You can't stretch that, can you?' Esmé asked.

'Certainly not. I understand you are both nurses, so you know the hospital stays on a strict routine.'

Minnie came in, all smiles, and planted a kiss on her forehead. 'Oh, you look heaps better. Not quite so pale . . . in fact, quite rosy. I wonder why that is,' and she threw Leo a grin. 'Now . . . everything we own is covered in grit, Es, but I borrowed one of Ma's nightgowns for you to wear until I've washed yours. It's rather large, but it opens down the front and you'll be able to slip it on and off easily.'

She indicated the starched linen hospital gown. 'It's fractionally better than the one you're wearing. And I've washed your
hairbrush . . . and there's a soap bag and towel.'

'Thanks, Min. My hair does feel knotted.'

'I'll brush it for you. By the way, Leo, there's a message
from Alex for you.' She passed it on word for word.

He laughed. 'I'd better let you two have some girl talk. I'll
wait for you outside and see you home if you like, Min.'

'Oh . . . you needn't. The tram stops just a few yards from
the end of my street.'

'I'll come and see you tomorrow then, Es. I don't know
what time. It depends if I'm called out or not.' He stooped to
kiss her cheek and whispered in her ear. 'Be good.'

'Leo . . . thanks . . . for everything . . . and yes.'

'Right then.' His eyes lit up and so did his smile. He blew
her a kiss and was gone.

Minnie helped her into the voluminous gown, and then
began to pull the brush gently through the dark waves of her
hair, picking out bits of debris and grit. 'I can almost feel you
buzzing, Es. Tell me about it.'

'Leo was about to propose when the ward nurse came in
and interrupted him.'

'Ah . . . so that was what that parting "yes" was all about.'

'What do you think?'

'I think, congratulations, and I wish you all the happiness
in the world. Leo Thornton is the cat's whiskers, and the best
thing that could ever have happened to you. He'll be able to
handle your family, too, since he's on the same level.'

'Handle my family? I don't know what you mean.'

'Didn't you wonder why Liam turned tail and ran at the
first sign of opposition? No matter how he tried to fit in, Liam
would have always been an outsider.'

'Good Lord, I didn't give it a second thought. I should tell
them about Leo, I suppose. I wonder what they'll say.'

'Does it matter? It's your life.'

Esmé thought about it for a while, and then shook her head.
'I don't need their approval, and neither does Leo.'

'There . . . I told you he could handle them, and so can
you now. Leaving home has done you the world of good. As

for Leo, he has a lusty look to him. He'll have you wedded and bedded in no time at all, though perhaps not in that nightgown . . . it's a real passion killer.'

When colour rose to her cheeks, Minnie grinned. 'You've got to lose it sometime, Es, and at least you'll have a ring on your finger. Not like me.'

'I wonder if it's too soon after Liam.'

'Liam was a good-looking chap, and I fancied him myself at first sight. But he was self-absorbed. You don't still hanker after him, do you?'

'Of course I don't . . . although I was upset at the time.'

'We were both silly and jumped at the first thing in trousers that took an interest in us.' Minnie giggled. 'Matron kept us both on too tight a rein while we were training, so we didn't get any time to practise the art of male watching.'

They ignored the bell that said visiting hours were over. 'Is there any sign of Wally?'

'No, but I think Ma knows where he is. He's in trouble. He's taken up with the young sister of a local thug, and she's expecting his child. John Teagan thumped her before he tossed her out. Ma has had extra bolts fitted inside the doors . . . just in case.'

'Heavens, what are you going to do about Wally?'

'Divorce him when I can afford it. I do have grounds.' She shrugged. 'He told Ma that he loves me, and I think he tried to do the right thing by marrying me. I was willing to give it a second try, but it didn't work out. I'll never be able to trust him.'

Glumly, Esmé gazed at her friend. 'Be careful, Minnie. With thugs like John Teagan hanging about you should have allowed Leo to take you home.'

Airily, Minnie said, 'Oh . . . I'll be all right. John Teagan doesn't even know me. Anyway, forget my troubles, just make sure you get better.'

It was twenty minutes before the sister came back. She gazed at her watch, tutting with an assumed ferocity, since she'd chosen to ignore the chattering pair. 'Didn't you hear the bell, young lady? It's time you went home, since my patient needs to rest.'

They exchanged a grin at the familiar words, and then

Minnie gave Esmé a kiss. 'Bye, love. I'll see you tomorrow. I'm going to the agency in the morning to register for work.'

Leo didn't turn up for two days. When he appeared he loped into the ward with a bunch of flowers in his hand and a smile on his face. 'I can only stay for five minutes, I'm on my way to the airfield.'

Esmé blinked at the ring he slid on her finger. The two small diamonds flanked a larger one set in a platinum band, and they winked in unison back at her.

He smiled at her expression. 'How do you like the handcuff? We can swap it for another if you don't.'

Tears filled her eyes. 'It's exquisite.'

'Only the best for my girl.' His smile faded, replaced by alarm. 'Why are you crying? Have you changed your mind?'

'Lord, no. I've decided you're a rare bargain. I'm crying because I'm happy, and I wish my family were here to share it with me.'

'Heavens, I don't want them all crying on my shoulder, as well. Shall I send Chad a happy-from-Esmé telegram?'

'I'd prefer to write him a letter, because I want to surprise Livia. I won't tell him about the accident . . . they'll only worry.'

'Chad's a doctor . . . well, almost.'

'Doctor or not, Chad is also my twin. He'll never be objective about me, we've been through too much together.'

'Ah, yes . . . the orphanage.'

'He told you? He doesn't usually like talking about it.'

'Neither do you. The best way of getting rid of something that sticks in your throat is to cough it up.'

'That's not a very romantic notion.'

Although she gave a light laugh, he didn't, and his sympathetic enquiry brought tears to the surface when he said, 'Was it a bad time?'

'We had each other, and Chad made himself responsible for me. We were babies when we were taken there, so we didn't know any different, I suppose. It wasn't until my sister was in a position to care for us that we realized what we'd missed. Chad found it hard to hand over my responsibility to another.'

'It gave him a purpose in life, I imagine.'

'I clearly remember the day when we went to be with Livia. She was living in Nutting Cottage, and was almost a stranger to us. It was a big change in my life and I reacted badly, because I was scared that Chad and I were going to be parted. Chad was angry about something. We had our own rooms, which was wonderful after sleeping in a dormitory. Richard Sangster, who was Livia's first husband and Meggie's father, gave a dog to Chad and a kitten to me. He was a nice man, and he helped Chad build a posh henhouse.'

'So Chad told me. Cackleberry House, wasn't it?'

'Cluckington Hall. When Richard married Livia we were pleased. It was tragic when he died. You get used to having family. You feel . . . owned.'

'Don't you mean loved?'

'That as well, I suppose. But when you're not used to being loved it can suffocate, as if the early lack of it needs to be compensated for by the giver. Then you have to estab-lish a place in the family for yourself instead of growing up knowing it. Poor Chad. He's so grateful and earnest at times. He's doing what's expected of him, and never seems to have much fun.'

'What a complicated creature you are. Chad is doing exactly what he wants to do, and you only see one side of him. And yes, he does know how to have fun. He has a lot of friends in medical school, and he's going to be a bloody good doctor.'

She squeezed out a smile.

Leo hesitated. 'We haven't had time to make plans for our future together yet, have we.'

'No . . . I don't suppose we have.' She gazed at the ring on her finger. He'd referred to it as a handcuff. She was sure she wanted to share her life with Leo, wherever that path took them. 'Do we need a blueprint?'

'Lord, no. I have no intention of running your life. In fact . . . I was hoping you'd help run mine. To start with, you could give me your opinion on this. At the end of the year I'd intended to return to England. I've been accepted for a position in a children's hospital in London, since my intention is to specialize in paediatrics. After that I was going to return to Australia. That was before you came into my life. How do you feel about it?'

It was perfect. Two years in England meant she and her family would have time to adjust to the parting of the ways. 'That's fine with me.'

'If you want we could get married in England, so your family can be part of it.'

'Then again . . . we could marry before we go, so *your* family can attend.'

'I won't argue with that, the sooner the better as far as I'm concerned. My mother will be pleased. We can have a honeymoon on board the ship taking us to England, and will be there in time to celebrate Christmas. That will be a perfect start to our marriage.'

It was also romantic, she thought, so she got the snuffles all over again.

'Why are you weeping, Es?'

'Because you were being romantic, and I didn't expect it.'

'Was I?' Head slanted to one side he gazed quite seriously at her. 'I have my romantic moments, you know, but generally I'm basic Australian male.'

'Yes, I know. You Leo the jungle boy, me Essie the tabby cat.'

He chuckled, and taking a handkerchief from his pocket, applied it to her tears. Picking up her undamaged hand he kissed the palm. 'My dearest tabby cat . . . I love you so much that I die a thousand times every time I think of you.'

'You're overdoing the lethal bit, Leo.'

Her retort brought a fleeting grin to his face. 'Stop complaining, woman.'

Odd how she felt totally at ease with Leo, but she gazed at the shadows under his eyes with some concern. 'You look tired.'

'There was an emergency. A couple of children wandered away from the mission two days ago, and we've been searching for them, me from the air and with an Aboriginal tracker on the ground. We found them this morning, scared and hungry, but safe.' He gazed at his watch. 'It's amazing how much ground two nippers can cover in a short time. I must go now. I've got to deliver some medication before I can have a sleep.'

'Take care. And Leo . . . I love you.'

His eyes took her measure, his grin came, then widened into a smile. 'You know, Es, it's about time you told me that.'

'Did you doubt it, then?'

'I have enough arrogance in me to know that you'd tell me some time.' Soft and leisurely, his goodbye kiss robbed her of breath and of her will. The back of her mind noted that her responses bordered on healthily indecent.

Wally put in an appearance after closing time. He had a small, scruffy beard and moustache. Minnie eyed him up and down. 'Look what the cat's dragged in.'

'Don't be like that, Min. Why aren't you at the homestead?'

'The little pig huffed and puffed and he blew the house down.'

He laughed. So did she, because the joke was on him.

'I need some money, Min.'

'Put your arm down a snake hole, you might find the pot of gold.'

She hardened her heart. His little-boy-lost expression didn't work with her any more. 'You've come to the wrong person. The small amount of money I've got has to keep me until I start work. And don't think you can steal any more from Esmé. She's in hospital.'

'Oh, come on Minnie . . . you're my wife. There's a game going and I only need a fiver to get me into it.'

He hadn't even bothered to ask what was wrong with Esmé. 'I won't be your wife for much longer, and I haven't got a fiver. But I have found a job, and as soon as I've got some money together I'm going to divorce you. I'm given to understand that I have grounds.'

'What you've heard is lies. Lillian played up when her brother was in the cooler, but I doubt if she's expecting a baby. I . . . um . . . acted as Lillian's minder, more than anything. We went out dancing, and stuff. Somebody told John Teagan and he got the wrong idea.'

'You were her pimp, you mean.'

He winced, then lowered his voice and gazed towards the stairs. 'Lillian isn't a slut, whatever my mother thinks. She's a nice, ordinary girl. Aw, come on Minnie, you know it's you I love. Why else would I have married you?'

He'd married her because of the baby, and because she'd nagged him, she thought, and really, that was the only thing he'd had in his favour – that he'd been willing to support her and the child. It had soon become obvious he didn't have the wit to support either. Perhaps he was telling the truth and Lillian wasn't pregnant. She doubted it. Ma knew what a pregnancy looked like. It was about time Wally learned what responsibility was about, and she wasn't going to finance him in his folly.

'Minnie,' Ma bawled from above. 'Is that my Wally?'

'Yes, Ma. I'm on my way,' he said.

She watched him go, her eyes narrowing. Wally was up to something, and whatever it was she didn't think it included her. Even if it did, she wouldn't be a part of it. She was through with him.

She turned her back and slopped water on to the floor, feeling resentful. Wally should be doing this. He'd soon get some money out of his mother.

He did, and came down with a smile on his face, looking confident. Before he left the hotel, Minnie asked him, 'Where are you staying?'

He hesitated before shaking his head. 'If you don't know, you can't tell anyone. As soon as I've got a good stake I'm getting out of town and going over to the west coast. You can come with me. We could make a fresh start. Come on, Min, think about it. As soon as we're settled I'll sell the homestead. The mining company offered my uncle a good price for it.'

She wondered how she managed to keep her face straight; she wasn't going to be the one to tell him the homestead was now a heap of rubble. She couldn't imagine what use that salt lake and scrubby bit of land would be to the mining company, now the stream had been diverted. If there was gold there, she'd never seen any. Ben had said the mine wouldn't buy it now, and besides, the company had closed until the economy picked up.

'Do you expect me to leave everything and go off with you? What about my new job and my friends? And then there's your mother? She's not been well. Her heart isn't what it should be. She needs someone here to help her, and you're all she's got left. If you leave it will break her heart.'

'Ma has had that heart problem for years; she just hasn't seen anyone about it. She's told me she's as strong as a horse. Besides, Reg will help her out. As soon as we're settled she can sell up and join us. I'll find myself a regular job, and perhaps we'll buy a hotel of our own when everything's settled. And we'll have a baby or two, to make up for the one we lost.'

His statement lacked the ring of truth. He was telling her what he thought she wanted to hear, making it up as he went. 'What about Lillian?'

He looked troubled and avoided her eyes. 'I told Lillian I was coming back to you. I promise I won't stray again, love.'

Did he really think she'd take him back, or even wanted to? As for his promises, they tripped too easily from his tongue and had as much substance as a fart in a colander. She grinned as she wondered what Esmé would say to her using that vulgar expression, even in thought.

Wally misinterpreted the grin and went to hug her. 'I knew you'd see sense.'

She stepped back, keeping him at arm's length. *See sense?* She'd seen that weeks ago. She wasn't going with him, and that was that.

'I do love you, Min. Honest. Things will work out, you'll see. Lady Luck is on my side and I'm going to win big money tonight, I feel it in my bones.'

And Wally did win. But there was a price to pay for that slice of luck – a price neither of them expected, or would have wanted.

Sixteen

'Wally is dead?'

Esmé's eyes widened. No wonder Minnie was wearing a black armband. She also had dark circles under her eyes, and looked tired and pale. 'Oh, Min. I'm so sorry. I mean . . . I know you and he didn't get along, but dead . . . how did it happen?'

'The police told me that Wally was at a poker game. Someone accused him of cheating. He left with his winnings and was waylaid by two men, who set about him. One hit him from behind with a brick, and when he went down his head bounced on the kerb. The assailants fled when some people appeared. Wally was still breathing, but unconscious. He died on the way to hospital. The hospital gave me his personal effects.'

'Poor Wally. How is Ma taking it?'

'As you'd expect, she cries a lot. Losing Wally so soon after her husband has been a bit too much for her. She tries to be strong but she keeps breaking down. The police think Wally was set-up.'

'John Teagan?'

'Apparently he has an alibi, but anyway, nobody is talking. Ma is blaming herself for giving him the stake money to gamble with in the first place. I feel guilty about it. He'd asked me to take him back, and I said I'd think about it. I knew I wouldn't forgive him, though. Wally meant well . . . but he was as shallow as they come, and I know he was lying to me.'

'When's the funeral to be?'

'Next week.'

'Is there any good news?'

'Yes . . . I've got a part-time job, right here in the hospital. I'll be in the emergency department at weekends, Thursday night through till Sunday. Apparently it's busy. The sister in your ward put a word in for me. It will be enough to keep us in essentials until your bones are healed and you're able to help out.'

'I won't be able to lift, or do much to help round the bar.'

'Reg will help on the days I'm not there, and it's only for about a month. There are always the accounts to do. Have you and Leo decided on a wedding date yet?'

'We snatched a few minutes together yesterday evening. All being well the wedding will take place towards the end of October in that little church around the corner. We'll be boarding the ship straight after and heading for England. Leo is making all the arrangements, and we'll be in England for Christmas. I'm so looking forward to seeing everyone again. It seems like ages. We won't be gone for good though, and will eventually return to Australia. Promise me not to lose touch. You will be all right here on your own, won't you, Minnie?'

'I won't be alone. I'll have Ma to look after. We get on well together, and I have nothing to go back to England for. Have you decided on a wedding gown, yet?'

Esmé shrugged, saying wryly, 'It will be something simple, I imagine. I'll make it myself.'

'What about those dresses you used to dance with Liam in.'

She shook her head. 'It wouldn't feel right.'

'Wally had some money on him . . . quite a lot, in fact. I can give you what's left of what he owed you. The rest will pay for his funeral. For Ma's sake I thought I'd have a nice one.'

'I don't like the thought of taking money from a dead man.'

Minnie was sharp with her. 'Do stop being so squeamish, Es. I wish I hadn't mentioned it now. After all, money is only bits of paper with numbers on, and goodness knows how many dead people's pockets it's been in.' She gave a slightly hysterical giggle. 'Besides, it's the only way Wally will be able to repay you now . . . so just accept it and shut up, will you.'

'Only if you stop being cross and give me a hug . . . just a gentle one. I'll be glad to get out of this place. I'm sick of staring at the ceiling.'

'That will be tomorrow. It's all arranged. Leo will bring his car for you, and deliver you to the hotel.'

The funeral was well attended, mostly by bar patrons, who donned their Sunday suits and hoped to get a free beer out of it. Ma looked haggard in her grieving, and she didn't bother to hide her trickle of tears. Leo and his brother, Alex, attended and the four of them gathered around Ma in support as the coffin was lowered into the grave.

Leo put his arm around Esmé and she turned into his body as far as comfort, and her arm cast, allowed. Unthinkingly, Leo pressed a kiss against her hairline, and she looked up at him and they exchanged a smile.

Minnie smiled to herself at the sight, and then she had the feeling of being watched, and caught Alex's thoughtful gaze on her.

Minnie reminded herself that this was her husband's funeral, and not the time and place for the tingle of awareness that sang through her body. Feeling guilty, she swiftly averted her gaze.

She couldn't keep her attention on what the reverend was saying . . . not like Esmé who appeared to be absorbed. Then she noticed that her friend's eyes had glazed over. Es was dreaming of her wedding day, no doubt.

Her glance then lit on a young woman who stood on the fringes of the mourners. Tears trickled down her face. She was no more than seventeen, and was pretty in a bold sort of way. Her dress needed a wash and her hair was stringy. Her stomach had a tell tale roundness to it. She was in her second trimester, about four months along, Minnie guessed.

Minnie whispered to Ma, 'Is that Lillian?'

Ma sniffed. 'That's her. I don't know what Wally saw in her when he had a classy wife like you to come home to. What's she doing here, anyway? I didn't invite her.'

'It's not her fault, Ma. Look how young she is, and she's crying over Wally, I imagine. For what it's worth, unless my training is at fault, that's an infant she's carrying. It's probably your grandchild – the only one you'll ever have.'

She received an aggrieved look from Ma for her trouble. 'You know when to stick the knife in. You're not going to let this go, are you?'

'I know right from wrong, Ma, and so do you. Lillian is just a kid. Look how gaunt she is. She's sleeping rough by the looks of her, and you have a spare room. Now I'm at work, you could do with the help, especially until Esmé gets back to normal.'

'Who do you think you are to be filling my home with down-and-outs . . . Florence bloody Nightingale?'

'Nobody asked you to invite me and Esmé to stay.'

'I didn't mean you two. You give the place a bit of class. Not like that Lillian . . . she's a bag of bones.'

Minnie conjured up a lie and whispered, 'I wasn't going to tell you this, but now it doesn't matter. Wally and I had a good chat the last time I saw him. We were going to try to get our marriage annulled and just remain friends.'

'How?'

'You know how . . . pretend we didn't get on with marital relations. When we were free he intended to marry Lillian.'

Ma stared at her. 'Are you telling the truth?'

Fingers crossed behind her back, Minnie nodded.

Ma had just needed to be given a reason, and she capitulated more easily than Minnie had expected. 'Invite her home for something to eat, while I think about it. But if that brother of hers comes sniffing around I'll feed him rat poison.' She sniffed. 'Perhaps you're right, love. I wouldn't want Wally's kid to grow up with that crook Teagan for an uncle.'

'The child will probably end up in an orphanage if it survives the pregnancy and birth.'

A peeved expression appeared on Ma's face, and she folded her arms across her chest and said stoutly, 'Over my dead body.'

With Ma standing a little way off, Minnie approached the girl when the mourners began to move away. 'I'm Wally's widow.'

Lillian flinched, as though she expected to be hit, then gazed dully at her.

'Wally's mother wants you to come home with us.'

'Why should she?'

'Because you look as though you need help.'

'I went to her for help once, and she shouted at me . . . though she did give me some money. Why should she want to know me, especially after what happened to Wally? Why should you?'

She fed this girl the same lie as she'd offered Ma, since it would help them both feel better. 'My marriage to Wally was only on paper. We were going to seek an annulment, and he was going to return to you and the baby.'

Tears trembled on her eyelashes and hope filled her eyes. 'Is that what he said?'

'That's what he told me the night before he died.'

'What about his mother . . . does she know?'

'Yes. Think about it, Lillian, you're carrying her grandchild. That's all the family she has left. Ma might be noisy, but her bark's worse than her bite and she's got a heart of gold.'

Ma joined them, saying indignantly, 'Who's noisy?' She scrutinized the girl, her gaze lingering on her stomach. She sighed. 'You are telling the truth, aren't you?'

'Course, I am,' and her hands went to her stomach. 'What d'you think this is, a suet pudding?'

Ma glowered. 'It could be for all I know, and that's enough of your lip. I meant, about my Wally fathering it.'

Lillian's voice took on a despairing note, but her eyes shifted away from Ma. 'I haven't been with anyone else. He gave me a drink or two, and said he loved me. It just happened, and I didn't know how to stop him. I didn't know he was married then.'

That sounded about right for Wally, who'd hardly been the last of the great lovers, Minnie thought unkindly, but it still struck a false note with her.

Ma shrugged. 'I suppose it's not the kid's fault. Well . . . we can't stand around here all day. Are you coming or not, Lillian Teagan? If you are, you might as well know that I'll expect you to do your share of the work. And be warned, there will be no hanky-panky with the customers.'

Minnie chuckled as one of them walked past, respectfully doffing his hat and leaning heavily on a stick. 'I don't think you need to worry about that, Ma. I doubt if your customers have any hanky-panky left in them.'

'You might be right. As for you, Minnie girl, less of your cheek, too. Off you go and join your friends while I sort this one out. And be careful of that sheep farmer. He's got a wicked gleam in his eye, and will have your drawers down around your ankles before you can say Jack Robinson.'

Ma smiled approvingly at Lillian when she giggled, and Minnie left Ma with the satisfaction of having the last word.

Lillian's presence took the pressure off Minnie. The girl

wasn't frightened of getting her hands dirty, and she could cook.

Minnie roped Esmé in to do volunteer work at the women's shelter, three mornings a week. Money was donated to provide a fund of emergency money for women who had no husbands as support. Esmé was kept busy issuing dockets and keeping the records, anything that didn't tax her as she gained strength

There was only a small amount of relief to go round, and much of that was donated from the better off for those female victims of the Depression, who were ineligible for government support. Some women had been forced to go on the streets to stop their children from starving. Some were evicted from their homes because they couldn't pay the rent and had to camp along the river in makeshift tents.

Esmé and Minnie shared what they had. Ma kept a roof over their heads and fed them. Esmé didn't know how she'd be able to afford a wedding after she gradually gave all the money Wally had owed her to those more needy.

A month later Leo removed the plaster from Esmé's arm. She lightly scratched the skin, sighing with relief, then held them both out at his request. 'One's brown and one's white. I'll have to even up the tan.'

'Wriggle your fingers,' he said. She wriggled. Gently Leo edged his fingers down the bone to lightly press his thumb against the nerves in her wrist. 'Any pain?'

'None.'

She found herself gazing into the blue intimacy of his eyes when he whispered, 'Hold your arms out, Esmé, my love.'

His fingers walked along her collarbone in more of a caress than an examination and skated lightly up over her ribs, leaving a trail of raised bumps that prickled against her skin.

'Mmmm,' she murmured when he took the weight of her small breasts in his palms, and ran a thumb over the sensitized nub. Sliding her arms around him she melted into his body.

He kissed her, a deliciously long, lingering and infinitely sensual kiss. Afterwards he gazed down at her, saying nothing.

When she fluttered her eyelashes at him, he grinned. 'Sometimes I can't believe my luck. You wouldn't like to come to bed with me, I suppose?'

Heat rushed into her cheeks. 'I'd love to, but I'm . . . oh, I don't know.'

'Scared?' he suggested.

She touched his cheek with a fingertip. 'No . . . I'm not scared, Leo. I know how things work between people, and why. I'm just not ready to take that step. I'm enjoying the chase, though.'

He groaned. 'So am I in a way, but it's playing havoc with my sleeping habits. The trouble with you, Es my darling, is that you think too much.'

She laughed.

There came the sound of a throat being cleared and they jumped apart when Ma appeared. Looking from one to the other, she grinned. 'You Thornton men are becoming fixtures around the place. If it isn't one, it's the other.'

Leo's eyes sharpened. 'Alex has been here? How did he manage to escape from the farm.'

'He brought young Minnie home a couple of times from the women's shelter. He's courting her, I reckon. Not that she's got much time to be courted in. She's always rushing around doing things for people.'

'Alex is seeing Minnie . . . the sneaky hound,' Leo breathed, and a grin spread over his face. 'Did you know about it Es?'

She shook her head. 'No . . . she hasn't said a word. I work mornings at the centre, doing paperwork and dishing out advice, and Minnie does nights. I'm hoping to get a paid job now this cast is off. The agency has my details, but I can only take a temporary position, so that sets my chances back.'

Ma had been shopping and she handed Esmé a parcel. 'I've bought you a present. I found a length of damask that would make a classy wedding dress, with a little jacket. I went to see a dressmaker and pretended I was a prospective customer, and I looked at their designs. I used to be a seamstress before I married, and I reckon I can make you one. Apparently, long dresses worn with hats with lace are fashionable this year.' She grinned in triumph. 'The material came from the market, and it was really cheap. There's a sewing machine somewhere. I'll see if I can dig it out.'

'Thanks, Ma. That's kind of you. I've spent all my savings.'

'I know. You and Minnie both. The pair of you are getting names for yourselves as soft touches.'

'What can you do when a child is hungry and has nobody to turn to?'

'You can't feed them all.' Ma's face softened. 'Your heart is in the right place, I'll give you that. Now . . . where's that Lillian got to?'

'I sent her upstairs to have a rest before the bar opens.'

'Good. I'll leave you lovebirds alone and go and peel some potatoes for dinner, it will save doing it later.'

'Leo was just about to leave, anyway.'

He frowned after Ma had gone. 'The fact that you might be short of cash had never crossed my mind. You must allow me to pay for the wedding expenses. I'll go to the bank and get you some money tomorrow. I'll drop it off.'

'Why didn't you tell me you were seeing Alex?' she asked Minnie that same evening.

'With it being so soon after Wally's death, I didn't want people to gossip. You know what those men in the bar are like when they get together. Besides, I'm not seeing Alex, at least, not officially. I'm allowing him to see me. He's taken me home from the shelter a couple of times, that's all. Oh . . . and he's invited me out to the station and has offered to teach me how to ride a horse.'

Esmé laughed. 'He'll have you shearing sheep and tossing them over your shoulder before too long.'

Minnie grinned. 'I'm quite enjoying the display of his male skills. Alex is quiet and shy by nature, you know.'

'He won't be when it gets down to brass tacks, I imagine.'

Minnie dissolved into laughter. 'Lady Esmé, you surprise me sometimes. Don't you say another word, and before you ask: Yes, I like Alex . . . a lot. Yes, he knows the circumstances of my marriage to Wally. Yes, he's kissed me goodnight and yes I enjoyed it. And if he happens to ask me . . . the answer to that question will also be yes. But I don't want to rush into anything yet, or do anything to frighten him off.'

'So we might end up as sisters-in-law, if you survive the riding lessons.'

'We might. Would you mind, Es?'

'I'd welcome it. Alex is such a solid, hard-working man, one who takes his responsibility seriously. Leo has a great deal of respect for him. You know Min, in all seriousness, Alex is just the type of man you need, and you'll suit each other perfectly. As for him, he'll get an absolute gem to share his life with.'

Tears misted Minnie's eyes and her voice thickened. 'Thank you, Es. I'm really going to miss you.'

'Think of it this way. When you snag your farmer we'll be related, and so will our kids, so we'll see a lot of each other in the future.'

They hugged each other tight, then Esmé said as they pulled apart, 'Good luck. Ma will miss you.'

'Oh, Ma will manage. She gets on famously with Lillian, and has the baby to look forward to.'

'I do hope Lillian has the baby before I leave for England in October. I think she might have the dates wrong. Which of us will deliver it?'

Ironic laughter trickled from Minnie. 'I shall claim that honour because she's carrying my former husband's child. But you can assist if you like, and if I'm not here at the time, then it will all be up to you.' She spread her hands. 'I think you're right about the earlier date. If I dare utter the unspoken . . . I have my suspicions.'

'I think we need to give Lillian the benefit of the doubt. I'm curious to see the baby, though.'

'Lillian's young to have the responsibility of a child.'

'She might be young, but she has a sharp mind, and is shaping up to be a real asset. And haven't you noticed how Ma's been doing herself up a bit lately, especially with Reg paying her more attention. If you ask me she won't miss either of us for long.'

With the money question resolved, and a budget set, Esmé was able to get on with arrangements for her wedding.

'If I smarten the bar up we could have the reception here, one of those help yourself affairs,' Ma said halfway through September. 'I haven't polished the brass for years.'

Everything took off after that. Reg layered two coats of whitewash over the smoke-stained ceiling and painted the inner walls a golden yellow and the outer walls cream. The maroon tiles outside were given a wash. The final result was dazzling, as though they'd let the sunshine in. The bar fittings were polished, as were the brass handles on the two oak entrance doors. Mirrors and windows were cleaned, and the flypaper swapped for a new curl.

Ma went down to the cellars and rummaged around, coming back up covered in dust and staggering under the weight of a sign.

'The chains broke in a storm some fifteen years ago, and nearly flattened one of the customers. My Harry promised to put it up again, but he never got round to it. Fetch us a dish of soapy water and a cloth, Lil. I'll give her a good dowsing.'

From under the dirt emerged the picture of an over-endowed woman in historical clothes, and the words, *Red Rafferty's Inn.* She had a leery face, flaming red hair; a low-cut green bodice and a tankard of ale clutched in her podgy fist. The other side showed her in the same position but painted from the back view.

'What do you think?' Ma said.

The four of them contemplated Red Rafferty in silence.

'She's a bit on the vulgar side, but she has something,' Esmé said cautiously.

'Big whatsits?' Ma suggested.

Minnie added her opinion. 'That aside . . . she's certainly no Van Gogh.'

Cocking her head to one side, Esmé countered that with, 'Actually, it's an original William Cheeseman, painted in 1902.'

Ma's eyes widened as she gazed at Esmé. 'And how do you know all that arty-farty stuff, Miss Clever Clogs?'

Esmé's smile had an edge of smugness to it. 'It might look like an inscription, but the details are painted on the side of the tankard.'

Peering closer, Ma squinted at the tankard. 'I can't see what it says.'

'Try putting your glasses on, Ma!'

'Another know-it-all. Still, you can't help it, being nurses, and all. It's trained into you.'

Lillian gave a trill of laughter. 'I like Red Rafferty. It's a bonza of a name for a hotel.'

Ma sent her a smile. 'So do I, love, though she looks like a bit of a baggage. I'll send Reg to buy some new chains and hooks, and he can go up the ladder tomorrow and hang her back up.' Her eyes went to Esmé. 'Shouldn't you be prettying yourself up for that man of yours? He'll be here before long to take you to the flicks. You might as well take advantage of the courting while it's going, because it stops when the honeymoon is over.'

When they all laughed it struck Esmé as peculiar that the others understood the nuances of the honeymoon – while she, who'd never experienced a relationship with a man of any physical depth, didn't really have a clue what would be expected of her.

'I wonder who Red Rafferty was,' Lillian said.

'Some old convict tart, I expect. She's no lady, that's for sure.'

Lillian began to laugh, and they all joined in, dancing about in a spontaneous and relaxed manner that said they were comfortable with each other.

Lillian began lumbering about, cradling her stomach with her hands. She knocked over a chair. Righting it, she seated herself.

Soon they were all out of breath. They sank on to the chairs and gazed at each other, giving sporadic spurts of giggles, though none of them knew what they were laughing at.

There was a sudden trickling sound and they gazed at each other as a small pool spread across the floor. Then their glances turned towards Lillian.

In a scared, but excited voice she told them what they already knew. 'I think my water may have broken.'

Seventeen

It didn't take long to change Lillian's bedroom into the delivery room, since it had been scrubbed and disinfected a few days before.

A rubber square was laid on the mattress, followed by an old flannel sheet that had been almost boiled out of existence. Folded up, it would serve as a birthing pad.

Minnie performed the necessary preparation on the patient, like an enema, a shave and a good dose of castor oil – all designed to encourage a sanitary birth environment. Esmé lined up bowls, pads and a warm shawl made from the same flannel sheet to receive the baby. From the cellar, Ma had dug out a pair of shop scales to weigh the child on.

'Ma's cellar seems to be a bit of a treasure trove,' Minnie whispered as they washed the dust from the scales, and placed a square of towelling on the metal tray for the infant's comfort.

Minnie smiled at they tied clean white aprons around their middles. 'I'm really looking forward to this. I love babies. When I marry . . . *if* I marry, I want four children of my own. What about you, Es?'

'Two . . . perhaps three, but not straight away.' And they would look like Leo.

They checked that all was ready. There was a wicker cradle ready to receive the child, with a mosquito netting hanging from a metal bar curving over the top.

Lillian gave a little whimper and Minnie gazed down at her. 'Has labour started?'

Lillian nodded.

Minnie's capable hands probed carefully over Lillian's distended stomach, and she smiled. 'The head's well down. Did you have any pains before these?'

'No . . . but my back hurt a few times when I was having my rest and I couldn't get comfortable. Then I fell asleep and forgot about it.'

Minnie exchanged a smile with Esmé. 'Let me know the next time you have a contraction so I can measure how strong they are. Afterwards, Esmé will swab the area so you're nice and clean for the delivery.'

Esmé went down to fetch some hot water to add to the cold she already had. She found Leo in the sitting room sipping tea with Ma, and remembered they'd been going to the cinema to see the Hitchcock film, *Thirty-Nine Steps,* with Robert Donat.

She gave him a quick kiss, then took the cup from his hand and helped herself to a gulp. 'I can't stay, but the way things are going, I shouldn't be too long. We might catch the late sitting.'

'If you need me I'll be here.'

'It's going to be one of the easy births, and shouldn't take long. Minnie's in charge and I'm the fetch and carry nurse. But thanks anyway, Leo.'

Ma's face took on a worried expression. 'Lil will be all right, won't she? She's only a kid.'

'All the better, since she's nice and flexible.'

'Shouldn't she have a doctor?'

'Goodness, Ma, will you stop worrying. Minnie and I are qualified midwives. We've done this many times before, and this is going to be one of the easy ones. We have Leo to call on if a doctor is needed . . . but I promise you, he won't be.'

Lillian was having a contraction when she went back up. A few minutes and several more contractions later, Minnie told Lillian, 'Your contractions are strong. This baby is in a hurry and will come into the world fairly quickly. You'll get some strong pains one of top of the other when we near the actual birth. Try to stay relaxed, so it won't hurt so much.'

Esmé patted her hand and smiled at her. 'Don't worry about anything. Dr Thornton is downstairs if we should need him.'

The baby's head began to appear fifteen minutes after Esmé had swabbed Lillian.

Lillian grunted and groaned, and worked long and hard through the constant contractions. Perspiration covered her, but she was being carried along on the surging tide of her labour pains without too much effort.

Minnie talked Lillian through it. 'The baby has fair hair . . .
and a little wrinkled forehead. Try not to push for a minute
while I feel for the cord . . . good . . . I want you to turn
on your side, put your foot against my shoulder and push hard
with the next contraction.

Esmé acted as a brace to her friend.

There was a prolonged grunt and the baby's head was out.
A few minutes later, the infant turned and slithered into
Minnie's waiting hands. She smiled at Lillian. 'You have a
darling little girl . . . so perfect and pretty. Wally would have
been proud.'

Tears prickled behind Esmé's eyes. Although her friend's
marriage to Wally had been a mistake from the start, she knew
Minnie had been upset when she'd lost her own child. It said
much for Minnie that she could be so generous of heart towards
this girl.

The baby was placed on Lillian's stomach, the afterbirth
delivered cleanly, and the cord cut and tied.

Handed into the waiting sheet, Esmé made sure the airway
was clear and washed her little screwed-up face with cotton
wool dipped in warm water. A rosebud mouth and pert turned-
up nose gave her a dainty look. The infant was placed on the
scales and the weights adjusted. She gave a wail and began to
quiver as she stretched her arms and legs. She was a good
colour, as sweet a newborn as Esmé had ever seen. 'Six pounds
and four ounces at birth.'

Esmé couldn't see anything of Wally in the child, but it was
early days yet, and she hadn't had all that much to do with
him.

Minnie took up the child and gazed at her. Her eyebrow
lifted a mere fraction, signalling that she'd been looking for a
similarity too, and couldn't find it. Esmé held her breath,
wondering if the straightforward Minnie would say anything.

There was a fraction of a shrug, as though her friend had
reminded herself that it wasn't mandatory that a child should
resemble its father – and she didn't really care, either way. 'She
looks like you, Lillian, though I can see a bit of Ma in her.'
She placed the child in Lillian's arms. 'See if you can get her
to attach to your breast. Some babies need encouragement

before they can suck. I'm going to look below to see if you need any stitches, so don't jump.'

While Lillian admired her daughter, Minnie briefly examined her patient. 'Everything seems to be in order. You did well for a first child. What a wonderful birth, four hours from start to finish, and hardly a groan.' She gently cleansed and dried the area. 'I wish they were all like that. Pass over those pads, please, Es. And then we'll change the draw sheet.'

When Lillian was comfortable, Minnie asked her, 'Have you thought of a name for your daughter? And don't you dare suggest Red Rafferty! Her appearance has created enough excitement for one day.'

Lillian giggled, then thought for a moment before giving a big smile. 'Shirley, I think, after Shirley Temple, that child film star . . . and after Ma, as well. Shirley Marlene.'

'That's a pretty name.' Esmé picked up the soiled sheets and the afterbirth, which was wrapped in the morning newspaper, and would be burned with the rubbish in the rusty oil drum that was used as a backyard incinerator.

A name jumped out at her. The article was short. Crime boss, John Teagan captured after an armed hold up, and faces fourteen years in jail for robbery with violence. Other charges are pending.

Esmé crooked her finger at Minnie and they moved to one side. They exchanged a smile when she read it. 'I'll ask Ma to tell Lillian tomorrow. I'll go and put these sheets in to soak, and I'll get you a cup of tea.'

Minnie took it from her hands. 'I can see to all that . . . don't keep Leo waiting any longer.'

She nodded. 'Don't wait up, Minnie, I've got my key.'

Minnie laughed. 'Why don't you do both of you a favour and stay with him all night.'

She surprised herself by saying, 'Perhaps I will.'

Washing her face and hands she brushed her hair. She was growing it, and it rippled to her shoulders, where it terminated in loose curls. Pulling on brown slacks and drawing a long pink cardigan over a chiffon blouse, she powdered her face, applied lipstick and dabbed a little perfume behind her ears and in the hollow of her throat.

It was Coty's Chypre. Chad had given it to her two birthdays ago, and although she'd been frugal with it, she'd shared the fragrance with Minnie, and now there was barely any left.

She hadn't used it for some time, and the perfume brought a sharp, nostalgic moment of delight that she'd soon see her family again. Minnie had been right . . . this trip to Australia had been an adventure for both of them.

Snatching up her coat, she smiled as she heard Ma cooing over Shirley. That was going to be one spoiled baby.

They took a tram into the city and made the cinema in time, managing to get a seat in the back row, where they held hands and exchanged occasional, but increasingly passionate kisses. Towards the end of the film Leo whispered in her ear, 'What's that perfume you're wearing?'

'Chypre.'

He gave a chuckle. 'It doesn't smell like any sheep I've come across. You smell good enough to eat, though, and I didn't have any dinner.'

'Neither did I.'

His stomach rumbled loudly, and she chuckled. 'If we left now we could take a tram to that fish and chip shop near your flat, then eat supper on the way to your place, where you can make me a cup of coffee to wash it down with.'

He raised an eyebrow. 'You've got it all worked out, then.'

Far from it, she was hoping he'd work it out when the time came.

They ate crisply battered fish and fried chips from newspaper wrapping as they walked. After they'd finished, Leo dropped the paper in a rubbish bin and said, 'That newspaper was probably full of chemicals.'

'The contents tasted good, though . . . and besides, we didn't eat the newspaper. It was only there to keep the food warm. It had that white paper lining.'

'Also full of chemicals.'

She laughed, sliding her greasy hand into his. 'It's best not to think about it. Chemicals or not, it was delicious, and I enjoyed it.'

It began to rain, a fine drizzle that soaked the pavements and picked up the reflection of the city lights and turned the ground into a kaleidoscope of colours. The gutters rumbled with miniature streams of running water, and now and again a car went past, the tyres hissing in a blur of fine spray.

'It will begin to pour before too long. We'd better run . . . the flat isn't far.'

By the time they got there they were both dripping. Long as her legs were, they were no match for Leo's, and soon she was out of breath. Collapsing against him when he used the key in the main door, she gasped out, 'I can't go another step.'

He swept her up in his arms, carried her up the stairs and balanced her precariously on one raised knee while he inserted the key into the door of his flat. Nudging it open he secured her under the knees and smiled down at her as they went inside and he set her on to her feet. 'The bathroom's through there. Hang your coat on the line over the bath. I'll make us some coffee.'

Leo's flat had two bedrooms, and was on the second floor of a four-storey red brick block. There was space to park a car behind the block. Leo had bought the flat with a legacy from his Thornton grandmother. The rooms had high ceilings, and the furnishings were sparse, with a masculine look of leather and some red curtains and matching cushions to soften it.

She supposed they'd live here eventually, though she'd prefer something with a garden so she could have a dog and grow vegetables.

When she was dry she joined him in the kitchen, towelling her wet hair. 'What will you do about this flat?'

'It's not much use trying to sell it while the Depression is on. When we've gone Alex will pack up my personal things and take them to Fairfield to be stored, along with the car. The flat can be let furnished, and we'll get ourselves a house when we come back.'

The kitchen was small and neat. 'What about the Moth?'

'The plane has its own shed at Fairfield, and there's room for the car. Alex can have the use of them both, especially while he's courting Minnie.'

'Is he courting Minnie? She likes him a lot, and I'd hate her to be hurt again.'

'Seriously . . . but it might take him a while to get round to asking her. I might have to give him a push.'

A smile sped across her face. 'I'm glad, because I want her to be happy. When we get to London where will we live?'

Stirring a spoonful of sugar into her coffee, he added milk and handed it to her. 'I've already had accommodation arranged for myself. It's an attic bed-sitter and will be a bit small for two. We can find something bigger once we're there. You're not worried about how we'll manage, are you?'

'A little . . . I imagine I can get a job though.'

He placed her coffee to one side and lifted her to sit on the edge of the table, so their eyes were level. 'We've never discussed finances, have we? I want you to know that I have enough money to support us comfortably, since I get a good income from the sheep station, and will have a wage from the hospital while I'm studying. You don't have to work to help support us, Es. You only need to work if you want to, until we have children who need mothering.'

'I do want to work.' Colour touched her cheeks, and she remembered that she'd decided it was time to surrender her innocence. She didn't really know how to go about broaching the subject.

'Leo . . . I want to ask you something?'

His glance went to her mouth. 'Ask away.'

'I don't know how to.'

The puzzlement in his eyes changed to dismay. 'You're not going to change your mind about getting married, are you?'

'Lord . . . no.'

'Well, what the heck is it? Stop keeping me in suspense and just say it.'

'Would you . . . will you take me to bed?'

She giggled when his eyes widened in shock and he said, 'What . . . now . . . this very moment?'

'Oh, no . . . not at once. You can finish your coffee first.'

His mouth twitched at the corner, and his eyes filled with such amusement that her blush deepened. He began to laugh, then roared with laughter before choking out, 'I had no idea you were churning with lust for me?'

'I am not churning with lust. I don't even know what lust feels like, never mind churning it. I don't like you any more, Leo Thornton . . . you've embarrassed me and I'll never forgive you.'

Her wail of frustration was muffled inside his mouth when he kissed her and said tenderly, 'Yes you will. I adore you, Esmé. I take it all back. You neither churn nor lust.'

The touch of his lips had a weakening effect on her and she caressed his face. 'I lied. I churn like a dairymaid and lust like crazy, and I meant what I said . . . it wasn't a joke. I just don't know how to flirt and be suggestive.'

'You don't need to with that direct approach. I got the message completely.' The laughter left him. 'Thank goodness for small mercies. I would suggest we go to bed *before* drinking our coffee, since coffee has a sobering effect.'

The breath inched from her lungs as his fingers walked up from her waist, undoing each button on her blouse. When he reached her breasts his palms gently caressed her, and then he bent his head and kissed each one. His hand slid under her buttocks and he lifted her and carried her into the bedroom, her legs wound about his body.

They had both seen naked people before, but this was different. His body was beautiful, long, lean and muscular, and she was ready for every caress from his fingers and tongue.

The bedroom was lit by a lamp in the image of a nearly naked woman draped in a cloth, and holding aloft a flame of opaque glass. It emitted a soft glow. Esmé was suddenly overtaken by shyness. 'Are you going to leave the light on?'

He laughed. 'If we're going to be wicked let's be brazen about it. I want to see your face.'

She soon learned what lust was, and triumphed in the way he responded to her tentative exploration of his warm body. Something gradually changed between them so the play became more intense, and Leo more commanding. His breath came in short bursts, and for a moment he reached into the bedside cabinet and removed a small packet with *Silver Text* written on the side and ripped the top off.

A condom! She'd demonstrated the function and purpose of such devices to expectant mothers at birth control lectures, to embarrassed giggles and ribald remarks. She'd never put one on living flesh. 'Let me, Leo.' Taking it from his trembling hands she rolled it down over his rigid penis, her palms gently caressing his skin as she went. It felt soft and silky against her fingertips. He made a strangled noise in his throat and rolled over on top of her.

She opened to accommodate him, and his hands lifted her. He impaled her with one movement, and the little jolt of shock she experienced was soon absorbed into a slow dance of advance and retreat.

'My darling Es,' he murmured against her ear, and shuddered when she gently bit the curve of his jaw in response.

She slid her hands over his backside, which was taut and powerful in its rise and fall, and he murmured something deep in his throat and the pace increased.

Now it was her turn to murmur. But there was a build up of raw excitement running through her that made her want to scream with the pleasure of him. Every nerve in her body was concentrated in that one place, and she felt reckless with her need.

His mouth explored hers, his tongue stroking in and out of her mouth. She was being made love to in more ways than one, consumed. It was sublime. Soon she became lost in a tumbling turbulence of thrusts and his breath began to pant from his mouth.

The excitement of the moment brought a sudden upward thrust of her pelvis that she hadn't expected, and he growled with her when she cried out. There was the sudden flood of heat inside her, and he relaxed.

She lay there, cuddled against his body, feeling his heart beat against hers. She traced her finger over the angles of his face, his eyelids and the curving mouth that had left a warm imprint on hers, and she whispered, 'I love you.'

His lashes fluttered and his eyes opened. He gazed at her, then lifted a strand of her hair from her face and tucked it behind her ear, smiling. 'And I'm crazy about you. Now we've got the awkward bit over with, how do you feel?'

'Perfectly wicked,' she said.

★   ★   ★

The time passed quickly, and soon it was Esmé's wedding day. Ma had made a good job of her wedding gown, and it looked lovely. Minnie wore a pink dress, and acted as her bridesmaid. Both of them carried a spray of pink silk roses to match the ones pinned to the lace on their hats.

Leo was waiting for her at the altar, elegant in a light grey lounge suit with double-breasted waistcoat. His eyes caught hers as she was escorted down the aisle on his father's arm. Esmé couldn't help but wish it were Denton Elliot giving her away.

The vows were exchanged and photographs were taken with Leo's camera, so they could get the film developed on the ship.

Ma had done her proud and she hugged the woman. 'Thank you for everything, Ma.'

'Don't forget to come back. Good luck, my love. Doc has got himself a treasure.'

On the stroke of eight, Alex and Minnie brought the car around. There was another round of goodbyes.

Leo's mother gave her a tearful hug. 'Look after my boy, and make sure he wears a vest in the winter. I don't trust the cold weather in the old country.'

His father kissed her. 'Welcome to the family, my dear.' His eyes briefly speculated on Minnie. 'I hope Alex does as well. It needs someone practical to be a farmer's wife.'

Alex drove them to the ship in Leo's car.

Tears in her eyes, Esmé hugged her friend. It would be a long time before she saw her again, 'I'm going to miss you, Min. You won't forget to write, will you?'

Minnie blinked back her tears. '*Bon voyage*, Es. I'll see you in a couple of years. The time will fly pass, you'll see.'

The brothers shook hands and they exchanged hugs all over again.

Gruffly from Alex, who'd shuffled his feet and cleared his throat now and again. 'Look after her, Leo.'

'Go on then, while you've got your best suit on,' Leo said, elbowing his brother in the ribs.

'What . . . you mean, now?'

'Of course I mean now. The ship sails in a couple of hours, and if you want to come on board and share a glass of champagne with us, you'd better get it over with.'

Alex cleared his throat, then glanced round at them. He gave a resigned shrug and mumbled, 'I reckon I'll be getting married myself soon . . . that's if she'll have me.' His embarrassed glance settled on Minnie. 'Will you, Min?'

Minnie smiled. 'I was beginning to think you'd never ask.'

Eighteen

The day was cold, but sunny. Rimed with frost, the grass sparkled. Steam puffed from Meggie's mouth as she pedalled her bicycle along the lane.

It was nearly Christmas, and she was looking forward to it. The only sad thing was that her Aunt Esmé wouldn't be there to share it with them.

Major Henry seemed to be out of breath when he let her in. Shuffling back to his chair, he seated himself and tried to draw in a steady breath. It ended with a cough.

'Are you all right, grandfather?' she said with some concern.

He pressed his hand against his chest. 'I've been hurrying, and the pressure in my chest is being stubborn today. Pass me that bottle of pills, I'd better take one,' he said.

Meggie snatched up the bottle and tipped one into his palm. 'Do you need the doctor to call on you?'

'No . . . he'll look in on me later on his rounds. Don't fuss over me, Meggie.'

The cottage was cold, the ashes in the grate told their own story. 'Have you had anything to eat?'

'I'm not hungry. I could do with a cup of tea, though. And perhaps you could light the fire. How are you, my dear? I haven't seen you for a while.'

She tucked a colourful crocheted blanket around his knees. 'I've been studying for my end of year exams, and my stepfather has asked me to help my mother around the house more often. I think he suspects I'm seeing you.'

'Your visits have made an old man very happy.'

She fished in her bag, taking out a pencil sketch that she'd mounted in a photo frame. 'I've drawn this for you. It's a copy of the photograph of my father on the piano at Foxglove House. It's your Christmas gift and I hope you like it.'

She left it in his lap and went to the kitchen. There was gas for cooking, but the kitchen range was usually lit to provide warmth as well as hot water. It was barely warm, and hadn't been built up since the night before. She fetched coal and kindling from the bunker and built up the fire.

When she carried the scuttle into the sitting room he was still gazing at the sketch, his eyes blurred with tears. 'It's a good likeness. Richard was strong then, and had just finished his law degree. You have a good eye, Meggie. I had such high hopes for my boy. I never thought he'd go off to fight when he could have spent the war in a desk job.'

'It was brave of him. Everyone says he was a hero.'

'He was frail when he came back . . . his health ruined by the gas in the trenches. His nerves were shot, of course. He cringed every time he heard an unexpected noise. Your mother and his man, Beamish I think his name was, looked after him. I had no idea Richard had fallen in love with your mother, otherwise I wouldn't have done it. I don't know what came over me. She was such a lovely little thing, and she tried to push me away. But Rosie was being a nuisance, and I'd been drinking, and I needed to hurt someone.'

Meggie looked up from her task, wondering if she'd over-heard what he'd said. 'I don't understand, grandfather. Who did you hurt?'

'Poor little Livia.'

'You hurt my mother?' No wonder she wouldn't have anything to do with the major, Meggie thought, bewildered by this odd confession. Was his mind wandering? 'How did you hurt her?'

'Nothing you're old enough to know about, my dear.'

'I'm sixteen.'

'Yes, I know, you're still a child in that way. You should ask your uncle . . . he saw . . . though he was just a lad.' His smile was far away. 'I used to watch Livia as she worked. She was such an innocent young woman, and kind. Margaret . . . my first wife, adored her. I couldn't stop myself, you know. After that, she never spoke, or smiled at me again. Not even at Richard's funeral.'

Meggie wasn't so young that she didn't understand what he was telling her, and the blood rushed to her ears. Surely her mother wouldn't have let him do that to her. Although she didn't want to hear such dreadful things said about her, she couldn't stop herself from listening.

'I had an argument with Richard when he discovered what I'd done, but by then I think it was too late . . . he told me to get out, and it was the last time I saw him. I bitterly regret what I did. But he didn't have to marry the girl because of what I'd done.' A tear fell on to the glass and he wiped it away with a swollen, arthritic finger. 'I miss my son, but I'm sick of living with this secret. I have you as compensation for my sin . . . my sweet daughter. You've filled my life with happiness, but I don't deserve you.'

He meant she was his *granddaughter*, of course, Meggie determined, as she put a match to the kindling. Unease set in as she remembered her early birth. That was followed by a shock of realization that slammed her in the midriff, leaving her breathless as his words sank in.

She leaped to her feet, denying what he was suggesting. She had to deny it; else it would be too sordid to bear. 'Surely not. You're lying. Richard Sangster is my father. It says so on my birth certificate. He married my mother because he loved her and she loved him. My stepfather told me that, and he'd never lie to me. He was your son's best friend. Stop blackening my mother's name . . . stop it at once! You're being hateful.'

It was as if she'd never spoken. 'The medical report said he couldn't father a child, you know. Dashed silly to pretend he could. It doesn't make him more of a man.'

'You must have read it wrong.' She remembered the major could be odd at times and tried to pacify him. 'I think your mind might be wandering. I'm your granddaughter. My mother told me you might make mischief, that's why she doesn't want me to see you. I won't come any more if you're going to get upset.'

'I'm surprised she allowed me to live in this cottage, then. She must have known I'd see you. Perhaps she was taunting me, daring me to let the truth out.'

She pulled in a breath and counted to ten. 'You're very lively today. Have you taken your other medication . . . the stuff they give you for bad nerves?'

He pressed a hand against his chest and his smile had a sly edge to it. 'I've stopped taking it. It made me feel drowsy, as though I was only half alive. I couldn't have needed it because I'm still ticking. I can hear it beating through my body. It's so strong that I could keep you here and tell everyone that my daughter was in her rightful place. That would wipe the smile off the housemaid's face.'

For the first time since Meggie had got to know him, she experienced a moment of irrational fear. But the major's body was old and feeble and the man couldn't run, despite his feeling of strength, she reasoned. 'I'll go and make your tea, then I must go.' She wouldn't come here again. Not ever.

Remembering the letter she'd picked up from the mat at home, she handed it to him.

'It's from America, your wife I expect. I removed the stamps for the boys. I didn't think you'd mind, since you never read them.' Indeed, there were several letters from various people in the drawer that he hadn't read. Curiosity burned in her as to the contents of the letters, but she'd never been brave enough to summon up enough nerve to ask him. 'Shall I put it in the drawer with the others?'

'You can read it to me if you like.'

She stared at him, half believing.

'The letter isn't from Rosie. I haven't heard from her for some time.'

Meggie read the return address. 'It's from Maxwell Henderson and Sons, Attorneys-at-Law,' she said.

'I suppose the woman's after a divorce again. Perhaps we should just throw it away, like all the others.'

Meggie opened the letter before he could change his mind.

Dear Major Sangster,
It is my sad duty to inform you that your wife, Rosemary
Sangster (née Mortimer) has died after a short illness. As per
her instructions, her body has been disposed of by cremation.
Mrs Sangster's estate was small. After sale of her worldly goods
and settlement of her debts, there was a small amount of money,
which was donated to charity, as was her wish . . .

Meggie's voice faltered when the major made a strangled noise in his throat and his shoulders began to shake. As usual, when he coughed or exerted himself, his lips turned a darker shade of blue and he struggled to take a breath. Gently, he rubbed his arm, muttering, 'Damn the pins and needles.'

Meggie stared at him. 'I thought you were crying, but you're laughing. Don't you care?'

'Good Lord, no. I outlived her, that's why I'm laughing. The woman was a vulture. She married me, and she couldn't wait for me to die so she could pick over my bones. Only she wouldn't leave me alone. First it was money, and then it was men. Then she wanted to come back. Then she came up with some scheme about getting custody of you, so we could control your fortune. Then she met someone else and wanted a divorce. Oh, don't look so shocked. Make yourself useful and go and fetch the tea, there's a good girl.'

The old man had changed over the last month or so, Meggie thought, setting the cups and saucers on a tray. He was much more demanding of her time, but then, so was everybody now it was nearing Christmas. It worried her that there seemed to be a new strength of mind to her grandfather. What if it were true that he hadn't been taking his pills? She worried over whether to tell her stepfather.

When she went back in with the tray he was reclining in his chair, his head against the wing. His mouth was open and a string of dribble hung from it. She set the tray on the table and, filled with dread, touched his shoulder. 'Grandfather.'

His head rolled on to his chest. She stared at him, feeling panic well up in her. One minute he was alive and talking to her, the next minute . . . Was he dead?

She knew how to take a pulse, her stepfather had shown her several times, and he'd allowed her to practise on him when she was going for her first aid badge at Girl Guides. She'd even listened to her own heart beating through his stethoscope.

Carefully, she reached out to touch the pulse point under Major Henry's jaw, ready to jump back if he moved. There was no reaction. His skin was an awful colour, a greyish purple. His eyes were open, but slitted, as though the lids weren't big enough to cover the eyeballs, and they made him looked secretive. She avoided looking at them.

What if somebody thought she'd killed him? A panicky cry came from her when his arm slid from his lap to dangle loosely at his side. The letter fell from it to the floor.

Backing away from him she grabbed up her coat and ran from the house as fast as she could, riding home like the devil himself was after her as she sought the safe haven that was her home.

Her mother was in the kitchen, and her first glance was followed by a second, sharper one. 'Oh, there you are, Meggie, are you all right, my love?'

'I went out for a ride.'

Concern filled her mother's eyes. 'You look pale, and you're trembling all over. Are you all right?'

'I feel a bit sick.'

'You'd better go and get into bed then. I'll bring a bucket up, just in case, and ask your grandfather to look in on you. It might be something you've eaten.'

She imagined her grandfather coming up the stairs, all dead, grey and purple with his limp hands and sly eyes. My grandfather is dead! She wanted to scream, but her tongue was stuck to the roof of her mouth. Just in time she remembered that the grandfather her mother was referring to was old Dr Elliot.

Changing into her nightgown she got into bed, and, pulling the sheet over her head, she curled up into a ball. Major Henry's image wouldn't go from her head. She began to sob, and eventually cried herself to sleep.

She jerked awake, feeling threatened when her door creaked open.

Her stepfather came in, and she gave a sigh of relief. He sat on the edge of the bed, felt her pulse, listened to her heart and took her temperature. 'Your signs seem to be good. Are you feeling a little better?'

She nodded, though his voice was so filled with concern over her that she wanted to tell him about it, and be hugged and comforted, as though she were still a child. It was hard to act like an adult, when you weren't quite one, but everyone expected you to be.

'From what your mother said, you seemed to be suffering from fright when you came home,' he said. 'Has anything happened we should know about?'

Vehemently, she shook her head. If she told them what had happened, both of them would be furious. After all, she was sixteen. She shouldn't be sneaking behind their backs. But then, she'd been doing it for such a long time that she didn't know how to tell them the truth now.

When her grandfather was found they'd say it was old age, and they'd bury him and he would be forgotten. Nobody would know then that she'd been seeing him.

But what if his body was never found?

She avoided her stepfather's eyes. 'I expected Dr Elliot to come. Has he finished his rounds?'

'I saw no point in calling my father out when I was having a day off. Though if you'd prefer to consult with him I'm sure he'd come over when he's finished what he's doing.'

'No. I expect he gets tired at his age. He has plenty of patients who are worse off than me, and some must be at death's door, I expect. I imagine his patients die every day.'

He didn't fall for her ruse, merely chuckled. 'I don't think my father would like it if you told people that.'

A giggle tore through her. 'No, I don't suppose he would.' She tried again, treading cautiously so it wouldn't sound obvious. 'Do you lose patients?'

'Now and again, but none of us can live forever. Enough of this morbid talk now, young lady. It's not healthy to dwell on dying while you're still young and able to enjoy what life has to offer you.'

'It must be horrible to die young, like my father did.'

His hand covered hers. 'I've got no answer to that. I just wish he'd lived long enough for you to have known and loved each other.'

'I had you instead. You made a good father in his place, absolutely wizard, and you're a jolly good doctor, too. Everyone says so. I don't deserve you.'

Wiggling his eyebrows at her, he smiled and said, 'Thank you for the reference, cherub, but what brought it on? You're not usually quite so demonstrative.'

'Sometimes I don't feel very safe. Will you give me a big hug.'

'Like I used to when you used to feel twenty inches tall, and needed reassurance?'

She nodded. 'It's hard to get hugs when you look grown-up, but don't feel it.'

He obliged by hugging her tightly, and then he kissed the top of her head. 'There, does that make you feel better?'

It made her feel safe, and loved, and she was sorry she'd deceived him. She nodded. 'I must have pedalled too fast, that's all. I'll get dressed and help Mummy with the dinner, or do the ironing.'

'Good girl.' He turned when he got to the door. 'Your mother will be relieved to know you're healthy. She was worried about you. By the way . . . I've got some news that might interest you.'

Half-dreading it, she gazed at him, sickness roiling in her again.

'Your uncle Chad rang when you were asleep, and he'll be home in a few days. He'll be staying until after New Year. Oh yes, and he's invited that Australian friend of his, the one we all liked, Leo Thornton. Apparently he's married now, and he's bringing his wife down with him so we can meet her. He's going to be working in London for a while.'

Meggie almost collapsed with relief. 'Oh . . . that's super news. I do wish Aunt Es would come home for Christmas, too. It won't be the same without her. You know, I always imagined Dr Thornton would marry Aunt Es. He seemed to like her a lot and they had heaps of fun together, teasing each other.'

'People can like each other a lot and have fun together without getting married. That's a different thing altogether. Your aunt and her friend will be lying on some warm beach getting a tan, I expect.'

'Like the bathing beauties on the postcard she sent me.' She laughed. 'Esmé's awfully pretty, isn't she? I wish I looked like her.'

'My dearest, Meggie. You are perfectly formed. You resemble your mother, and she's the most beautiful woman on earth.

You'll have to be contented with being the second most beautiful woman in my life. I'll award Esmé third prize.'

'It's ages since Aunt Es wrote, and I miss her. She didn't even send us a Christmas card. Do you think she's forgotten us?'

He laughed. 'So that's why you're so jittery lately . . . because you haven't heard from Es. I know you got on well with your aunt, but she's an adult now, and must live her own life. Australia is a long way away and I expect her letter and card have been held up by bad weather. There are a couple of weeks to go before Christmas, so they still have time to get here. Now, I must go to the boys. I've promised to help them with their stamp collection.'

Esmé had indeed been caught up in bad weather, and the ship had wallowed in it for a couple of days. Neither she nor Leo had been affected by it, since they'd got over their seasickness early in the journey.

Now they stood, arms round each other's waists, and like other travel-weary passengers, gazed across the wind-whipped choppy grey sea towards the coast of England, the lights of which were just visible on the murky horizon. They'd be tied up at Tilbury Docks before too long, but it would be morning before they would actually disembark.

Excitement quivered through Esmé. 'I'm so looking forward to seeing everyone again.'

'I know, love.' Leo's breath shivered warmly against her scalp. 'Let's get settled into the flat first, then I'll put out some feelers to see if there's something bigger available.'

'I'm used to confined quarters now. Our cabin was quite cosy, I thought.'

She giggled when he said, 'The bed certainly was.'

'We can do our Christmas shopping in London before we go down. You know, Es, I do think we should either tell your sister that we're coming, so she can cater for us, or take some wine and tucker with us.'

'Yes . . . I suppose we should, but Chad will be doing it for us.' She grinned. 'By now Chad would have told her he's invited friends. Goodness, it's been two years. Meggie will have grown up, so will the boys, and Chad must have finished his

training by now.' She shivered and moved closer to him. 'Brrrrr
. . . this wind is quite chilly.'

'Let's go down to the cabin. I'm sure I can think of a way
to warm you up before dinner.'

'Leo Thornton!'

He placed a smacker on her lips and laughed. 'I love it when
you blush. Afterwards we'll put our glad rags on and enjoy the
party. We might as well make the most of our last night on
board.'

The following day they said goodbye to the acquaintances
they'd made on board the ship, already distancing themselves
with a handshake rather than a hug, because the possibility of
them meeting again was highly unlikely, and one didn't become
too familiar with strangers.

London was grey and misty in the morning light, and it
began to drizzle. After they'd cleared customs, Leo headed for
the phone box to let his new landlord know they were on
their way, and explain the position they were in.

'We're in luck. He has a basement flat available in the New
Year.' They hailed a taxi and were driven to a roomy house in
Finsbury Park.

'I was going to put up new wallpaper and lay some fresh
lino first,' the landlord told them. 'And I've got a new mattress
for the bed being delivered.' He gave them an apologetic look.
'You can take a look at the flat if you want, but don't expect
too much. The last tenants were a dirty lot, and went off
during the night owing rent. I'll soon set it to rights though.'

'We'll bear that in mind.'

'You're an Australian, aren't you? My brother and his family
went over there a few years ago . . . he grows oranges in the
west.' He consulted a piece of paper in his hand. 'What did
you say your occupation was, Mr Thornton?'

'I'm Dr Thornton. This is my wife. Mrs Thorton is a nurse.'
He looked impressed.

While Leo came to arrangements about the lease and rent
with the landlord, Esmé wandered around. It was dirty,
extremely so, but the kitchen was big enough to accommodate
a dining area. The equipment was greasy, the lino torn and
the facilities would need a bucket of disinfectant to make them

anything close to hygienic. A scrubbing brush would be needed for the bath. Two roomy bedrooms led off a large room that doubled as both sitting room and dining area. A door led into the back garden. She felt a small thrill of possessiveness over what was to be her first home with her husband. She'd soon make it comfortable.

Leo said, 'We'll be going away next week, and will be back after New Year. Can it be cleaned up by then?'

The landlord nodded. 'I'll get the wife to give me a hand, and she can check all the pots and pans while she's at it and make a new inventory. Everything's included except linen. You can stay in the vacant bedsit until it's ready for occupancy, seeing as it's only going to be a week or so. And if you want to leave your luggage with me when you go away, I'll make sure it's kept safe.'

The deposit of a month's rent in advance had been paid, and they moved into the bed sitter, which didn't seem much larger than the cabin of the ship had been. Esmé scoured the local flea market for cushions and lamps, as well as gifts.

The landlord was a wizard. By the time they were ready to travel to Dorset he'd transferred all the facilities to Leo's name, and the telephone would be installed and ready for service by the time they returned.

Chad was waiting for them at the station, and Esmé flung herself into his arms. 'I've missed you so much. You haven't told anyone, have you?'

'No . . . but Meggie was suspicious, I think.'

'How is she? I'm dying to see her. She must be quite grown-up now.'

'Physically, she's changed. I must warn you, though, she's been a bit difficult lately.'

Head to one side, she gazed up at him, thinking that he'd lost a little weight. 'Difficult? What do you mean . . . how is she difficult?'

'Denton said she seems to be moping, and her eyes are often red, as though she's been weeping. She has nightmares, and also snaps at Livia, who loses patience, like she does on occasion. Livia's much better with boys.'

'Because you boys are big babies, and don't mature as quickly as girls.'

'Sometimes Meggie goes off by herself. It's probably female stuff . . . you know how your species go all soft in the head sometimes. She's at that difficult age.'

'Hello, is anyone out there? This big baby has been forgotten,' Leo said from behind a carton of gifts, and sounding rather disgruntled at being ignored.

Chad swept their luggage up. 'Sorry, old chap, I'm glad to see you, of course. We'll get together and have a chat later on. I might give you a quick thump for running off with my sister without consultation. I'm very fond of her.'

'So am I.'

'The car's this way. I say, sis, you look rather elegant with your hair up like that. '

'And you've lost weight.'

'I've been doing time in emergency. Livia's cooking will soon fatten me up. Leo and I have a lot to catch up on. I intend to do nothing over the holidays, except be waited on hand and foot by you women.'

'Me too,' Leo said.

'That's what you think. Leo Thornton. Livia has rules, and so do I.'

They dumped the luggage in the back seat and Chad turned, gazing from one to the other with a wide smile on his face. 'My congratulations, you couldn't have picked a better girl, Leo. As for you Es, my love, well done. You've managed to keep up the family tradition.'

She drew close to Leo, accepting his arm around her waist and his kiss, gently possessive against her cheek – allowing him to claim her. She couldn't bear to think of Livia snubbing him, like she had Liam.

But, she rationalized, without Livia to fall back on she and Chad might not have turned out as they had. Livia had remembered Liam from the orphanage when they'd first met. He'd been Billy Bastard then, the boy Liam had tried, and succeeded, to leave behind.

The sharp reminder of it from Livia had wounded him enough to make a quick retreat into his shell. The fact that she'd reinforced that wound when they'd parted now filled her with shame. But he'd had the strength to bounce back into the role he'd set for himself. Livia had reminded him of it just in time, and he'd seen the danger in reliving the past and had moved on.

'So you think our sister will approve,' she said.

'It's your life, and she doesn't have to approve. I think Livia has learned that the hard way . . . so try not to judge her, Es. Besides, she's met Leo a couple of times before, and often asks after him.'

'Livia always struck me as being a good sort,' Leo said amiably, and Chad and Esmé exchanged a grin.

As they were under way, Chad said, 'By the way . . . Major Henry died a few weeks ago. His heart has been failing for some time, and he went quickly. There was a letter from the solicitor of his former wife, advising him of her death. They think the bad news was just too much for him.'

Esmé remembered the secret Meggie had sworn her to before she'd left for Australia. She hadn't given her niece's relationship with the old man much of a thought. She'd been too wrapped up in her own life. Now the reason behind her troubling behaviour was clear, and her heart went out to the girl.

Nineteen

Meggie had hugged Esmé when Meggie arrived, and although she gave a little squeal of delight it had been a restrained sort of hug.

Her niece had grown into her woman's body over the last two years and was taller than both her mother and her aunt. She was graceful with it, Esmé thought, and she could see Richard Sangster strongly in the hauntingly delicate, fey quality of her face, and the brilliance of her smile.

'Hello, Meggie Moo,' she said.

Meggie's smile was more polite than spontaneous. 'Aunt Esmé, it's wonderful to see you again. Mother will be surprised.' Since when had Meggie started using the formal when referring to Livia? Her smile slipped and tears trembled in her eyes. 'I've missed you so much, Aunt Es. You look happy.'

'I've missed you too, my love, but I'll be living in London for a couple of years. Perhaps you can come and stay with us now and again. Are you well, you look a bit pale.'

She flicked a glance towards the kitchen, lowered her voice and shrugged. 'Oh, I'm perfectly all right. I daren't be anything else in a house full of doctors.'

'I've brought another one to add to it. You remember Dr Thornton, don't you?' Esmé looked up at him and smiled. 'We were married a few weeks ago.'

Shock filled Meggie's eyes and she gave a peculiar little smile. 'Heavens, and without consulting Mother. What will her reaction be to that, I wonder?'

Leo kissed Meggie's cheek and offered her a smile designed to charm. 'Call me Leo, you always used to the other times I visited.'

Meggie dashed the tears from her eyes and her smile warmed. 'You don't want a hug as well, do you? If so you've come to the right place. It's a hugging sort of household.'

'I've noticed. I never say no to a hug, especially from a

good-looking type of girl like you. By the way, was that a statement, or is it an offer?'

Meggie sounded more like her old self when she giggled spontaneously. 'It's an offer.' She seemed to relax as she hugged him. 'Welcome to the family, Leo.'

Livia appeared in the doorway, patting her hair into place. 'I heard voices; has Dr Thornton and his wife arrived?' Her eyes widened and a smile came and went, then came again. 'Esmé? How wonderful a surprise this is. We weren't expecting you.' Her glance went to Leo, puzzled. 'Where's Mrs Thorn . . . ton? Es, how did you get here? Did you travel down on the same train?'

Esmé held out her hand and wriggled her ring finger, knowing the gesture was a sweet revenge for the way her sister had treated Liam. 'Yes . . . I did. I am Mrs Thornton, Livia.'

Completely astonished now, Livia gave a little cry. 'Oh . . . my goodness . . . Esmé has married Dr Thornton. Chad, why didn't you tell me it was Esmé?' Her eyes fell on her son, waiting in line for the duty hug. 'Luke, where's your father?'

'In the attic playing trains with Adam.'

'Go and tell him that Esmé is here and to stop pretending to be the station master for five minutes, and to come down at once. What a wonderful surprise for Christmas. Come and give me a hug, Es, and you too, Leo. I knew something was going on.'

Everyone began to laugh.

Leo seemed to fit into the household like an old shoe, becoming one of the males found in the hall removing their coats and scarfs, or lounging in an armchair hidden behind the daily newspaper, or in the kitchen reaching for something from the tall shelf.

Or indeed, they could be found playing unseasonal cricket on the lumpy lawn, with the two boys, yelling 'howzzat' every time someone hit the ball, or sent the bails flying, or reaching a long arm into the air to pluck the ball from its trajectory in mid-flight.

Sometimes they gave each other fiercely challenging stares over the chessboard before a move, or managed inscrutable smirks if they won.

They stole newly-baked mince pies from the kitchen table, chased house spiders back up into the attic, fixed punctures, carried in the coal, drove to the shop for previously forgotten groceries, and were generally useful in a fiercely competitive way, giving each other no quarter when there was a task to be done.

Shadow hung around them, leash in his mouth, tail flagging hopefully, in case someone took pity on him.

Esmé found a little time to be alone with Leo, who seemed to enjoy being part of the family.

They were using her usual room, a space to sleep that was now only on loan. It was tidy. The paraphernalia Esmé had left behind had been packed into a box and stored in the closet in order to make room on the dressing table for the mythical Mrs Thornton they'd been expecting.

She could either take it with her when she left, or store it in the attic, never to be seen again. She would take it. Esmé had lived three lives. One had been in the orphanage, gone, but not forgotten, because she'd learned she couldn't escape from the past. The second had been with Livia, who'd wrapped her so tightly in love that she'd almost smothered in it. Now she had found herself. She belonged with Leo, and their life together had just begun. Marriage had reclassified her status. This was no longer her home. She was a visitor.

The room was about to become Luke's private domain. He would move in when it was emptied of her existence, and he would fill every available nook and cranny with his boyhood treasures and young man's dreams.

She felt a wrench at the thought of having been evicted from her own bedroom.

Luke offered her a bone. 'Of course, you can use it the next time you come to visit if you like, Aunt Es. That's if you want to. Mummy said that now you're married to Uncle Leo, it might be easier all round for you to sleep on the new couch in the sitting room. It unfolds into a bed, you know. It's a jolly clever idea.'

'Yes, it is . . . and that would be fine.' She kissed his cheek to reinforce the concept that, being a permanent member of the household, his comfort took precedence over hers.

Luke looked like his father. Both of the boys did, but Adam had a strong dollop of the Carr family in him. He sometimes reminded her of Chad. She wondered if they'd become doctors too, and carry on the tradition.

Leo helped her open her cards. There was one of skaters on a lake. A photograph was enclosed of Liam Denison in a sailor suit. He was leaning on a ladder, one foot on the bottom rung, and casually, but obviously posed. Across the bottom of the photograph in a carefully constructed scrawl was the name: *Denison Williams*. On the back was written: *First step on the ladder, chorus line . . . on the set of 'Follow the Fleet'.*

'So you finally made a name for yourself, even though you gave it a twist,' she whispered, pleased that he'd possessed more grit than anyone had given him credit for, including herself.

Leo raised an eyebrow when she smiled.

'It's my former dancing partner. He went to Hollywood to try his luck and it looks as though he succeeded.'

'And you didn't want to go with him?'

'It would be fairer to say he didn't want me to go. My dancing wasn't up to his standard.'

'Was this the man you were getting over when we met?'

'I was getting over the break-up, not the man. It was messy. It left him embarrassed, and me feeling inadequate.'

He drew her into his arms and kissed her. 'Tell me about it.'

'I was in a position where I had to choose between Liam and my family. It doesn't make me feel any better knowing they were right. And I don't think it made my sister feel any better either.'

'Livia takes her responsibilities seriously.'

'And doesn't know when to let go of them.'

'Do you wonder what your life might have been like if she'd been less responsible?'

She grinned at him. 'Often. I probably wouldn't have met you.'

'That's my girl.' He kissed her and there was no more to be said.

Christmas came and went and they headed towards the New Year.

Meggie, it seemed, had learned the art of dumb insolence

towards her mother, usually when the men were out of earshot. She'd developed a casual shrug, a cutting line of sarcasm. Livia put up with her daughter's barely disguised rudeness with remarkable patience, but now and again mother and daughter argued, and Livia was forced to lay down the law. When that happened, Meggie stormed off.

Then there were the dreams. Meggie's room was next to Esmé's, and she'd been jerked from sleep by muffled whimpering on several occasions. Esmé had gone to her, and she'd been trembling.

On the couple of times Meggie had woken, she'd said she'd had a nightmare, and on this occasion her eyes were wide and staring and she was rigid. Coming awake when she spoke soothingly to her, Meggie said in a panicked voice, 'Thank goodness you've come. He was coming for me, and I couldn't move.'

'Who was coming?'

'I don't know, but I was scared. Will you stay with me tonight, Aunt Es? Please.'

It was nearly dawn. Leo had turned into her warm patch after she'd vacated the bed, and he was still sleeping soundly so wouldn't miss her.

Things came to a head later that day.

The men had gone down to the local, and the boys were up in the attic, adding bits of rail and landscape to the model railway. Esmé had bought them a second station with an extension of rails that led to a siding – a bridge, and some black and white cows to populate the hills with.

Esmé found her sister in the kitchen after voices had been raised, in tears. Throwing caution to the wind, she said, 'What on earth is going on between you and Meggie, Livia?'

'Oh, she objected to helping me with the vegetables, said that she was being used as a slave. Denton said it's just her age, and she'll get over it.'

'People say that when they don't know how to handle the problem. It's a convenient fob off.'

'Yes . . . I know. But Denton has enough on his plate with his job, without me bothering him with family problems. Meggie has always been a bit on the rebellious side. But she's been like this since Major Sangster died. I've suspected for some time that she's been visiting him behind my back. It was the stamps, you see.'

'Stamps?'

'The American ones in the boys' stamp collection. They told me they came from Meggie. I think they were on the letters that Rosemary Mortimer wrote to the major. There were several of her letters in the drawer. They hadn't been opened, but the stamps were missing. And when the major died, they found a letter from her solicitor that had dropped from his hand. It was to advise him that she'd died. The stamp was missing from that envelope too, and Denton said there was a tray of tea with two cups on the table. I found the stamp in the pocket of Meggie's skirt. There was also a picture of Richard on the major's chair. Meggie had sketched it.'

'Why didn't you have it out with her then? She knew Major Henry was her grandfather.'

'Yes . . . she did. But I told her that she mustn't visit him. She'd been seeing him for some time behind my back, I think.'

'Perhaps you kept Meggie on too tight a rein, Livia. She was bound to be curious, and was seeing her grandfather so bad?'

'You know how unstable he was. He tried to kill himself.'

'That was after Rosemary Mortimer left him, and Richard kicked him out. If you thought he would do any harm to her, why did you allow him to live in the cottage?'

'It was Denton's idea. The major was a friend of old Dr Elliot, as well as being Richard's father. They both felt some responsibility towards him. So they asked me if I'd let him live in the cottage. The alternative was a home for the mentally ill. I couldn't really say no, after all he was my former father-in-law, and people would have talked.'

'People have always talked. You worry too much about what other people think. What was the real reason you didn't want Meggie to get to know him?'

'I don't know what you mean?'

'Yes you do. Not once did you go to see the old man, and you nearly had hysterics every time he was mentioned. What did he do to you, Livia? Why did Richard send him packing?'

'Do to me . . . I don't know what you mean.'

The door creaked open and Meggie stood there, her face pale and determined, as if having Esmé involved had given her courage. 'Tell her, mother. Tell her what the major did to you.'

'Meggie . . . this is none of your business.'

'Of course it's my business. After all, the major is my father. He told me so.'

Her sister dragged in a breath so painful that it reached out to Esmé, who was almost floundering with her own amazement at hearing such a statement coming from Meggie.

'He lied to you.'

'Did he? I've always known there was something about me that wasn't quite right. You didn't treat me the same as you did the boys, and you used to gaze at me, as though I was a stranger.'

'You're being ridiculous.'

'Did the saintly Richard Sangster know you were having a relationship with his father as well as him?'

When Livia's hand connected with Meggie's face the girl cried out and her eyes widened with the shock of it. So did Livia's.

'Livia, that's enough,' Esmé spluttered, moving between them.

Mother and daughter stared at each other, bristling like cats, then Livia said, 'That's what comes of listening at keyholes.'

Meggie placed her hand against the reddening patch on her face, and between sobs, choked out, 'I think I hate you.'

Ashen-faced now, Livia whispered. 'You don't know what you're saying. Meggie. I'm sorry . . . so sorry.'

The girl turned and walked away. The front door slammed shut.

Livia lowered herself into the nearest chair and buried her face in her arms.

Pouring a measure of brandy into a glass, Esmé handed it to her sister and waited until the colour returned to her cheeks before saying, 'I'll go after her.'

'No . . . she'll come back when she's cooled down. I'll tell her then.'

'Tell her what?'

'Something that only Richard, Denton and myself have ever

been aware of . . . that the major raped me when he was drunk, when I worked at Foxglove House. I've never been there since. Neither have I been to Nutting Cottage. I hated allowing him to live there. We were happy living there, and now, it's as though everything the major touched was soiled. I was scared he'd do the same to Meggie – harm her in some way. And he did; only, he got to her through her mind.'

'You've been carrying this with you for all this time. I wish you'd told me. What will you tell Meggie when she calms down?'

'I don't know. I'm not sure which of them fathered her. Richard married me to provide her with a name. He wanted to be her father so much, and despite his medical report, he did manage to be a husband to me on occasion. I closed my mind to the other possibility, and convinced myself that Meggie is Richard's daughter. She looks so much like him at times that my heart aches. That can't just be my imagination, can it?'

Esmé didn't want to wreck Livia's conviction. 'She does look like Richard, except for her eye colour, and she looks like you, as well. She's a good mix. Oh my God! I never suspected all that had taken place there without me noticing.'

'You were only young.'

'You can't tell her that her parentage is in doubt . . . that will just help to confirm in her mind what the major told her. Meggie's only sixteen. It will ruin her life.'

'What else can I do? Not content with encouraging her behind my back, that horrid old man decided to ruin her life as well as mine, by laying claim to her. If he wasn't dead already, I think I could kill him myself. I'm not sure what to do.'

'You can invent a lie. You've got to, Livia. And it's got to be convincing enough for her to believe it. I can't bear seeing you estranged from her like you are. With Meggie so angry and upset, and you so remote from her, things can only get worse unless a solution is found.'

'I don't know how to close the gap.'

'Remember when she was a baby? Meggie was such a sensitive and curious child. We all loved her so much. You can't ruin her by leaving such an uncertainty on her shoulders . . . you mustn't. She needs to be reassured, and made to feel as though she's loved.' She placed a hand over Livia's. 'Would you like me to talk to her first. It might be easier for both of you.'

Livia drew in a deep, shuddering breath, and a wry smile twisted her mouth. 'We had an argument the last time you advised me on how to raise my daughter.'

'I'm willing to risk another one to bring together two people I love so much.'

Livia kissed her cheek. 'This time I'm listening, but no, Es. This I must do for myself and for my daughter. I just have to run her to ground.'

'Try Foxglove House . . . you'll need a torch.'

She received a reproachful look. 'How long have you known?'

'Since before I left for Australia. Sorry, Livia. Meggie needed me and I couldn't break her trust. Besides, I'd already been told to keep my nose out of your affairs . . . remember?'

Livia nodded. 'Keep an eye on the boys if you would. They'll be down for something to eat before too long. There should be some bacon and egg tart left in the larder, if the rest of the wolf pack hasn't discovered it first. I hid it behind the bread bin.'

'Good luck, Livia.'

'Thanks, I think I might need it,' she said, and was gone.

Twenty

Meggie left the back door of Foxglove House unlocked. The air inside the house was cold and clammy.

She made her way up to the room that was her hideaway, the one her *father* . . . Richard Sangster, had used, and huddled under a blanket for warmth.

The house made all sorts of creeping noises around her.

She had never felt so miserable, or so mixed up before. She shouldn't have said that to her mother. Her mother would hate her now, and Aunt Es would hate her, as well.

She shivered, and wondered if she should light a fire in the grate. The fireplace in here was of black cast iron and had a curly pattern that looked as though it wore a moustache. Blue and white tiles formed a surround, and there was a brass fender, one that needed cleaning. Everything was stale, grubby and used up – even the ghosts.

Along the mantelpiece was a row of photographs of the Sangster family. Her family! Her grandmother smiled at her from a silver frame. Her name had been Margaret Sinclair.

Meggie had inherited her grandmother's name as well as her house. Foxglove House was hers. Nobody would mind if she lit a fire. She could do what she liked here, and nobody could tell her what she could do or what she couldn't.

Yet she felt lonely here, like a small, tender crab in a very large carapace. It was as though she hadn't yet grown into her armoured shell. The rooms were empty of sound, and of souls. The house could not be owned. Major Henry had told her it was tied to the will of the dead Sinclair who'd built it. The house was her master, and she a minion manacled to its will, as all the Sinclair heirs had been.

It would have her playing the bagpipes and dancing on crossed swords before too long. A thought entered her mind, one so astounding that she smiled at both the simplicity and the enormity of it.

'I don't want to be owned by a house,' she shouted out, and her voice was absorbed by the thickness of the walls. It was not listening. A draught made a little moaning sound as it forced its way under the door. One of the stairs creaked.

She shivered, and the hair of her arms stood on end as she remembered her recurring dream. But that spirit wasn't in this house, it was in her mind. And because she managed to ignore it during the day, it came to her at night, so sometimes she was forced to stay awake.

She found some kindling, and some coal in a scuttle in the other room, and soon had a blaze going. Dragging a wing chair in front of it she curled up on the seat with her head on the arm and gazed into the leaping flames. Gradually, she fell asleep, but not quite, for it was a shallow one, more like a daydream – an escape from the remorseful thoughts crowding in on her. She saw the old man coming, his face terrible – and he'd come for her.

The spirit dragged her in deeper. She tried to avoid his eyes but she couldn't. They were red-rimmed. His face was purple and his mouth hung open. She wanted to get up and run, but she couldn't move. 'Get away from me,' she screamed out.

Somebody shook her. 'Meggie, my love . . . stop it, you're frightening me.'

'Mummy?' Half-awake and half-asleep, she mumbled. 'Don't let him take me.'

'It's a dream. Open your eyes, Meggie.'

The nightmare faded, and she found herself looking into the worried eyes of her mother. 'Tell me about it, Meggie. I want to know everything.'

'I was there . . . in the cottage when he died. He told me I was his daughter, not his granddaughter. I was shocked, and scared. I wanted to run away, but my legs wouldn't take me. I went to make him some tea, I was going to make some excuse and leave after that. When I came back he was dead. His face was all blue and his mouth was open. I knew Dr Elliot was going to visit him, so I ran away. Now I keep thinking, what if he was still alive, and if I'd told someone, his life might have been saved.'

'Oh, my dearest girl. It wouldn't have made any difference.

His heart was worn out and he was living on borrowed time. I wish you'd come to me with this.'

'Was he my father? I must know.'

'Of course he wasn't your father.' Her mother was stroking her hair, and it was soothing.

'Why would he say such an awful thing?'

'Remember that I'd been employed here. When Richard and I decided to marry, the major thought I was beneath his son. One day, when he'd had too much to drink, he assaulted me. Do you know anything about the relationship between men and women?'

'Only what I've read in Daddy's medical books.'

'Then this is a secret between you and me, since you are growing up. Men often react physically to women. That's what happened to the major with me. But he was too old and too drunk to . . . well, he passed out. Chad was there and he fetched Richard's servant. Beamish helped me up and sorted the major out. When Richard learned of what had happened, he asked his father to leave the house.

'After that the major's wife left him. He tried to kill himself. I was so worried that he'd attempt to hurt you. He tried to take you once. He escaped from the mental hospital and came to the cottage. I'd just finished hanging out the washing, and found him holding you in his arms. He was confused, and thought you were Richard. I was scared stiff until Denton came and rescued you.'

So that was why her mother hadn't wanted her to know her grandfather. 'So, Richard Sangster really is my father.'

'He really is. I loved Richard dearly, you know. And he was so proud that he'd fathered a child. I wish he'd lived long enough to know you. I can tell you that he loved you as much as I do. Sometimes I look at you and it's like looking at him.'

'How could he have loved me, when he never met me.'

'He just did. He left you a letter, but you're not supposed to have it until you turn eighteen. It's in his journal.'

Curiosity filled her. 'Have you read it?'

'No . . . it's sealed, and it's for you. I didn't know it was there until after he'd gone. He wrote me a poem, too. I'd like you to have that. It will tell you exactly how he felt. I was so privileged to have read it. '

'Do I have to wait until I'm eighteen?'

Her mother smiled. 'Not if you'll accept my apology and we can forget all this nonsense going on between us. I love you so very much, Meggie. I wish I'd been able to show it better.'

'I love you too, and I've been such a brat over the past few years.'

'I guess we both were. It's time you started being the graceful young lady that you are. Resenting the past won't make it change. Now, if we're going to kiss and make up, let's get it over with. The men will be home soon, and I've got dinner to prepare. I've never seen men eat so much. They're like a herd of bulls munching their way though a field of clover.'

Meggie giggled. 'I'll give you and Aunt Esmé a hand with it.'

They stood for a few minutes and Meggie enjoyed the closeness of an intimate few moments of such love and warmth that it shut out the rest of the world. Then they moved apart. Her mother went to the writing bureau. She slid a couple of panels aside and opened a compartment. Pulling out a bulky, leather-bound journal that filled the secret space, she kissed the cover and placed it in Meggie's hands. 'You can keep the journal as well. This is very precious, so look after it. It will give you an insight into your father's mind, and he can tell you his story much more eloquently than I can.'

Her look of enquiry was met with a tremulous smile. 'It's Richard Sangster's journal. I think you're old enough to read it. He made a monthly entry all through the war, and up until his death. It will help you to understand him. Are you ready to come home now, my love? The fire has gone out and it's cold here.'

Meggie nodded.

To my unborn child, whether boy or girl, I take with me into the unknown the thought that I've created and left behind a unique and beautiful child who will take its rightful place on this earth.

Tears blurred Meggie's eyes.

> *It grieves me that I won't be here to support and guide you*
> *over the years to come. I've left that task to the sweet and*
> *generous lady who filled the last months of my life with such*
> *joy, and gave me you.*
>
> *You will be grown when you read this, child of mine, and*
> *your mother will have guided you through the uncertainties of*
> *growing into maturity without me.*
>
> *There's not much else I can say, except you were created by*
> *love, and your presence, even though unseen, is a miracle to me.*
> *I love you, my infant. If there's a window in heaven, you might*
> *catch a glimpse of me in the starshine now and again.*
> *Your loving father,*
> *Richard Sangster.*

Meggie crossed to the window and gazed at the sky. It was a
clear night, with a white moon riding high in a circle of mist.
She held her breath when a star shot across the sky, then smiled
at the coincidence.

She smiled again and whispered, 'Not a coincidence, I think.
The star was created especially for me. Thank you, Daddy.'

Downstairs, the party was getting under way. She smoothed
down the blue satin folds of her calf-length gown, and adjusted
the flounces at the shoulder line. She was wearing the garnet
ring her aunt had given to her, and had spent hours practising
in her grown-up shoes with the heels. She was nervous.

A knock came at the door, and her aunt came in with her
mother. Aunt Es looked wonderfully wicked in a long, black
satin cocktail gown, with diamanté clips resembling miniature
chandeliers dangling from her ears. A matching one was clipped
daringly to the low point of her bodice. Her mouth was a red
pout to match her nails.

Her mother was in an ankle-length gown of tangerine silk,
that was old-fashioned, but breathtaking.

'Where have you been hiding that gown?' Meggie asked
her.

'It was designed by our mother . . . your grandmother,
Eloise Carr. I felt like wearing it in her honour tonight, though

I'm surprised it still fits. But never mind me. As the only women in the family, we felt we should offer you support on the occasion of your first New Year party.'

Meggie smiled at her mother, because she knew she'd understand when she said, 'I've just seen a shooting star.'

'I think you're going to be the star yourself tonight, my Meggie. You look quite grown-up. Hmmm . . . I must remember to keep an eye on the local boys.'

'Mummy, you're making me squirm. Boys my age are all so impossibly . . . well you know . . . impossibly gauche and terribly *spotty!*'

'You're right of course. I recall that your Uncle Chad was as spotted as a Dalmatian once. Now he's quite handsome.'

Esmé laughed. 'By the way, I believe he's invited a local girl tonight. I'm dying to meet her.'

Meggie smiled. 'I know who it is, Aunt Es. It's a girl who used to be your best friend at school. I can't remember her name, and Uncle Chad wouldn't tell me. He said it was a surprise.'

They exchanged grins, then linked arms and went down the stairs to celebrate the coming of the New Year.

Their appearance brought them a barrage of wolf whistles.

'Oh . . . for heaven's sake,' her mother said, but she turned pink and laughed and looked pleased, anyway.

Remembering the shooting star and its brief, but oh-so-glorious journey across the heavens, a lump rose in Meggie's throat, and she slipped one hand into her mother's and raised the small glass of champagne to her lips. She wrinkled her nose at the taste of it. Like most grown-up things, she discovered that forbidden fruit didn't always taste as sweet as it looked.

Later, her stepfather raised his glass in toast. 'To absent friends, and to whatever the New Year may bring.'

The church bells began to ring and everyone raised their glasses.

'To 1937,' they said, and they began to count. 'Fifty-nine . . . fifty-eight . . .'